ABOUT THE AUTHOR

Ralph Thorpe left school at 18 and went straight into business. By the age of 22 he was the youngest Brand Manager in the U.K.

At 25 he gave up this career to see the world. After a year in Italy and six months in Greece, once sleeping in the ruined temple at Bassae, he spent ten years travelling east of Istanbul, learning several languages.

His experiences include: being stoned at a mosque in Turkey; being prevented by the Secret Police from joining the nomads in Persia; rescuing from lynching a western girl, who butted into a religious festival in Peshawar; swimming past corpses in the Ganges; catching a (very small) shark with his bare hands in Japan; getting drunk with sumo wrestlers; spending five days each month meditating from 4 in the morning till 9 at night in a Zen Temple – and in Jerusalem standing on the recently excavated steps of Herod's Temple that Jesus trod.

International Praise for The Dreamer

'A timeless novel that empowers you to change your perception of the meaning of life,' Dave Clarke, director.

'A fascinating mystery with an unpredictable ending,' Lewis Hosegood, author of *The Birth of Venus*.

'A powerful and deeply imagined novel,' Dr John Hatcher, Easter scholar and writer.

'A great talent . . . a great tale,' Ffyona Campbell, world walker and author of *Feet of Clay*.

'Striking and revealing and for some it might be challenging,' Maurice Rowden, author of *Perimeter West*.

'*The Dreamer* is a little masterpiece . . . displaying simplicity, truth and love. I have been completely gripped by it . . . it will be hailed as a classic,' Robert Tennant.

'The novel of the decade!' David Kubiak, American film producer.

'A moving, sensitive novel I will long remember,' Albert Wallace, British Academy Award winning producer.

'A book for those who ask, "What am I doing?" "Where am I going?" Read it and find yourself,' Christine Wilde.

'No western writer I know has absorbed the wisdom of the East so profoundly,' Junko Suwa, Japenese writer.

'I enjoyed the thrill; the suspense was breath-taking. During my second reading I dived into the novel to collect pearls of wisdom, which I had underscored earlier. He has very well succeeded in bringing forth the quintessence of the Wisdom of the East through the poetic melody of *The Dreamer*,' Sri Saumitra Mullarpattan, closest disciple of Sri Nisargadatta Maharaj.

'A thoroughly good read. I was gripped by it,' Brother Bernard, author of *Open to God*.

'*The Dreamer* thrilled me. I couldn't put it down. I loved it,' Ma Prem Shunyo, author of *Diamond Days with Osho*.

The Dreamer

A VOYAGE OF SELF-DISCOVERY

RALPH THORPE

ELEMENT

Shaftesbury, Dorset • Rockport, Massachusetts
Brisbane, Queensland

© Ralph Thorpe 1996

Published in Great Britain in 1996 by
Element Books Limited
Shaftesbury, Dorset SP7 8BP

Published in the USA in 1996 by
Element Books, Inc.
PO Box 830, Rockport, MA 01966

Published in Australia in 1996 by
Element Books Limited
for Jacaranda Wiley Limited
33 Park Road, Milton, Brisbane 4064

Reprinted June 1996

Cover illustration by Telegraph Colour Library
Typeset by Dorchester Typesetting Group Limited
Printed and bound in Great Britain by
Biddles Limited, Guildford and King's Lynn

British Library Cataloguing in Publication
data available

Library of Congress Cataloging in Publication
data available

ISBN 1-85230-779-X Hardback edition
ISBN 1-85230-838-9 Paperback edition

FOR
MY MOTHER, DOROTHY
AND FATHER, DOUGLAS

'Our birth is but a sleep and a forgetting,'
William Wordsworth

1

. . . and she danced.

The waves were galloping across Shark Bay. She rode them, mounted their crests and dived into the arms of the ocean. She swam through the spirals. It was her element and she loved the liquid embrace of the sea.

The sun rose. Time for her to return home and go to the well. The women in the village took it in turn to fetch the water at daybreak.

Lina swam round Shark Rock, which reared up out of the cliff as if some monster shark had been metamorphosed into granite. She swam to the line where the waves were breaking. Her legs beat, her arm arched over and pulled, catching a wave – and the surf carried her to the sand. She ran out of the water.

A shadow flashed past her. She knew it was a sea-hawk, even before she heard its cry. Lina watched the sea-hawk fly to the pine tree at the top of the cliff above Shark Rock. It perched on a branch, trilling its high-pitched call.

Then she saw him.

A man lay sprawling on the beach.

Lina started to run towards him. Then she stopped, shading her eyes and looking closely. Her forehead furrowed. She saw that the man was not lying there comfortably: his body was contorted, with his arms stuck out behind him. And he was naked.

In the fishing village of a hundred thatched homes nudity was not unusual. The pearl-divers dived bare-breasted. And before dawn at the winter solstice the entire village

1

assembled on the beach; when the sun rose, they stripped off their clothes. The young dashed forward, throwing themselves naked into the sea with the elderly bustling after them.

But this man was a stranger. And Lina was wearing only the white briefs of the pearl-divers. As dawn flamed into the sky, she turned and ran home to tell her father.

'So you've found a man at last!' Martin exclaimed with a laugh, looking up from the keel he was planing in the boat-yard. He stood six foot three and was massively built. Martin was a boatbuilder and the owner of the village tea-house and ship-chandler's shop. 'Let's go and take a look at this fellow of yours then,' he gave Lina a wink.

'I have to fetch the water,' Lina replied, turning to go to the well.

'Katha can do that.' Martin laid the plane down on its side on the work bench and called out, 'Katha!'

A young woman ran into the boatyard from the house. She was the wife of Lina's brother, Ken, who had left to go fishing while it was still dark.

'Lina's found a body on the beach. It sounds like a ship-wreck. We're going to take a look at him,' Martin told her. 'Go and fetch the water, will you, Katha?'

'Of course,' Katha nodded.

'I'll do it for you tomorrow,' said Lina.

Martin walked to the chandler's shop. He picked up a yellow fisherman's cape and slung it over his arm.

Birds were singing as he and Lina stepped into the lane, where thick hedges and walls of rocks protected the houses from typhoons. The boatbuilder did not hurry, nor did he waste a moment. He strode through the lanes, smelling of the seaweed and gutted fish left out to dry in the sun.

'Where is he?' Martin asked, glancing at the sun rising above the horizon, when they arrived at the wild grass on the edge of the beach.

'There,' Lina pointed towards Shark Rock.

'Ah!' Martin gave a nod. He looked over the fishing

2

boats drawn up on the sand, facing the sea, to those at anchor in the bay, floating like gulls. His step lengthened as he walked towards the man.

Lina had to break into a run to keep up.

The sea-hawk launched itself off the branch of the pine tree, squawking, and flew away with easy wingbeats to circle over the blue bay.

'At least he's not drowned,' the big man said, throwing the yellow cape over the man's lower half and going down on one knee beside him. 'I have seen those bloated bodies only too often.' He took the man's pulse with one hand, laying the other on his heart. 'He's alive. No doubt about that. Ticking away merrily.'

Martin placed his hand on the forehead of the unconscious stranger. The man was about 30. He was bent forward at the waist with both arms sticking out behind his back. 'What a weird position! He looks like a mating dragonfly.'

Lina blushed.

Her father shook the man's shoulder. Nothing happened. 'Wake up, my friend,' he said, slapping the stranger's cheeks. He tried to pull forward the rigid arms. 'I've never known anyone sleep like this,' Martin said to Lina, taking both shoulders and shaking vigorously. 'We'll give him a swim. That might do the trick.'

Martin picked up the man and carried him into the sea until he was waist deep. Then he let go – and stood there with his hands on his hips, watching the body sink.

'Father!' Lina cried, running forward as a wave rushed over the helpless man. 'He'll drown!'

'Dragonflies can hold their breath for hours underwater,' Martin laughed, catching the body up into his arms.

Lina smiled painfully.

Martin threw the man into the next wave as it was breaking. The surf tossed the sleeper several yards towards the shore before Martin leapt across and fished him out.

The stranger did not wake – and his arms remained

3

behind him in the awkward position that had put the boat-builder in mind of a mating dragonfly.

'We'll take him home.' Martin carried the man out of the sea. He laid him down on the beach and wrapped the fisherman's cape round the unconscious body. Then he hoisted it over his shoulder as easily as a sheaf of rice. 'I never thought I'd have this much trouble finding a husband for you.' He shook his leonine head at Lina as they started walking back across the sand. 'I didn't think I'd have to carry one home unconscious.'

'Oh, you'll have to do better than that, father, if you want to get rid of me,' Lina said, skipping to keep up. 'Do you expect me to take whatever the tide washes up?'

'Nothing is chance in this world of ours.'

They both laughed.

Martin seldom missed an opportunity of teasing Lina about marriage. Most of the girls in the village of Shark Bay got engaged as soon as they reached 13; they married soon after. Lina had refused to meet a prospective husband in a formal interview. This was considered perverse by some of the women. Lina was 17 and they would have criticized her mercilessly if the tea-house owner had not been the most popular man in the village.

The priest's wife said that Lina was obsessed by the Great Shark: 'That's why the creature spends so much time swimming at Shark Rock.'

Shark Rock lunged out of the sea, shaped like the head of a shark, jaws open for the kill. The cliff formed the snout of the shark, overhanging the jagged jaw. High tide submerged this lower rock, which emerged balefully as the tide went out. The shark's mouth then appeared to open – and the waves shrank away from the granite as from some Jurassic malevolence.

The villagers greeted Martin and Lina with looks of surprise as they returned and walked past the thatched houses with their wooden storm shutters. Young boys

4

stopped playing and old women looked up from their spinning to stare at the body in the yellow cape slung over Martin's shoulder.

The grin of pride vanished from the face of an adolescent fisherman, swaggering home, carrying his harpoon over his shoulder with four sea-bream skewered through the gills.

'Come to the tea-house and we'll reveal all we know!' Martin called out with a wave of his free arm, in answer to the questions called out over the village symphony of cocks crowing, hammers banging, donkeys braying, children shouting, cows mooing, women singing, seagulls calling . . .

Everyone knew everyone else in the village. Most of them were related – and the elderly delighted in pursuing the family connections through the maze of marriages. People would spend hours in the tea-house – the men particularly, when they had time due to storms or injury – the thought never occurring to them, or even to Martin, that they should buy something.

Children skipped ahead, chasing chickens and squealing questions. They darted into the tea-house then out again to call their friends. Sparrows flew in and perched chirruping on the cedar beams. So many people crowded into the tea-house that they overflowed into the chandler's shop.

Conversation buzzed. Apart from those who had already gone to work, either fishing or in the fields, most of the village had now come to Martin's tea-house: from the dignified, silver-haired giant Headman to the giggling children, jumping up and down, hoping to spin things out and have an excuse for not going to school.

Even the swallow, sitting hatching her eggs, looked out from her mud nest on the cedar beam.

When Martin carried the stranger in, he had laid him down on the carpet, pillowing his head on a cushion. However, the fisherfolk gestured at the body, covered by the yellow cape, as if the boatbuilder had dragged up some

5

weird denizen of the deep in a fishing net.

One woman put her finger into the stranger's mouth and drew down his lip; she peered at his teeth and announced, 'Strong and even.'

Unusual though the circumstances were, the stranger was his guest. Martin picked him up and carried him inside to the family room.

His daughter gave him a look of gratitude, which he did not notice – fortunately for her. Picking up her swimming mask, Lina left to go pearl-diving.

'That's it. I've told you all we know. The show's over,' Martin called out, returning to the tea-house. 'Only the Headman and the Elders may go inside.'

The Headman, the only man in the village bigger than Martin, clapped his hands together, 'Off you go, children. School calls. You're late already.' He shooed the giggling children away like chickens.

The women chatted together about the man from the sea. He was about 30, they reckoned, well-built, but without the bulging muscles of a fisherman, or the scars and calloused hands. He had not spent his life fighting marlin and hauling in nets. He did not have the pallor of a town-dweller, nor the roughness of a farmer. He had a day's growth of beard.

'He's been shipwrecked. The only survivor,' said a woman, sitting at one of the tables in the tea-house.

'He's a sailor. He was knocked out and fell overboard,' said another.

'And carried ashore by a dolphin!' exclaimed a woman sitting on a lobster pot in the chandler's shop, which was packed with rods, sea-knives, harpoons, masks for the pearl-divers, and all manner of ropes necessary for the fishermen.

'Hunh. Stranger. Mountains. Down come. Hunh. Old road.' The slurred speech of Danny, an angular man of 20, standing on a buoy, showed that he believed that the stranger had come down from the mountains that cut

Shark Bay off from the rest of the world.

'He's a merchant. Rich!' said one woman, getting up from the pile of nets she was sitting on. 'Pirates robbed and stripped him.'

'Throwing him over the stern.'

'With his arms tied behind his back!'

'The ropes were cut by – cut by . . .'

'Slashed by a swordfish!'

'Hunh!' Danny stood with one hand clutching a net that was hanging from a beam, in case he fell over. His mouth open, he swung his head to gawk at whoever was speaking.

'His ship sank with all hands. He's a ghost!'

'No. He's got feet.'

It was a mystery! They looked forward to the man waking and telling them what adventures he had had.

They had longer to wait than they expected. The stranger did not regain consciousness all day.

'We can't keep calling him the stranger,' Martin said, coming into the family room that evening and sitting down at the head of the table. He had just given the unconscious man a shake and splashed a bucket of water over him.

Martin's fisherman son, Ken, was sitting, arms folded, at the other end of the table. He was eight years older than his sister. Their mother had died giving birth to Lina. Martin did not marry again.

Ken's wife, Katha, who had fetched the water for Lina, was preparing the evening meal. She was the mother of two children: Older Brother, aged five, who was often found, when not playing with his friends, thrusting beetles into the face of his sister, Anna, aged three.

'I suggest we give him a name until he wakes up,' said Martin.

'If he does wake up,' said Auntie, an elderly woman, who lived with them. She had lost her husband and son in a typhoon. Auntie looked across from the sea-bass, whose scales she was scraping off. 'This is no ordinary sleep.'

'What do you mean?' asked the boatbuilder.

Auntie gave him a lofty look, as much as to say 'You would never understand.'

Martin turned to look at Older Brother, who had forced his sister to give him a piggyback with threats of thrusting a dead starfish down her blouse. Now he was kneeling down on all fours, telling Anna to take her turn.

'Would anyone care to make a suggestion?' Martin chuckled.

Lina realized that her father had conjured up a name. She sat down on his left, looking at him expectantly.

'If no one else has any ideas,' Martin folded his arms, 'I suggest we call him "Hari", because the first thing that struck us was that he looked like a mating dragonfly.' Lina looked away to Ken at the other end of the table. 'And he must be having a dream to end all dreams.'

'Hari' meant dragonfly in their language, but it also meant 'dream-bringer', since it is the dragonfly that brings dreams to sleeping minds from the bosom of the Infinite. That is why, legend says, the dragonfly has no voice – unlike his cousin the cicada, whose ringing chorus sings in the trees all summer – for it is only in starlit silence that dreams can blossom in heart and souls.

'Call him "Neru",' said Auntie, nodding as if this was a pearl of wisdom. Neru meant 'twice-born' in the language of Shark Bay.

'Good idea,' Martin's eyes twinkled.

Katha set the bowl of fish stew before him, and the big man began to ladle out generous portions.

That night, in the excitement, lamps were not trimmed properly as the fisherfolk sat up late discussing the mysterious arrival. When the men had gone to bed – they had to get up early to row out to the fishing grounds before sunrise – some of the women even began weighing up the merits of the stranger as a husband.

'I think he is good-looking,' said the wife of a fisherman called Tao.

'He has an honest face,' said the priest.

'He will do for that creature, Lina, since no one else will have her,' Rita, the priest's wife, replied scornfully. 'That's why Martin is keeping him. I'll bet he's some fugitive from justice. Martin collects garbage.'

The priest looked at the floor at this reference to the frail Auntie.

Rita's close-set eyes narrowed, 'That creature swims by Shark Rock for pleasure.'

'Lina says she likes watching the sun's rays underwater,' the priest volunteered. 'And the dancing seaweed.'

'Nothing could be more perverse!' Rita snapped.

No one else swam near Shark Rock. Even the pearl-divers did not dare dive into the 'jaws', unless four of them swam down together, with a man above in a boat. Although it was said that the best pearls could be found there, maybe even the fabulous Dragon Pearl, the pearl-divers said that diving at Shark Rock gave them night-mares. They dreamt that fierce currents sucked them down into dark caves, where the Great Shark ripped them apart.

Next morning a strange thing happened:

Lina returned from the well and set the two water buckets down in the kitchen. Then she went up to see the stranger. Martin had given him a room on the upper floor.

The pearl-diver knocked, waited, then opened the door and walked in, glancing out of the open window at the mauve flowers of the jacaranda tree. She knelt down beside the quilt they had laid out on the floor.

It was the first time she had seen the man since they had brought him home from the beach. She gazed at the face of the sleeper, who had remained unconscious all this time in that strange posture.

His eyelids opened.

They found themselves staring into each other's eyes –

9

and the man smiled, as if he was seeing a long-lost friend. Lina smiled back. This was improper. She knew she should avert her eyes and leave the room, but an inner force compelled her to hold the stranger's gaze with her own. She felt a singing in her heart she had never heard before.

'Ah! Awake and shining!' Martin broke the spell, walking into the room. 'Did you sleep well?'

The man's eyes clouded over.

'Are you all right?' Martin asked.

The stranger looked round as if in a dream.

'Can you understand our language?' Martin went down on his knees beside Lina.

The stranger nodded, 'Who are you? Where am I?'

'This is the village of Shark Bay.'

The stranger's eyes closed.

'It means nothing to him,' Martin looked at Lina.

'Where is he from?' Lina addressed the question to her father – it being impolite for a woman to speak to a stranger directly.

The man opened his eyes and looked at Lina, trying to remember. He shook his head, a bewildered look on his face. His body began quivering. 'My arms. I can't move them.'

'Bring him a towel,' said Martin, seeing the sweat on the man's forehead. Lina left the room to get one. 'Take it easy, my friend. You've been unconscious for at least one day. Relax and leave it to Time, the great healer.'

Lina returned with a towel and handed it to her father.

'You'll recover before long, I have no doubt,' Martin said, dabbing the stranger's forehead. 'What's your name?'

The man's body went tense. In a voice they could hardly hear, he replied, 'I don't know.'

'Oh no,' Lina gasped.

'You don't know!' Martin took away the towel, glancing at Lina. 'Don't worry. It will come back to you. You've had a tough time. You're lucky you weren't drowned.' He dabbed the stranger's forehead again. 'Bring him some tea

10

and something to eat, my darling. We must build up his strength. You rest, my friend, that's the best medicine. We'll look after you.'

The tea did not restore the stranger's memory.

He did not know his name, his age, his family or even his country. Some horror had thrown a shadow across his mind so that he could not face that memory again.

But what amazed the villagers was that 'Hari' spoke their language as though born and bred in Shark Bay. Each of the villages on the Coast had its own unique dialect. It was impossible for a foreigner to speak with their accent and idioms. Hari had never been to Shark Bay before – they were sure of that – yet he could recall no other tongue.

This they would ponder, while they sat under the bougainvillaea in the lanes outside their homes in the warm evening air, enjoying the sunset and the slim sickle of the new moon. They chatted contentedly, watching the children playing, and the swallows flying low over the ground, then darting up to their nests under the thatched eaves.

Shark Bay was cut off from the other villages along the Coast by wooded cliffs that were pink with wild azaleas in the spring. However, Ken, Tao and the other fishermen, when sailing out into the deep waters where the dolphins played, came within hailing distance of the fishermen from other villages. Standing on the prows of their boats and cupping their hands to their mouths, they yelled out enquiries – sounding not unlike the mountain wolves howling at the moon.

But no one knew of anyone missing. No one had seen any broken masts, rigging or floating cargo from a ship-wreck. Nothing emerged to give the fisherfolk any clue to the identity of the man Lina had found on the beach.

2

Wingbeats of summer heat flew over Shark Bay – blue days and lacquer-black starbright nights.

The villagers were always busy, wresting their livelihood from the soil and the sea. They rose while it was dark and worked through the day until the sun set. Then columns of smoke climbed from the chimneys in the thatched roofs and the smell of wood fires permeated the village. Exhausted by the day's work, they would sink into wooden bath tubs, relaxing in water so hot it was the most excruciating of pleasures.

No one was more busy than Martin and his family – with the boatbuilding, the tea-house, the chandler's shop, Ken's fishing and the two children. Yet they found the time to look after Hari and show him round.

The man with no memory spoke their dialect flawlessly, but his mind worked so differently that he had to concentrate to keep up with what the fisherfolk were saying: dialogues of tides and currents, catalogues of brides and cousins. Sometimes they spoke in front of him as if he was not there; sometimes they expected him to follow every word.

At low tide Ken took Hari and Older Brother octopus hunting amongst the rocks. Hari did not find an octopus, let alone catch one. Yet Ken spiked 15 on a pole. Even Older Brother found one; without a word Ken caught it for him. When they returned home, the little boy scampered ahead to brandish it in his sister's face.

'How many octopus did you catch, Hari?' Martin called,

coming out to greet them, when they reached the tea-house.

'None,' Hari shrugged with embarrassment.

The next day the stranger went digging for clams with the women, including Auntie, stooping, and Katha, with her little girl, Anna, slung over her hip.

Hari dug up only nine shells before the tide came in, but the women filled their baskets.

'He always was the same,' Auntie winked at Katha, stopping for breath, as they walked back along the beach.

The following morning Hari woke to the sound of hammering. He washed quickly, and hurried to the boatyard, where Martin was working on the keel of a new boat.

'Can I help?' Hari offered.

'Find out who you are, my friend. That's your work,' said Martin, putting down his hammer and taking out the nails he was holding between his lips. 'Walk around. Something might spark off a memory. How can you speak our dialect? Yet you know no one's name. Not even your own!' His arm fell like a collapsing mast round Hari's shoulders.

The stranger picked up a mallet, as Older Brother ran into the boatyard on his way to school. He leapt into Martin's arms.

'Off to school, Older Brother? Fill yourself up with knowledge till you're bursting like a pufferfish,' Martin counselled, taking the little boy's hands and whirling him round. He set Older Brother down on the prow of the unfinished boat and turned to Hari, 'Try another tack: why were your arms stuck out behind you? They're all right now?'

'Yes,' Hari nodded, stretching his arms. 'As soon as they straightened out, they were back to normal. I can do anything.' He shook the mallet meaningfully.

'Ready to lift the universe, are you?'

Katha came round the stern of the boat, carrying a basket of figs she had just picked in the orchard. 'Hurry, Older

13

Brother, or you'll be late for school.'

'Watch, Marty!' the little boy called, jumping off the boat. He did a cartwheel across the boatyard.

'Brilliant! I couldn't do that!'

'Bye bye!' Older Brother ran off to school.

'Help yourself, hunter of the octopus,' said Martin, taking a couple of figs from Katha's basket and popping them into his mouth.

Katha held out the basket to the guest. He took a ripe fig, as Martin continued, 'Wait till the new moon. If you haven't woken up by then, we'll send you to the Dreamer.'

'Who's that?' Hari quivered, an echo tingling in his lost memory.

'The Dreamer is one of those great sages, who has found himself in the journey of life. The Dreamer sees things we can't see and answers the questions we don't know how to ask.'

'Sounds just what I need,' Hari smiled.

'Suit you down to the ground, my friend. And the rest of us too, if we but knew it.'

A fisherman, aged about 30, came into the boatyard. 'Can I borrow a saw, Martin?'

'Help yourself, Tao. You know where they are.'

'I'll bring it back.'

'Did I doubt it?'

Tao ran his hand through his dark, curly hair.

'One Dreamer came to Shark Bay – a delightful man with long hair and a white beard,' the big man added, as Tao went into the workshop to collect the saw. 'Halcyon – that was his name – baffled the grown-ups. Rita, the priest's wife, called him a buffoon. But the children loved him. "Where have you come from?" they would ask. "The Hills of Heaven," he always replied. "Where's that?" "In your dreams. See you there tonight." '

Thrills ran up Hari's spine. *I know that name!* Echoes vibrated in the abyss of his memory. *Who am I?*

'Halcyon gave me the will to live when my wife died. He

14

was holding her hand when Lina was born. In fact Halcyon gave Lina her name,' Martin waved goodbye to Tao. 'He left as suddenly as he came. Some say he's living in the mountains.'

Lina came into the boatyard, returning home after pearl-diving, carrying her weighted diving belt.

The boatbuilder turned round to see what Hari was staring at. 'Hallo, my darling! Find the Dragon Pearl?'

'Not yet, father,' Lina laughed. 'Have you?'

Hari watched Lina go inside the house, singing. *She smiled at me!* He could not take his eyes off her.

'All this brainwork's making me tired,' Martin said cheerfully. 'Come on, hunter of the octopus. We'll go for a swim. Wash away the cobwebs.'

'Shall we have something to eat first?' Hari suggested, taking a step towards the house.

'I like to start the day with some labour, then come in for breakfast when I've worked up an appetite. Today we'll have a swim,' Martin replied, putting his hand on Hari's shoulder. 'I'll finish this keel after breakfast.'

They left the boatyard and walked to the beach.

Martin watched as Hari dived in. The stranger swam hard, frustrated at not being able to be with Lina.

'My word, it looks as if you're quite a swimmer. I'll race you to that skiff,' Martin shouted, pointing to a boat riding at anchor in the bay. 'Off you go, my friend. I'm giving you a start.'

Martin plunged into the waves, but he could not catch up with the man no one knew.

'Hari can certainly swim,' Martin said, when they came home and were sitting down to breakfast. 'I dare say he could swim to your island, Auntie.'

'Of course he could. He always was a good swimmer, weren't you?' The old lady nodded at Hari, who kept looking round. 'Martin's the best swimmer in the village, Humi.'

'The most powerful, maybe,' Martin agreed, his mouth

full of egg. 'Lina is much more graceful.'

Lina! Hari sat up. Where was the lovely girl who had found him on the beach? How lucky they were who were with her! He took a gulp of seaweed soup. Why had he come to Shark Bay? *To meet Lina!* What other reason could there be? Fate had brought them together!

'Where is Lina?' he asked casually.

'She'll have gone pearl-diving again,' Martin replied.

Hari walked down to the beach, stopping to watch the old men, their weather-beaten faces creased with ancient laughter, as they played bowls on the hard ground between the palm trees.

He passed the well with its thatched roof. It was shaded by palm trees, under which women stood chatting, watching another woman pulling up her bucket.

A fisherman was hauling his boat over the greased logs that ran up the sand to the wild grass beyond the tide's reach.

Hari offered to help pull, but the fisherman waved him away as he might a well-meaning child, his crow's-feet eyes crinkling with merriment.

Other fishermen were checking their nets – hanging some to dry over bamboo poles, then sitting down on the burning sand to mend those that were torn, which they held taut between calloused toes, talking and laughing.

A fisherman walked by, his shoulders rolling as though already out at sea. He stopped and gazed at Hari, running his hands through his tousled hair. It was Tao, the man who had borrowed Martin's saw.

'Heh! I'm going fishing!' he shouted, as if Hari was on the other side of the bay. 'Do you want to come, stranger?'

No one called him 'Hari.' Martin had taken to calling him 'Hunter of the octopus!' Auntie called him 'Humi.' Ken had not said one word to him. Nor had Lina, alas. Katha attracted her unknown guest's attention, when required, by clearing her throat.

'Yes, thank you,' Hari smiled. This was the first chance he'd had of going out in a boat. 'I'll give you a hand. Will you be fishing near the pearl-divers?'

'My name is Tao,' the fisherman replied, as they walked to his boat.

'They call me Hari.'

Together they pulled Tao's boat down the logs, over the sand and into the waves.

Tao barely glanced at the pearl-divers. A breeze filled the sail. Looking towards the horizon, his hand on the tiller, he crossed his legs with the confidence of years of experience. Perfectly at home on the water, the fisherman wove his way between submerged rocks that would have ripped the bilge out of the boat if Hari had been steering.

Before long Tao cast anchor and they were riding on the swell of the open sea. Hari became aware of the might of the ocean. Tao's boat seemed like an insect that skims across the surface of a pond.

Now Hari saw that the hills circling the village were ringed by heat-hazy mountains, cutting Shark Bay off from the world. He sat at the prow with his fishing line dangling into the water. Looking up, he sighed: his personality had no more substance than the creatures formed by the clouds before they melted into the blue sky.

Hari caught a tiddler, which Tao told him to throw back. Then he lost a hook. He thought he'd been as useless as he had been with the octopus and the clams.

However, Tao made a great catch of yellowtail and saury. 'I caught nothing last month,' he gloated, rowing back since the wind had dropped. 'I asked you to come with me, stranger, because I hoped it would break the bad spell. And it worked!'

The next day Hari went out in the boat again. From then on, Tao would not go fishing without the stranger.

Tao would not let Hari do any work – not even dangle a line over the side – in case that broke the luck.

'Don't touch!' the fisherman shouted, when Hari bent to

17

pick up a sea-bream Tao had netted. 'Excuse me.' Tao stuck his calloused fingers into the eyes of the fish, where he could get a grip without it slithering out of his grasp; he threw it from the bilge into a wooden bucket.

The man with no name was content to act as a good luck charm. At least he was doing something! His mind on Lina, he watched the awed pleasure on Tao's sunbaked face as fish rained into the boat.

Left with nothing to do, he dived off the prow and swam until he was exhausted.

A dolphin swam up to him and, having terrified him as it raced towards him, sported with him for a few minutes. Its mate joined them. Then the dolphins swam away, smiling, leaping out of the water.

Hari floated on his back, listening to the rattle of the pebbles fathoms below and watching the seagulls flying above. And dragonflies! What were they doing out here? *What am I doing here?* What was his past? Where was his future? Nowhere. Unless it was Lina. If it wasn't Lina, it was nothing. *Lina!*

Tao watched the stranger with wonder. 'Excuse me. Was he calling the dolphins?' he asked, when Hari swam back to the boat and heaved himself in over the side.

Hari smiled uncertainly.

'He was!' Tao grinned at the stranger as if he was a god. 'Excuse me.'

As great catch followed great catch, day after day, Tao was confirmed in his belief that Hari's arrival was due to his prayers to the Dreamer, perceived by the sea-folk to be a fisherman god. A stone statue of this well-fed Dreamer, brightly painted and clasping a huge sea-bream under his arm, laughed fatly from the cliff on the point of the bay opposite Shark Rock.

'For all we know, the stranger is an incarnation of the Dreamer,' Tao told his wife.

'He is not fat enough.'

'He is not portly like the statue,' Tao conceded, 'but the

Dreamer is not bound by men's ideas. God can descend to this world in whatever shape he pleases.'

His wife grunted, salting fish away against the next lean season. She did not intend to be bound by the caprices of the Dreamer, portly or otherwise. But she said nothing to contradict her husband – until the stranger came, she had had to spend the day digging up lug-worms for Tao to use as bait.

Apart from the nagging worry of his lost memory, Hari found peace in this fishing village, where the only messengers from the rest of the world were the swallows and the wild geese – and the fish that came in their season.

In autumn the jellyfish would come, Martin told Hari. The pearl-divers did not swim then – except for Lina, who would come running out of the waves with purple welts lashing her legs. Autumn! He could not stay till then. As each day passed with the moon waxing fuller, Hari felt something within telling him he must be on his way. But where to? And why? *She* was here.

That afternoon the half moon hid in the heavens, only its circle edge giving it away amongst the wisps of white clouds feathering the sky.

'It is the evenings I like best: when the sea sails from azure into amethyst, and veils of violet twilight fall across the cliffs,' Hari was saying, back on the beach with Tao after another huge catch. 'Between worlds. When one reality gives way to another, as the sky lays its cheek on the sea and seems to dream.'

'Between worlds,' the fisherman echoed, looking at the stranger with reverence, then bowing low.

Hari noticed two women by the pine tree at Shark Rock. They clapped their hands twice, then threw a bunch of flowers into the sea. They steepled their hands together in prayer.

The god had ceased to speak. Tao permitted himself to begin, 'Excuse me. Tomorrow we'll go net fishing . . .'

19

The two women bowed. Then they started walking down to the beach. One of them, stumbling and stooping, was Auntie.

The other was as lithe as – *it was Lina!*

'Fine. See you tomorrow!' said Hari. 'Goodbye!'

'Wait! Excuse me. We'll go net fishing. Don't!' The fisherman straightened in alarm, as Hari put out a hand to speed him up by helping him shoulder the bag full of fish. 'Excuse me. Nets – not the rod. If he does not mind.'

'Not a bit!' Hari looked towards Shark Rock.

'Thank you,' Tao bowed to the stranger with a devotion he had never shown in the Temple. He began mumbling details about tomorrow's fishing.

'I understand,' Hari interrupted. Lina would have left the shore by the time Tao finished. 'Tomorrow then. Goodbye.'

'Excuse me.' Tao no longer called Hari 'stranger'. He did not even clear his throat to attract Hari's attention. If he wanted to speak to Hari, he went motionless as a lizard sighting its prey; he waited until Hari looked his way. His eyes fell immediately. He mumbled, 'Excuse me'– which, in the dialect, literally meant 'I do not breathe.' Then Tao would speak, running his hand through his hair and using the politest forms of language he knew.

'I must go now,' Hari said to Tao.

'Thank you,' Tao murmured, shouldering his joyfully heavy burden. 'Excuse me.'

Hari ran towards Lina, his toes sinking into the cool sand – followed by the respectful gaze of the fisherman.

Lina had given Auntie her arm. The old lady was breathing heavily. Although Auntie lived at Martin's, Hari knew only that she was a widow who came from a nearby island.

On the clam-hunting expedition Auntie had stared at Hari. He had felt foolish, crouching and digging, but not able to find any clams at all.

When they returned home, Hari had sat down at one of

20

the tables in the tea-house with his head in his hands.

Auntie shuffled in from the family room carrying a plate of raw abalone, thinly sliced, which she pushed in front of him.

'Eat this, Humi. I only eat shellfish. Raw shellfish and boiled rice. Nothing else. That's why I never have a day's sickness. Eat the same, and you'll live to be a hundred.'

'If that's the cost,' Martin called out with a laugh, walking in from the chandler's shop with a coil of rope over his shoulder and a crab-trap in his hand, 'I'd rather die straightaway and have done with it.'

'Don't tempt fate,' Auntie chided him. Her fingers dug into Hari's shoulder. '*They* can't be expected to understand, Humi.' She added, 'I can still work.'

Every day at low tide Auntie hobbled down to the shore. Hari had seen her scooping the seaweed (which she never ate herself) out of the waves. Puffing, Auntie laid the harvest of the sea out to dry in the sun, then piled it up until her stack of dried seaweed was the largest in Shark Bay.

'What were you doing?' Hari asked, having run across the beach to catch up with Lina and the old lady. Beaming, he stared at the pearl-diver, ignoring Auntie.

Lina gave Hari a smile of welcome, but did not reply to his question. She turned towards Auntie. *How beautiful she is!*

'You see those men going out to fish tonight, Humi?' Auntie asked, breathing heavily. She pointed at the boats heading out into the darkening ocean. Soon torches would blaze from their sterns to attract the fish, and the horizon would glitter with a garland of flares.

'Yes,' Hari said, tearing his eyes away from Lina.

'They go fishing for squid,' panted Auntie, scowling. 'Detestable squid. I never touch them.'

Lina patted the old lady's skinny arm.

'One night the sea was as calm as a Temple pond, but typhoons spring up so suddenly. They can snatch a house and hurl it over the mountains!' Auntie's arm swept

21

round. 'My husband was the most skilful fisherman on the Coast. He knew the movements of the fish, Humi, as you know your own home.'

Hari looked at Lina. Her eyes did not leave Auntie.

'Every day he came back with a great catch,' Auntie nodded. 'We came to Shark Bay – if only we hadn't – for a new boat, which Martin had built. It was the biggest on the Coast. How their faces shone. I waved them goodbye.'

'Her husband and son,' Lina explained, looking at the horizon. 'It's bad luck for women to go on board a fishing boat, so Father was going to take Auntie home to her island the next day in the boat he uses for supplies.'

'Is it? Bad luck? Why is that?' Hari stared at Lina. She would not meet his eyes. *Oh, I would defy any superstition for you. You are more radiant than the dawn.*

Auntie had got her breath back. 'They were going night-fishing for squid. He said they would return home with a great catch, the first in the new boat. Suddenly a typhoon screamed out of hell.' Her voice choked in a sob. She sniffed and regained her composure, touching the crystal pendant in the shape of a crescent moon on her silver neckchain. 'The men of this village managed to return safely, but my husband was half-way to the island. The typhoon drove them out to sea.

'All night they fought the waves. Such was his skill that he succeeded in bringing the new boat back to Shark Bay. In the grey dawn I could see their faces . . . ' Auntie broke off.

'She had roped herself to the pine tree.' Lina pointed to Shark Rock without looking at Hari.

Hari gazed at Lina, but for once he was not seeing her. He could hardly believe Auntie's courage; lashed to the gale-whipped tree, praying for her men. The typhoon might have uprooted the tree.

'They did not scream for help,' the old lady said as her hand clutched his arm. 'Brave, brave men. My husband grasping the tiller, shouting instructions to my son above

22

the blast of the storm. A wave washed my son overboard.'
Auntie let go of Hari and put her hands to her face. She
groaned. 'Then a colossal wave crashed into the boat. It
turned it broadside on. Before he could straighten out, the
next wave smashed it against Shark Rock. It broke the boat
in half. Right under my eyes!'

Lina put her arm round Auntie's shoulders. The old lady
looked as if she was going to collapse.

'Auntie never forgets them. She brings them flowers
every month,' Lina said softly, gesturing to where the flowers had now sunk under the waves.

Hari glanced at the sea by Shark Rock. A lump formed in
his throat.

'Since I had no man to look after me, Martin took me
into his home. He has been a father and a son to me.' Auntie nodded to herself at the justice of this paradox.

'And you have been a mother to me,' Lina added, patting Auntie's arm, smiling.

'Your eyes are the eyes of my son, Humi.' Auntie stared
into Hari's face. 'It is 16 years since they died. Their bodies
were never found. I longed to see their faces again, if only
in a dream, but the Dreamer never gave me that comfort.'
Tears filled her eyes. 'Only that terrible wave, picking the
boat up and smashing it against the Rock. I prayed for the
Dreamer to come to Shark Bay – but no one ever came.'

'Halcyon came. Didn't Martin say he was a Dreamer?'
asked Hari, puzzled by *the* Dreamer and *a* Dreamer.

'Now, at last – you! Washed up on the beach after all
these years, Humi. Alive and well.'

Hari became quite intimate with the old lady after this.
He realized that the son of fact had eloped with the daughter of fantasy. They lay together in the secret chambers of
her heart, drinking the soup she made from the magic
mushrooms growing in the damp ground beyond the bulrushes, where at night the fireflies danced, crystal bright.

Sitting naked from the waist upwards in the oppressive
heat – as was the custom of the elderly women – Auntie

stared at Hari, though her focus was so uncertain he wondered if she was seeing him or an apparition from some less tangible world. Once she barked, 'Rita, that so-called priest's wife, says it was the reward for his pride in building such a big boat. May her gossiping tongue be blistered!'

Auntie would shuffle into the tea-house with chuckles of pleasure. Ignoring everyone else there, she would sit down beside Hari: 'You are a good boy, Humi.' She told him time and again how 'more than pleased' she was that he had returned from the dead. 'These days, not many sons come back to comfort their weary mother.'

He was the age of her son when he died. 'Even though *they* call you Hari, I know you are Humi. I was sure when I saw you digging for clams. Just the same as always. You never learnt, you silly boy.' She was surprised that even *they* did not see he was Humi. 'But *they* are so blind.'

Hari's growing beard did not disguise him from her motherly eye.

When Martin had given him a razor, Hari had taken it. Then he had handed it back, 'No, thanks. I won't shave until I've discovered who I am. It will be a constant reminder.' He turned to stare at Lina, who came into the family room carrying a wooden bucket full of oysters.

Martin gave him a jovial clout on the shoulder, 'Good for you, hunter of the octopus!'

Sometimes the passage of the years proved too subtle for the hectic activity of Auntie's brain. 'I was sure you never died, but . . . ,' she asked, tears filling her eyes, 'why did you stay away so long, Humi?'

Martin had trained a grape-vine beside the house, inter-lacing it with a gourd to make a shaded arbour.

As the sun sank to the horizon, Hari sat down on the bench Martin had made. Looking at the yellow gourd flowers that had furled up for the night, Hari caught a glimpse of the moon, nearly full in the sky, shining between the evening star and the red planet.

Suddenly Hari's body jerked. A memory burst in his head. He had to be there in a month! *Where?* He had no idea. But he was sure. *There!* The moon, measuring the month across the heavens, was warning him, counting down the days like some celestial timepiece. If he wasn't *there* in a month, disaster would strike. *Who?* He had to get there. *Where?* He thrust his head between his hands. *Why?* His shoulders quivered. *Who am I?*

'You always were a good boy.' He felt a maternal pat on the head. Auntie had shuffled into the arbour; she was thrusting a plate of raw shrimps under his nose. 'Eat them up.'

Hari stared at the plate.

'Now don't be fussy, Humi.' Auntie raised the plate till it touched his chin, digging the scrawny fingers of her other hand into his neck, either to prevent him running away or to assure herself that he was not some fragment mushrooming out of her skull. 'Eat them up. You'll live to be a hundred.'

3

Of course it was with someone else that Hari was hoping for an intimate relationship.

From the moment he had awakened and found himself staring into her eyes, Hari had thought of her often.

Going out with Tao in his boat, Hari shaded his eyes and scanned the pearl-divers. Ah, there she is! He always fancied it was Lina. Often it turned out to be a woman twice her age, thick at the waist. At home Hari would steal glances at her when he thought she was unaware of it.

At night Hari would lie on his back, looking out of the window at the jacaranda tree, sweating in the heat, swatting at the mosquitoes. And then, on the heady scents of the night jasmine, Lina would come to him, tip-toeing through the silent house. Their hands touched in the darkness, their lips met, their bodies entwined.

Such fantasies were interrupted by the spectre of the door crashing open and Martin bursting in.

Hari's eyes caressed her hair, rested on her breasts, luscious hillocks pushing out the white cotton of her shirt as, returning from pearl-diving, she sorted the shells, then helped Katha prepare the evening meal.

Hari did not know what Lina felt for him, even though Auntie, while mending Martin's shirt, had called her boy over to give him the benefit of her worldly wisdom on the subject of connubial bliss.

'There is a saying at the Betrothal Ceremony that precedes an arranged marriage, Humi,' she had told him, threading a needle. 'The eyes speak more than the tongue.'

The fact that Lina's soul-deep eyes never met his for more than an instant spoke eloquently to the heart that sees.

It was inevitable that *she* should have found him on the beach. Fate had decreed that he should end up here – and be discovered by this sweet-natured, wonder . . .

'Would you like to marry her?' Martin's gale of laughter and the shove of his arm rocked the smitten stranger like a boat in a storm.

They were sitting at the table in the family room, waiting for Ken to return home from the day's fishing so that the evening meal could begin.

Hari went red. He sat up straight, rubbing his shoulder and mumbling, 'I . . . er . . . I mean . . . if only . . .'

'Out with it, hunter of the octopus!' Martin clapped his hands together as if to spur Hari on. 'Either you do, or you don't. Which is it to be?'

Hari saw that Lina's father was serious. His heart leapt. He couldn't believe it. But would she . . . ? Hari looked at Lina.

The pearl-diver had finished washing the rice; she handed the bowl to Katha and dried her hands on her apron. Then she turned her face to Hari. He gazed into her eyes. For once she did not look away. It was as if no one else existed.

'Well?' said Martin.

'Humi?' Auntie prompted, hovering between the dining table and the kitchen sink, neither joining them nor doing the drying-up she had started for Katha.

'Well?' The boatbuilder tapped the table.

'Yes, Martin. I want to marry Lina.' Hari's eyes never left hers. His heart glowed. 'If she will have me.'

In a land of arranged marriages Martin's proposal was not unduly sudden. Lina showed no surprise. It was her father's duty to find her a husband – though usually the parents arranged it more adroitly, through a go-between with exchanges of poems and flowers.

'I don't imagine there'll be any problem about that,'

Martin said, giving the table a thump, as much as to say, That's settled. At last!

'An ideal match!' Auntie chuckled.

'I can't marry Hari,' Lina looked at her father.

'Why not?' Martin demanded.

'I am promised.'

'Promised?' Martin exclaimed. 'Who on earth to? This is the first I've heard of it.'

Hari's eyes went sullen with jealousy.

'I don't know,' Lina answered.

Auntie frowned at her, while Martin said, 'What are you talking about, Lina?'

Lina sat down at the table opposite Hari.

'I had a vision,' she said. 'An old man with "eyes that shine like the knowers of God" told me, "You are Anil. You can only marry the one who knew you before you took birth." '

'You are a kneel,' Martin exclaimed. 'What in the name of all that's holy does that mean? Do you go down on your knees for the rest of your life?'

'A.N.I.L,' Lina spelt it out for him. 'Lina backwards.'

'Lina backwards!' Martin banged his fist down on the table. 'A vision? You mean a dream! Do you mean to tell me you've refused to get married all these years, just because of some silly, girlish dream?'

'It's because I knew you would call it a silly dream that I never told you,' said Lina, laying her hand on Martin's massive forearm. 'There was no one I wanted to marry then anyway. I'm sorry I've upset you, father.'

The boatbuilder took a deep breath; he let it out. 'Now Lina, some old man told you – what was it? You can only marry the man who knew you before you were born?' Martin shook his head at Lina. 'It doesn't even make sense. Why do you feel bound by it?'

Lina answered Martin with an unwavering look.

'I've got it! The whole village knew you before you were born. You were inside your mother.'

'Whoever it may be, father, it can't be Hari, since we've known him less than two weeks,' Lina replied, patting Martin's arm. 'We don't even know his real name.'

'Since you don't know me, you can't know that I didn't know you,' Hari said, staring at Lina.

Auntie nodded eagerly. She was at home with such thought patterns. Well worthy of her son.

'I mean,' said Hari, rubbing his stubbled cheek. 'I might have been born here and taken away as a small boy. That would explain how I speak the dialect.'

Auntie shook her head, dismayed at this denial of her own maternity. Her mouth opened then closed.

'Since Lina is 17, you would have been a very large small boy,' Martin came to Auntie's assistance without being aware of it. 'I would certainly have known you – and a little rascal, I'll be bound, almost as bad as this one.' The big man's arm shot out and seized Older Brother, who was rushing by chasing his sister. Martin held the boy above his head – giggling and making shrill protests.

'He meant something more profound than seeing me in the womb,' Lina smiled. 'It was the Dreamer.'

'Oh, now it's the Dreamer,' Martin rumbled, setting Older Brother down on his knee. 'What makes you think it was the Dreamer?'

'I know it was,' Lina looked into his eyes. 'His meaning will become clear when the time is right.'

The time was right for Auntie. She chuckled as her imagination laid bare one hidden meaning after another.

'The Great Shark will take you,' Martin growled.

'Martin!' Auntie gasped, clutching her crescent-moon crystal neck pendant. 'How could you say such a thing?'

'What is the Great Shark?' Hari asked.

'Don't you know what you'll bring down on yourself?' Auntie went on at Martin.

'Hasn't anyone told you about the Great Shark, my friend?' Martin turned to Hari. 'We-ell, once beyond a time,' he made the beckoning gesture of the professional story-tellers in the tea-houses of the cities.

Anna skipped across and jumped onto his knee opposite Older Brother.

Auntie put down the bowl she was still holding. She came and sat at the table, leaving the rest of the preparations for the evening meal to Katha.

'Every village on the Coast has its own festival. I think our Shark Festival is the most awesome, though not everyone will agree.' Martin nodded at the old lady.

Auntie leant her elbows on the table, shaking her head as much as to say: no reasonable person could deny that her island's festival was supreme; still, you can hardly expect logic from *them!*

'On her island they make a giant straw sandal every year.' Martin stretched his arms out wide. 'Twice this size.'

'It's as big as a boat, Humi. You can't have forgotten!'

Martin smiled. 'They take it out to sea, and abandon it so that the incoming tide washes it up on the next island, where ogres live.'

'They *swim* the great sandal out to the Island of Ogres, Humi. *We* can swim.' Auntie jutted out her jaw with the plain implication that *they* couldn't.

'Of course you can. Superbly too!' The strongest swimmer in Shark Bay agreed. 'The ogres see the colossal sandal. Fearing that giants live on her island, they never attack them and ravish their daughters, of whom Auntie was the loveliest.'

Auntie's mouth opened, toothlessly grinning at the compliment and at the intelligence of her islanders in outwitting the ogres. She might have gone on to make a scornful comparison with *them!* – but Katha put a pile of spoons in front of her. Leaning on the table to help herself up, Auntie started getting to her feet.

Lina rose, placed her hand lightly on Auntie's shoulder, took the spoons from the old lady, and set the table.

The evening meal would begin as soon as the strong, silent Ken returned from fishing.

'Once beyond a time,' Martin repeated, 'a beautiful pearl-diver lived in this bay, when it was a small bay, long before it grew into the big bay it is now.' Martin winked at both children and smiles spread across their faces.

'One sunset the pearl-diver dived down. She cut her last oyster away from the rock. Coming up for air, she kicked off the coral on the sea-bed. "Ouch! Kick someone your own size next time," said the coral.'

Anna giggled and snuggled up against Martin's chest.

'At that moment the pearl-diver noticed a huge Shark. She swam for the surface as fast as she could. The Shark lunged forward and caught her in its jaws. It carried her away into the ocean. However, it did not so much as scratch her skin between its teeth, which were like rows of sharp knives.

'The Shark raced to an undersea palace. Swimming through its golden gates, the Shark turned into a prince, carrying the pearl-diver in his arms. He set her down. Everyone made way for them as they walked through the jewelled rooms of the palace.

'They came before the King, who was seated on a ruby throne; it was sculpted out of one enormous Dragon Pearl. Both knelt. The prince asked the pearl-diver to marry him, but warned her that he could only sleep with her if she promised never to ask his name. She consented. The prince embraced her. The King smiled. The courtiers cheered, and the couple were married straightaway.

'However, on the seventh night, the pearl-diver asked the prince his name.' His eyes wide with alarm, Martin threw open his arms, toppling the children. He hugged them both to him. 'Instantly she found herself back in the bay, kicking off the coral and coming up for air. She thought it was one of those hallucinations that come to pretty girls: they see old men who tell them strange things, which they regard as holy oracles.' Martin looked at Lina, who rose from the table and went to ask Katha if she could help.

'The pearl-diver swam to the surface. The sun had set. All the others had gone home. She swam ashore, only to discover . . . ' the story-teller paused dramatically 'that not seven nights, but seven *years*, had passed. The village had given her up for dead long ago. They looked at her with suspicion since they had grown older, but she had not aged at all.'

Lina placed a pile of soup bowls in front of Martin, then sat down at the table again.

'Years passed. The pearl-diver remained as youthful as ever, but she never married. Maybe the Shark told her she would marry an old Dreamer who met her after she died.'

'Father, sometimes you can be really silly.'

'I know,' Martin admitted with a shrug.

Lina shook her head at Auntie, smiling.

Auntie nodded, munching. *Them!*

'The villagers drove the pearl-diver out of the village. They were frightened she was possessed. She went to live in a cave where Shark Rock is now, eating only the shells she took from the ocean.'

'An excellent diet,' Auntie said, champing. 'That explains how she kept her youth.'

'She even ate sea-cucumbers, which are repulsive.'

'So good for the eyes.' Auntie's jaw jutted out with the suggestion that *they* never learnt anything. 'I always eat them, Humi. I can see perfectly. I do all the sewing.'

'And the mushrooms she found in the fields,' the owner of the tea-house and chandler's shop added innocently.

Auntie tossed her head.

'One full moon there was a typhoon. It blew away the cliff where her cave was, leaving Shark Rock as it is now,' Martin continued. 'The villagers did not see the pearl-diver again. They thought the cliff had crashed down and buried her.

'During the next month the Shark attacked so many times that the villagers lived in terror, mourning for sons, daughters, husbands. To find the cause of all these killings, they sent two Elders to ask the Dreamer.'

'I thought the Dreamer was a real person?' Hari queried. Something stirred in his lost memory.

'As real as you are, Hari,' Martin said with a laugh.

'A Dreamer is He-who-is-awake, Humi,' Auntie explained, deeming that the Dreamer demanded a more penetrating analysis than *they* were capable of giving. 'Although we think we are awake and all this is real' – she tapped the table with her finger, which was so skeletal as to hint at another world – 'We are only part of his Dream.'

Hari was wondering what this meant, when Lina added, 'When we wake up, we become the Dreamer – and realize that we have been him all the time.'

'There you are, my friend! He is you, and you are him. That makes it a lot clearer,' Martin laughed. 'Be that as it may, the Dreamer told the two Elders that the Shark was avenging the death of his beloved pearl-diver, whom the villagers had banished to her lonely cave.' He gave his daughter a nod, 'Lina, you're the poet of the family.'

Lina recited the words of the oracle:

'The Shark is mourning for his bride.
He wants some comfort for his pride.
Placate him with a naked girl.
In moonlight let her dance and whirl.'

'The two Elders returned and informed the villagers. They were indignant. They rejected the remote Dreamer, whose oracle sounded indecent.

'The shark attacks increased. This time the Headman himself journeyed to the Dreamer. The Sage told him that the villagers had offended the Shark by their stubbornness. The Shark now demanded not just a naked dancer, but a virgin sacrifice.' Martin turned to Lina. 'How did the oracle run, my darling?'

'The Rock is like the Great Shark's face.
Go bind a virgin to that place.

At midnight with the tide's last breath
His grace will bring her life in death.'

'The villagers were even more hostile to this than before,'
Martin tapped Hari on the arm.

'I'm not surprised,' said Hari, hastily removing his eyes
from the poet of the family.

'Nevertheless, this time they did as the Dreamer said,
fearing that the Shark would destroy the village,' Martin
went on. 'The Dreamer had convinced them with his
description of the Rock, which he could not have seen with
mortal eyes. They chose a girl and tied her to Shark Rock
at full moon. Next morning her body had gone.

'The shark attacks stopped,' Martin said, giving the children a hug. 'And that is the origin of our Shark Festival
and why this village is called Shark Bay. Awesome, don't
you agree, terror of the octopus?'

Auntie shrugged.

'Amazing,' Hari agreed. 'But how did the Dreamer get
involved in the legend? If he is real . . .'

The door burst open.

The children jumped off Martin's lap and scampered to
their places.

So well prepared was Katha that Ken had hardly time to
stride across the room without a word, wash his hands and
sit down at the end of the table opposite his father, before
she placed an earthenware tureen in front of Martin.

'A great catch?' the head of the family asked. He took off
the lid and raised it high. Then he started to ladle out the
steaming stew.

'Success? A great catch?' Katha asked, bringing across a
bowl and setting it before Ken. He began eating without
reply, as the smell of oysters and clams filled the room.

4

Hari woke with a start. *Where am I?* He had no idea where he was.

A crow was cawing in the jacaranda tree outside his open window. Oh yes. Shark Bay. *Who am I?* he groaned.

What was that dream? He turned over, trying to go back to sleep and continue the dream. Hunters were chasing him and Lina across a desert. Lina saw a magic stone: a ruby the size of a watermelon. Hari knew their hunters would flee if he could harness the stone's occult power: he had to pronounce his own name. His mouth opened. His name was N . . . No! He couldn't remember!

The harsh cawing shattered his attempts to get back to sleep. *No!* He couldn't recall the rest of the dream.

Hari got up and walked to the window. The crow flew away with ungainly flaps of its black wings.

Ken had long since left home to go fishing. Martin was in the boatyard; Hari could hear him sawing.

Hari thought Tao might be waiting for him at the beach. He did not want to keep the fisherman waiting so, after washing, he hurried out of the house without stopping to eat. He saw Tao waiting beside the sunflowers outside the tea-house.

'Excuse me,' Tao averted his eyes. He bowed his head, and turned to walk to the beach, as if preceding a deity.

Hari started following Tao, when Older Brother rushed across and caught his hand, 'Come and look at my newt!'

Anna caught his other hand. 'Today . . . today . . .' She

smiled, unable to remember what was going to happen today.

After admiring the red belly of the newt, Hari walked with Tao to the beach.

Cocks were crowing. Cicadas were flying through the air, screaming their sex calls for a mere three days, after 17 years as nymphs under the ground.

Tao's boat was already in the water, anchored at the waves' edge. The fisherman bowed as Hari put his leg over the gunwale. Then Tao jumped in and began to row out to sea. He had erected a shelter behind the mast to give shade to the luck-bringer. Hari noticed that it resembled the family altar to the ancestors in Martin's home.

With the legend of the Great Shark fresh in his mind, Hari watched for a dorsal fin cutting through the bay.

Shark Rock looked more like a shark than ever, glinting in the dawn sun with its white 'teeth', caused by the drop-pings of a pair of cormorants that lived in a cleft exactly where the shark's eye would be.

The pearl-divers' heads vanished when they dived. A minute later they bobbed up, gasping for breath with a plaintive whistle. Is that Lina? Is she? *Is she?* Was she lost to him forever because of that girlish dream? She couldn't be!

Tao stopped rowing closer to the shore than usual; he raised his oars and looked at Hari. Receiving the god's tacit consent, he cast anchor.

'Not nets,' he said, beginning to bait his hook. 'Excuse me. No time. I forgot.'

'Can I?' Hari asked, putting his hand out and picking up a rod.

'No!' Tao snatched the rod out of Hari's hand. 'Excuse me.' He went red and he put down the rod. 'If he wishes to take his swim and call . . . ' his voice trailed away.

After swimming, Hari hauled himself in over the side of the boat with some agility but, compared with the prac-tised movements of the fisherman, he was so clumsy that Tao, thrilled with having caught six sea-bream already, burst out laughing.

'Excuse me!' Tao clapped his hand to his mouth, horrified. He had mocked his benefactor – after all his kindness. Thanks to his grace, Tao had been more successful than ever before in his life. What punishment would the god now visit upon him? Tao would be reduced to eating lugworms, not merely using them for bait. The fisherman bent over and looked down at the rudder to check that no seaweed was caught in it. Finally he dared turn and glance at Hari.

The god was smiling!

Tao grinned. It was a joke. Of course it was! With his celestial humour the stranger was teasing the mortal he had seen fit to befriend. The god could climb into the boat as easily as any fisherman on the Coast. He could fly if he wanted to!

Tao laughed happily and said aloud, 'Excuse me.'

During Hari's second swim, Tao made a rope ladder and left it hanging over the side.

With a modest cough, Tao pointed to the ladder, when Hari swam back to the boat. 'If he wishes to *climb* aboard . . .' He left the sentence incomplete. The implication that he knew that the god could fly was clear. It would be insulting if he explained to the god, who could read every thought that passed through his mind. 'Excuse me.'

For the first time – so far as he knew – Hari climbed up a rope ladder. His clumsiness provoked more laughter from Tao, delighted that the god should continue to jest with him.

'We must finish now. The tide will soon be turning,' said the fisherman. 'Excuse me.'

A breeze enabled them to sail back. Hari watched the seagulls wheeling and calling in the blue sky.

With one hand on the tiller, Tao fixed Hari with his gaze until the god looked his way. 'Excuse me.' Looking at the bilge, Tao scratched his neck. 'Today we feast. I go to worship the god.' He pointed to the brightly painted statue of the fisherman Dreamer on the cliff, which he would feed, putting a blue bib over its portly stomach.

'Tomorrow, after the high tide, we hunt for swordfish in the deep sea where the dolphins play. Excuse me. Will he . . . ?' Tao broke off. He knew that Hari, whom he deemed it proper to address in the third person, spoke to the dolphins. Maybe he had called them to carry him ashore when his ship sank. Tao wanted the god to command the dolphins to drive the swordfish towards his boat, but he did not dare ask directly. He prayed inwardly for help.

'Swordfish is my favourite. Excuse me. After the high tide at dawn. I will bring my brothers. It needs three. My luck is such I can command. Excuse me! *He* can command.' Tao's sunburnt face went purple at this gaffe. However, his luck (another seven bream during Hari's second swim – and 'sea-bream' rhymed with 'good luck' in the dialect) was making him bold. He looked at the man whose name no one knew. 'If the god would deign to attend the feast at my home . . .'

Hari frowned, having no idea what Tao was talking about.

'Excuse me.' Tao's face fell. He had been presumptious, asking the god to visit his own insignificant dwelling – and straight after claiming the divine grace to be his own luck. The god had rightly rebuked him. He combed his fingers through his hair. He must worship the statue like everyone else. He would double the size of the dish he had planned setting out before the Dreamer. He might have lost his luck by this temerity. He had caught 13 fish that morning. Unlucky! The gods were fickle. I mean, capricious. That is . . . Excuse me! He must draw closer to the open-hearted Martin, whom the god blessed by residing with him.

Tao pulled the boat up onto the edge of the sand and bowed low to Hari.

The stranger walked away. There was nothing more for him to do that morning. If sitting in Tao's boat, floating between sky and sea, wondering who on earth he was, could be said to be doing something.

Something prompted Hari to take the half-hidden track beyond Shark Rock that led up into the mountains. If he had not been shipwrecked, he must have come to Shark Bay by this trail.

Hari had to push through as the path got more over-grown. Creepers clung to him. Thorns scratched. Wild grass cut his ankles. He couldn't have come this way. He would have been bloody all over if he had been naked, as Martin had said. *How had he come to be naked?* And they said there had been no salt on his skin. That had puzzled them all. Had they stared at his naked body? *Had Lina?*

Hari came to a stony clearing. What he did next amazed him. He saw a scorpion raising its head at him, blocking the path and brandishing its deadly stinger. Hari stooped, picking up a stone. His arm whipped back, then shot forward with ferocious accuracy: the scorpion's head and pincers slithered into the bushes, the body squirmed on the path in a macabre dance. He had cut it in two.

It took Hari a moment to realize what he had done. He reeled, all but falling over. Where had he been all his life to learn such skill in throwing stones? Not by the sea, since he knew nothing about life between the tide lines. Then how could he swim so well? It must have been in a river. *That dream!* The ruby stone. A flash lit the cavern of his mind. He'd caught something! He and Lina. A river in the desert. No! It was slipping away. Sweat broke out all over his body.

The man with no memory started clambering round to the next village, clinging to the cliff as precariously as the tiger-lilies. Crags jutted out into the sea with sheer drops and shell-encrusted overhangs. In places he had to swim, climbing back onto rocks storm-worn into jagged edges. Waves rustled round the shore. One wave, forced by the rocks into a fissure, knocked him off his feet. In rough weather the sea would be lethal.

Hari saw it would take him days to get to the next village. He clambered back along the cliff to Shark Bay.

The tide was ebbing. The lower jaw of Shark Rock gleamed, its black granite fanging out of the sea.

Looking for Lina, Hari noticed with surprise that the pearl-divers had all gone home. He saw only one boat in the sea. All the rest had been drawn up on the sand. Something else was wrong. The sun dried the shirt on his back before he realized what it was. No nets! He had never seen the beach without some nets hanging out to dry, reeking of fish. The bamboo poles had vanished too.

Were they preparing for a typhoon? He looked up. It seemed impossible. There wasn't a cloud in the sky. Only the gulls crying and the sea-hawks circling. But Auntie had told him how suddenly typhoons blew up.

Hari climbed the cliff up to the pine tree above Shark Rock. He sat down on one of the roots writhing above the rocky soil and looked across the bay. He could not see the cork buoys of the nets that were placed across the routes taken by the fish. Even the red flags signalling lobster pots had disappeared. What was going on?

A yellow butterfly fluttered round him, inscribing arabesques on the sultry air before it came to rest on the pine root, wings panting. Its wings stopped moving. The butterfly fell down the side of the root like a child falling over a cliff. It lay there inert.

Hari picked it up. It was dead! He marvelled at its wings. If he had wings and in proportion, they would be bigger than the pine tree. He could fly over the mountains. Caging the butterfly in his hand, Hari carried it home. He would give it to Lina.

He saw no one in the village as he walked through the lanes. It was so hot that the dogs did not bark, but lay in the shade, tongues hanging out, slavering. Only the blue-tailed lizards moved – darting to their holes like arrows of cobalt as the human passed.

Hari found the tea-house deserted, apart from the swallows in their mud nest on the cedar beam. Two fledglings peeped out, cheeping when he approached, hoping for food.

Hari walked through to the family room. He discovered them all sitting round such a mass of dishes that he could hardly see the table.

'Ah, there you are, hunter of the octopus! Just in time,' Martin called out. 'We were going to start without you. Where have you been? Come on. Sit down.' He waved his arm to the place at his side.

Grinning, Tao moved over to make room for the god. Tao had asked Martin if he might join them. 'The more the merrier! Bring your wife!' Martin replied. But the fisherman had not been sure about that. His wife's scepticism troubled him. She had snorted when he said, 'The dolphins sing to him.'

Tao had brought the two biggest bream he had caught that morning, but he attributed the god's delay in coming to his own presumption. He bowed his head until his forehead touched the table. His unruly hair went into a plate of fish.

Katha prodded him in the ribs, 'Sit up, Tao!'

'You had no breakfast, Humi,' Auntie wagged a finger at Hari.

'Naughty boy! You'll only live to 99!' Martin laughed. 'Let the Feast begin!'

Katha and Lina and Auntie had been working together all morning, singing (one of them making references to *them!* and the superiority of a certain island), preparing seaweed soup, amberjack in a sweet sauce, wrasse in a sour sauce, grilled eel with a soya sauce, and rice shaped into cubes, topped with slices of raw squid and octopus, abalone and scallop – and sea-urchin, Lina's favourite, tasting of cool ocean caverns.

Now, washed, combed and in clean clothes, Older Brother, the future head of the family, casting a look of scorn at his sister, lit sticks of incense before the memorial tablets of

41

the ancestors on the family altar.

Then he placed tiny brass bowls of rice before the black and gold tablets; the ancestors would partake of the spiritual essence, leaving the mortal remnant to their descendants. The family stood behind Older Brother, bowing – except for Anna, who looked up at the ceiling until Katha pushed her head down.

Auntie shook her head, grumbling and comparing *them* with the little girls on her island.

'Sit down! Eat, drink and be merry, for to . . . to make up for lost time. Sit down for Heaven's sake!' As Hari sat down beside him, the boatbuilder asked, 'And what have you been up to this fine morning? Have you been hunting the octopus, or have you found yourself?'

'Not quite,' Hari smiled, opening his hand. 'But I found this. It was at the pine tree by Shark Rock. I brought it to give . . .'

He broke off. Their reactions were utterly different from what he expected. They all craned forward to see. Then they jerked back with horror, glaring at the stranger.

'What's the matter?' Hari recoiled. The hostile silence was worse than shouts of rage. 'What have I done?'

'What have you done?' Martin echoed, his face going white as he stared at the dead butterfly. 'You've sealed her fate. That's what you've done.'

'Father,' said Lina.

Ken muttered to Katha, who was sitting at his side.

With a look of exasperation she jumped up, snatched the butterfly out of Hari's hand and rushed out of the house.

'Don't be so superstitious, father,' said Lina. 'I thought you were supposed to be above such things.'

Martin looked at her, then sat up erect, 'Yes, of course. You're right, my darling. What does it matter? Here! Have something to drink, stranger.' The big man's face was still pale, however. His hand shook when he passed Hari a tiny cup, then raised the gourd-shaped jar of warm rice wine.

'What have I done?' Pain pressed in on Hari's chest. 'I

didn't mean to offend you.'

'Of course you didn't. It's just an idle superstition, as Lina says.' Martin tilted the wine jar towards Hari, who held out the handleless cup while Martin filled it. Hari drank, then raised the cup for a refill, which he put down on the table.

'*We* call that butterfly "golden soul", Humi. That is its proper name. But *they* call it "virgin's soul",' Auntie explained, bringing across the rice cakes she had been toasting; she had burnt them while looking protectively at her boy. '*They* consider that bringing its dead body into the house is bad fortune.' Her tone declared that in the battle she saw coming, she would be on Humi's side whatever *they* said.

'Even if you didn't know its name,' Martin said in a voice intended to be detached, folding his arms, 'It was thoughtless to bring a dead body into the house today.'

'Why?' Hari asked. He looked at Lina. 'What's special about today?'

'What's special about today?' Martin brought his fist down with a crash that made the plates on the table clatter. 'We told you about the Shark Festival last night. Don't you understand anything? Tonight one of the girls in our village has got to die.'

'*Die!* Got to die! You don't mean? That's real?' Hari choked. 'That tale about the shark prince and undersea palace?'

'Of course it is,' Martin glared at him.

'How can it be?' Hari protested. 'I thought it was a fairy story, like Auntie's island with the ogres and giants.'

Auntie scowled at him. 'Martin spoke like that to ward off bad luck, Humi. Speaking of things can bring on the very fate we want to avoid.' She sucked her gums.

Katha returned. Glancing at the table to see nothing was wanting, she walked to the sink and washed her hands.

'Can we forget it now?' Lina asked.

'How can we forget it?' Martin turned on Hari. 'Tonight one of the girls in Shark Bay is going to be sacrificed to the Great Shark.'

'I don't believe it!' Hari's mouth fell open. 'A living girl? Sacrificed to a shark?'

Seeing the shock on Hari's face, Martin explained. 'That is why most girls get engaged as soon as they are 13. And why I get annoyed with Lina for refusing to marry. Today will be the fifth time she offers herself at the Betrothal Ceremony.'

'Betrothal Ceremony? Fifth time?' Hari's throat went dry. He looked at Lina with disbelief. 'Lina? *Lina?* offers herself to be married to a *shark?*'

'All the girls are offered to the Great Shark when they reach puberty,' Martin growled. 'There's no reason why Lina should be an exception.'

There's every reason in the world, Hari wanted to yell.

'Don't look like that,' Lina said to Hari.

Hari's face was twisted with confusion. 'She must be killed at once if she's thrown to this Shark.'

'That is when it begins,' Lina murmured.

'Their lives are not confined to this incarnation, Humi.'

'Nor their loves,' Lina agreed, adding with a smile at her father, 'Though I think the Great Shark would have chosen me by now if he'd been interested.'

'Yes. He's had enough opportunities. You may be safe.' Martin stretched out for a couple of slivers of raw fish. He dipped them into a sauce and popped them into his mouth, pushing the plate towards Hari. Mouth full, he added, 'He prefers them young.'

'That's better, father,' Lina tilted the wine jar towards him. 'The lofty equanimity we expect of you.'

Martin quaffed his wine, held the tiny cup out for a refill and drank that immediately. Lina filled the cup again. Martin swallowed the wine in one. Lina filled the cup again – and Martin set it down on the table.

Despite its gruesome ending, the day was a festival and

the owner of the tea-house liked to see his family enjoying themselves. Martin encouraged everyone to eat up and drink up. From time to time he left his place at the head of the table, angling the wine jar like a sail before a breeze. He filled the wine cups so enthusiastically that Katha was having trouble keeping the jar filled with freshly warmed rice wine.

Tao, bowing his head, and Katha also, filled Hari's wine cup whenever they saw it empty.

'Don't drink any more once you feel the warmth in your toes, Humi. You know how it takes you,' Auntie cautioned, digging her fingers into his arm. She pushed a piece of sea-cucumber into his mouth. 'Eat this. So good for the eyes.'

'And now, the moment we've been waiting for. The riches of the ocean! The feast that only the legendary hunter of the octopus could have trapped!' Martin boomed – and the warmth of the wine must surely have risen to his ankles. 'Katha! Bring it to Hari! A dish for the gods!'

Tao grinned: they openly admitted that the stranger was an incarnation of the Dreamer.

Katha hurried to the stove, while Martin drummed on the table with both hands, looking from one to another. She returned and set a covered bowl in the centre of the table.

'Open it, mightiest of hunters!' said Martin.

Hari, who was having difficulty chewing the rubbery sea-cucumber, stretched across and took off the lid – revealing a clear soup: in it, tentacles of octopus.

Martin burst out laughing. Hari looked bewildered, but Martin's laughter was so good-natured that Hari laughed too. Then they were all laughing, laughing till it hurt. Except for Ken and Tao. Tao had a troubled expression on his face. It was not right to mock the god. 'It was not my idea. Excuse me.' His forehead touched the table penitently.

Katha caught his tangled hair and pulled back his head: 'You'd better not have any more to drink, Tao.'

'A song! A song from everyone!' Martin called, pushing

a whole sea-bream in front of Hari and pouring lashings of sauce over it. 'A party's not a party without a song. Ken, you sing first.'

Ken, who did not drink, did not appear to hear his father. He helped himself to the octopus soup.

'Drink up, mighty hunter. You've hardly wet your whistle.'

'Just a minute,' said Hari, rising to his feet unsteadily.

'Call of nature?' Martin asked.

'Something like that,' Hari smiled. He wanted to go outside and spit out the rubbery sea-cucumber, which he couldn't chew and wouldn't swallow.

'Feel five years younger?' Martin welcomed Hari back, passing him a plate of ocean bonito, sliced on a bed of shredded radish and parsley.

'At least.'

'Plenty of room now. Drink up.'

Martin sang first: a love song charged with an emotion that surprised the stranger.

Auntie called upon Hari to join her in singing the song of their island: 'Don't say you can't, Humi!' It was the song the women sang at their spinning wheels, praying for calm seas and for their men to return in safety.

Hari followed as best he could, while tears welled up in Auntie's eyes.

'Well sung, terror of the octopus!' Martin clapped his hands. 'Drink up!'

However, Auntie frowned: 'You stubborn boy, just because it's the women's song!'

'Here!' Ken beckoned Older Brother. The little boy somersaulted across to his father, then stood beside him. Ken, Tao (gazing at the god) and Older Brother then sang the fishing song of Shark Bay.

Lina sang next.

Hari was thrilled by the purity of her voice as she sang the rice-planting song. He saw the vivid green of the paddy fields during the monsoon, when the women, backs

46

bent, sowed the emerald thread of the queen of the fields.

Anna, with a sunflower in her hair, sat in Lina's lap, eating a peach; its juice was running down her chin and onto her best frock.

'Do you hear that?' Martin called, raising both immense arms for hush. The swallows were chirruping from their nest in the tea-house. 'They are joining in with their own song.' He stood up. 'Come on, everyone. We'll give them a proper hearing.'

They all had to go into the tea-house and watch the two fledglings peering out of their nest on the cedar beam, cheeping as their parents flitted back and forth to feed them.

Hari walked carefully. The warmth of the rice wine had passed his ankles.

'Marvellous! In a few days they'll be able to fly.' Martin put his arm round Hari's shoulder and led him back to the family room.

Hari hiccupped. As Martin released him, he fell onto his chair, almost knocking it over.

Tao howled with laughter at the god's jest – until he caught a look from Katha. 'Excuse me.'

Auntie gave Humi a reproving look. She glared at his wine cup and wagged her finger. It was impossible, but Hari had the feeling that he knew Auntie from before, from *where?*

'Your turn now, Katha,' Martin called.

Ken had to catch Katha by the arm as she bustled about removing empty dishes and seeing that everyone had fruit. Her protests came to an end when Ken's hand landed on her buttock.

Katha sang the nursery song she sang to the children, when they went to bed: 'How you wax, Grandpa Moon, how you wax! How you wane, Granny Moon, how you wane!'

How right Katha is, Hari thought, rubbing his unshaven cheek, two weeks' growth prickling in the heat. It meant something, that tickle. What is it Katha sings? The moon. It wax and grax . . . then it . . . wanes and granes. Difficult language to get your tongue round. Own dialect much . . . shimpler. If only I could remember what it was. Who is Hari? Why am he? Full moon tonight. Must move on. Don't want to leave here, leave her. Can't. Must.

Lina stood up, 'It's time to go.'

Yes must go. Must go. In time. Got to go somewhere? There. Where to?

'We have plenty of time. All the time in the world. Sit down, my darling,' said Martin. 'That priest is always late. Learnt the trick from his father. Sit down.'

Lina did not sit down. She looked at her father. 'We must leave now for the Betrothal Ceremony.'

And the rosy world which Hari had been enjoying, whose warmth had risen to his knees and glowed in his head, was eclipsed by the nightmare of the Shark Sacrifice. His throat went dry. It could be Lina. Oh no! It couldn't be Lina!

'Are you all right, hunter of the octopus?' Martin put his hand on Hari's shoulder. 'Fit to walk to the Temple?'

Hari stood up – and fell down, knocking over his chair.

'Humi!'

Tao burst out laughing – then clapped his hand over his mouth.

Martin and Auntie helped Hari up. He found himself staring at the crescent-moon crystal at Auntie's neck. It looked like a leaping shark. He had seen her before. He knew it!

5

'God is One. Conceptions of God are many. The gods men worship are all masks of the Dreamer.'

Such was the legend over the double doors of the Temple, the only tiled building in the village. High in the amphitheatre of hills, it enjoyed a godlike view of the bay – the yellow tiles of its roof standing out against the wooded hillside.

Gigantic waves had destroyed the Old Temple near the beach when the typhoon that drowned Auntie's husband struck Shark Bay. The villagers had piously levelled the ground between great camphor trees in the hills, then built the new Temple, planting camellia trees beside it. With their deep roots, camellias formed the best wind-break against typhoons.

A jade statue on the altar dominated the interior of the Temple. It depicted the Dreamer as a young man, sitting cross-legged in the lotus position.

The inscription over the Temple doors quoted the words of this great soul, who had realized his identity with the Illimitable, but his followers did not understand his teachings, such as: 'The Kingdom of the Dreamer is within you.' They claimed that *this* Dreamer was the *only* Son of God.

It was almost midday when Martin led his family out of the tea-house, past the sunflowers, and into the kaleidoscope of bougainvillaea, throwing orange and scarlet shadows across the lane. Morning glories, which changed colour from deep-sea-blue at midday to magenta at sunset, arched up to garland the thatched roofs of the houses.

The boatbuilder was carrying two watermelons, his offering to the Dreamer. Ken, Tao and Hari each carried a pumpkin, and the women were taking chrysanthemums, gladioli and hollyhocks.

They were all sweating as they left the shaded lanes of the village and walked into the harsh sunlight – even the children, whom Martin held back to Auntie's pace.

Beneath a fig tree laden with purple fruit, most of which had been pecked open by the birds, Older Brother found a beetle, its shards glaring green-gold. He grabbed it and thrust it down Anna's blouse, which Katha had changed after she had finished eating. Anna screamed, sending flying the ladybird on her thumb.

Katha's scolding did not remove the smirk from Older Brother's face, so she called out, 'Father.'

Putting his pumpkin under one arm, Ken caught the little boy by the ear: 'Today is the Festival. Behave.' The look he gave his son made Older Brother burst into tears.

'There we are!' Martin nodded at the Temple as they walked across the bridge. 'Shark Bay's earthly home for the Dreamer.'

'Excuse me,' said Tao, looking at the man called Hari.

Other villagers, bearing offerings, were walking along the dusty road to the Temple, past allotments where vegetables were growing. Beyond them were the rice fields.

The whole village was going to the Ceremony, apart from the bedridden, known as 'Waking Dreamers', who waited, often with a tide mark of saliva round the mouth, for the summons to join their ancestors on the family altar.

'I don't know the difference between the Dreamer and God,' said Hari, as they walked along the track.

'If you truly knew, you would be the Dreamer, Humi.'

'My understanding, which is probably half-baked, is that the Dreamer is one who has realized the union of his soul with God, the One that is All,' Martin replied. 'Any man, who discovers his own soul, is the Dreamer.'

50

'Or woman,' said Auntie with a scowl. *Them!*

'I said it was half-baked,' Martin laughed, looking at Lina. She had given Auntie her arm and was singing softly. She smiled at her father.

'He has made the journey into the Now – only to discover he has been here all the time,' Hari said, glancing at Lina. She looked at the aubergine plants they were passing.

'What's that?' Martin exclaimed.

'I don't know!' Hari looked startled. *Who am I?*

'What matters is what you experience, not what you believe,' said Martin, walking past another vegetable plot, where soya beans were growing. 'Halcyon told me, "DOGMA is the opposite of Truth: AM GOD." Do you get it? Like ANIL, Lina backwards.' Martin grimaced.

Lina. Hari sighed. Lina, Lina, *Lina!* What an enigma she was! She was walking as cheerfully to this Betrothal Ceremony as if to a picnic, and helping Auntie. Yet it might be her execution. Who could reach her heart?

Before they began to walk up the hill, Auntie stopped to rest in the shade of a banana palm, digging her fingers into Lina's arm. Stooped and puffing, the old lady glared, like a fisherman staring into rough seas, at the road winding through an olive grove and up to the Temple. Stone lanterns stood on either side of the road, which was lined with palm trees. The Temple roof's yellow tiles glinted in the sunshine.

The most devout had already assembled in the Temple courtyard, where the Betrothal Ceremony would take place. They were wearing rice-straw hats and carrying waxed paper parasols. They stood sweating in the heat, mopping their faces with small towels.

Seagulls were mewing in the sky overhead.

Martin and his family were amongst the last to arrive and place their offerings before the jade statue of the Dreamer.

'Wake Dreamer!' the fisherfolk greeted the boatbuilder with broad smiles. 'Hot, isn't it?'

They chatted together, laughing more loudly than usual, for the warmth of the wine had risen to where the fishermen strapped sea-knives to their bulging calves. Some heads were beginning to ache, however, as the rosy glow wore off and the sun blazed down on the courtyard.

Danny staggered across to Martin, drooling, 'Huynh! Today, Sharsa. Sharcrify. Not Lina! Huynh-Hunh?'

'Certainly not, Danny-Dan!' said Martin, putting his arm round Danny's shoulders. 'Certainly not!'

Danny smiled up at the big man, then shambled to Hari and gawked into his face. 'Hunh. Stranger. Mou-huhn-tains. Down come.' Mouth open, Danny's head angled up at the sky, as if a cloud had been Hari's method of transport.

Flinging away the grasshopper he had caught, Older Brother cartwheeled across the courtyard to the Temple pond, where his friends were trying to stroke the carp.

Formerly, the children had been able to play as they liked in the Temple grounds, but the present priest had put a stop to that on instructions from a higher authority. His wife regarded the Temple as her own private property. Rita shouted at children who came to play; she cuffed any boys who went near the pond. But at the Shark Festival, she could do nothing. Her thin lips pursed, she trembled with rage. The boys *touched* her carp.

Anna skipped across to join the other little girls, who were blowing bubbles and running after the rainbow worlds, happy as if it was a holiday. As it was: Shark Bay's annual holy day. It was a compulsory feast too: from the low tide of midday till high tide next sunrise, no one was allowed to enter the sea and sully the Shark's union with his Bride.

This menacing undercurrent betrayed the joy of the Festival. The villagers all knew that when the full moon was at its height, the Shark would tear one of their relatives to pieces – and foul the sea with human blood. Although their minds accepted that it was a divine honour if the Shark chose his Bride from their home, their hearts felt as if he had ripped a limb away from their family.

The Betrothal Ceremony was supposed to begin when the sun was at its zenith – in contrast to the torchlit Marriage to the Shark when the tide ebbed at midnight.

'I don't know how much longer that priest is going to make us endure this heat,' Martin said to Hari. They were standing in the shade of a camphor tree. Martin wiped his forehead with a coloured handkerchief. 'I feel like a jellyfish washed up on the beach.'

'You look a bit like one too, father,' Lina's smiling voice came from behind them.

'Do I? Ha!' Martin laughed, his broad shoulders turning. 'And you look all right.'

Hari did not turn round to look at the girl he loved in case he gave himself away again, this time in public.

A mournful peal came from the bronze Temple bell. It brought the chatter to a birdlike twitter. A second peal – and there was silence. The bell tolled out five more times: once for each of the seven psychic centres of the body.

The double doors of the Temple opened. The shaven-headed priest walked out onto the veranda. Clasping his hands over his paunch, the priest stood at the top of the wooden steps and stared out at Shark Rock.

Hari gaped at the luxury of the priest's robes: the finest orange silk with lotuses embroidered in silver thread.

All looked expectantly at Lovegod.

Despite being the son of the village priest, he had been genuinely interested in 'the Way'. The young man had chosen his religious name, Lovegod, as his highest aspiration when he went to theological college. There he had lost hope. He had expected to learn how to pray; they had taught him what theologians said about prayer. He had hoped to realize the soul within; they had instructed him in rituals. 'It's regurgitated book knowledge,' said one of his peers, leaving in disgust. Lovegod had not had the courage to quit.

Facing the ocean, the priest bowed to Shark Rock. He turned round and bowed towards the jade statue inside the Temple. Then he intoned the legend of the Dreamer that gave rise to the Name of the Year in the 12-year cycle. This was the Year of the Deer:

A tribe of hunters in the desert wide
Had as their Dreamer, master, soul and guide,
A man of wisdom, power and boundless love.
He walked on earth, his heart in Heaven above.
This Dreamer, richer far than any lord,
Renounced the world by which he was adored.
In perfect solitude he found a cave:
To meditate on God his life he gave.
The nomad hunters stoned a pregnant deer,
Which hobbled half-dead to the lonely seer.
Her liquid eyes on his, with her last breath,
She bore a fawn. He called it 'Life-in-death'.
This holy man, who'd given up the world,
Adored the fawn that in his arms lay curled.
He lavished on the deer the sacred love
He'd kept for Truth within, the soul above.
The hermit died. His last thought on this earth
Was of the deer. And such was his rebirth.

Hari's spine tingled. The desert! That dream! What was it? Lina? Hunters? *Who?* His head pounded. Where did he have to go? If only he could recall something. In a month? *Why?*

The priest walked down the seven Temple steps to the bronze incense bowl in the centre of the courtyard; the sun shone on his shaven head and black clogs.

In twelve bunches of nine, Lovegod lit 108 incense sticks, standing them in the soft ash. A bronze dragon was mounted over the bowl. Smoke billowed out of its mouth. The villagers stared, trying to discover meaning in the phantoms of the 'dragon's breath'.

The priest bowed again towards Shark Rock. Then he turned to the Temple and called in his sonorous voice, 'Come!'

The drum inside the Temple boomed six times, its echoes carrying up into the wooded hillsides.

Six frightened girls edged out of the Temple. Each girl seemed to be trying to hide behind the virgin in front of her.

Hari's heart twisted when he saw her. He had thought she was still behind him and Martin with the rest of the family. He had avoided looking round. But she had slipped away at the first peal of the Temple bell. Lina stood last in the line.

Naked, apart from the white briefs worn by the pearl-divers, the six girls walked fearfully down the wooden steps. One girl looked as if she would fall if she did not hold onto the handrail. Everyone stood back as the girls formed a semi-circle in front of the incense bowl.

On his back the priest carried a silk quiver; in it there were six irises, upside down. Only one had a head. The girl who chose it was the Betrothed of the Shark.

On orders from his wife, Lovegod avoided looking at the girls' breasts. He waved his fan at the incense till it glowed, then he recited the prayer, which he knew by heart.

The villagers were silent, their faces showing their anxiety as the priest stopped speaking and the Betrothal Ceremony reached its climax.

A shudder snaked through the crowd when Lovegod spun round. He snatched the quiver from his back. With a sharklike lunge he thrust it at the youngest virgin, who chose first since they drew the lots in order of age.

The 13-year-old had to make a choice on which her life depended. Sweat was running down her neck. The priest held the quiver high above her head, so she could not see into it. She wiped her forehead with the back of her hand.

She stood on tiptoe, and reached up to withdraw the iris that meant life or death.

Lovegod and his wife had selected and cut the irises with meticulous care, so that they were all the same length, though only one had a flower at the end of its stalk.

The girl drew out one iris. Her lips parted, showing her teeth in a smile, as she caught sight of the iris she had picked. It was headless.

The crowd gasped.

Palms slippery, each of the girls in turn took an iris, upside-down, out of the quiver.

Schooled by his wife, Lovegod looked right over the girls' heads, but his breath was uneven. His pot-belly bulged and his silk robes brushed against the girls' sun-warm bodies.

Each of the next three girls withdrew a headless iris. When she saw it, she hunched her shoulders, putting her hand to her mouth to try to suppress laughs of relief.

Each time the crowd gasped; then another breathless silence followed as the next virgin made her choice.

The silence was tenser than ever when the fifth virgin, a girl with enormous breasts, approached to take her iris. It had to be her or Lina, who, as the oldest, came last. The Temple grounds were silent. Even the cicadas stopped screaming.

Hari felt his stomach contracting. Until Lina had walked out of the Temple, naked and ready to die, it had all been as remote as his own death, despite Martin's explanations. With horror the stranger saw it happening in front of him. One of these six girls was going to be a human sacrifice. Remorselessly the possibility was increasing that it would be Lina. He couldn't believe it! Sweat broke out on his forehead.

The fifth girl wiped the sweat from her neck and dried her hands on her white briefs. Trembling, she stretched up and drew an iris out of the quiver.

Lovegod jerked back so as not to touch the swaying

bosom. The green stem slipped out of her hand. Reddening, Lovegod snatched a glance at his wife.

Sweat poured down between the girls' breasts. Her breathing was staccato. She grasped at the iris again and pulled it out of the quiver. It was headless. She jumped into the air, stifling a shout of joy. She dropped the iris and put both hands to her breasts, squeezing them to control herself, but she could not help baring her teeth in laughter.

The fisherfolk murmured, pointing at Lina. Some glanced at Martin.

To Hari's surprise he saw a smile on Lina's face as she waited for Lovegod to come before her.

Lina slid her hand into the quiver. The others watched with mouths open. It had to be the fatal iris, since the other girls had taken all the headless stems, but Lina had to complete the ritual.

On one occasion, when all the irises but one had been taken, when something supernatural had happened: the last stem had had no flower either. The relief of the other girls and their families had been premature – and the whole ceremony, supervised by the Headman, had had to begin again. The Shark had intervened!

'It still might not happen,' Martin breathed. 'If only she had said "Yes" last night.'

Last night! How long ago it seemed. Hari held his breath.

Lina did not look at the stem as she withdrew her hand with a flourish. She held the iris at arm's length above her head for all to see. The indigo standards of the iris suggested the opening jaws of . . .

'The Great Shark has chosen!' the priest's resonant voice declared.

Hari gasped.

Veins stood out on Martin's forehead, but despite the pain in his heart he remained silent like the other villagers – more silent, in fact, for they were muttering, clearing their throats, shifting their feet. Martin stood still as a mighty cedar.

A crow flew overhead, cawing.

'Lina, only daughter of Martin,' Lovegod intoned, taking the iris out of Lina's hand and bowing low towards the ocean and Shark Rock. 'Follow me.'

In the solemn manner imposed by his black clogs, the priest marched back into the Temple. The sun glinted off his shaven head.

Lina followed Lovegod. She did not turn to wave good-bye or give one last look to her loved ones. She was not allowed to. Now she belonged to the Shark. The Chosen Virgin was isolated from the village, even from her own family.

From now on, in any conversation with the priest, the Shark's Betrothed would use the 'I' form of married women – and Lovegod had to address her by the formal 'you', even though he had called Lina 'thou' all her life.

The Temple doors closed behind them.

Otherworldly peals, as the priest's wife tolled the bronze Temple bell, announced that the Betrothal Ceremony was over. The Shark had selected his Bride. She had nine hours to prepare for his fatal embrace at midnight.

6

With hands to their mouths to silence screams of hysteria, the five virgins ran to their families as soon as they heard the bell tolling. They hurled themselves into hugs they would normally have found unbearably smothering.

Many people in the Temple courtyard were looking at Martin. Sometimes, after the Betrothal, the family of the victim would try to abolish the 'barbarous' custom. The fisherfolk feared this, because painful experience had shown that when the family was influential enough to have the Sacrifice abandoned, the Shark's retaliation had been pitiless, attacking fishermen and pearl-divers throughout the year.

The owner of the tea-house might wish to save his daughter – and plunge Shark Bay into a year of terror. They all knew how Martin adored Lina. The most popular man in the village had loved his wife so much that he had refused all proposals of a second marriage, explaining gallantly, 'I already have a woman living with me, her heart bright with the mature beauty of the maple in autumn.' Auntie had had more difficulty in recognizing herself from this description than when, standing under the palm trees by the well, she had overheard Rita criticizing 'that withered nettle'. Would Martin's love for his daughter wreck the village?

'And I thought her turn would never come!' the boat-builder called out with an attempt to smile, catching the eye of Rama the Headman, a silver-haired giant who bore himself with a kindly authority.

The villagers sighed with relief. Women looked with gratitude towards Lina's father. Fishermen nodded admiringly at each other. How noble of Martin to accept his tragedy like that. Always others before himself.

Martin gave Auntie his arm and was holding his head high, hiding his pain, which was all the more difficult because of the looks of sympathy.

The distinguished-looking Headman walked across and put his hand on Martin's shoulder. Big Rama stood six foot six, with a 54-inch chest and waist. He walked down the hill with his friend.

Ken and Katha were stooping, eyes glazed, pulling the children by the hand. Older Brother did not know what had happened, but he sensed it was a catastrophe. He let go of a cicada he had caught and stamped on it. Anna began crying.

Tao was walking woodenly, glancing at the god.

Hari's head ached. He wanted to do something. To make them stop it. To rescue Lina and escape. To wake up from this nightmare. Hari was well-built, but he couldn't take on the whole village. The men might not be accustomed to physical combat, but they were used to fighting the sea and its creatures. If Martin himself, or the giant Headman, did not lay Hari out cold with one blow, any of the fishermen with their bulging muscles could knock the stranger flat, without drawing their sea-knives. There was nothing he could do. One man against the mass will. And an outsider. He felt helpless in the face of this inexorable, meaningless . . .

'Think of all the girls who died to make the sea safe for others, Humi.' Hari felt a scrawny hand on his arm. It was all he could do to stop himself wrenching his arm away and yelling at her.

'One year they sacrificed a goat. The year we came here – if only we hadn't. You've forgotten it now, of course, like everything else, Humi.' Her back bent painfully, Auntie clutched Hari's arm for support.

'The Shark must have smelt the goat because it did not enter the bay. That year 52 people were killed by shark attacks. One a week. The Shark even knocked men out of their boats. A smell spread through the village, Humi. It was the smell of fear. Since then they have forbidden goats in Shark Bay. We live here now, so we must put the village before our own preferences.'

They reached the tea-house. Katha carried Anna, and Ken pushed Older Brother inside.

Standing by the sunflowers, Martin was shaking the hand of Big Rama. The Headman had walked all the way with Martin, saying nothing, but being there in a supportive silence, his hair tidy and his beard neatly trimmed.

'Curse this Shark!' Hari blurted out. 'How can it be the same one? How can it know when to come? It doesn't make sense. Why don't you do something?'

'I know you loved her, my friend. And I should have been glad to see you marry her,' said Martin, letting go of the Headman's hand and stepping forward to put his hand on Hari's shoulder. 'But we have to bow to the will of the Dreamer. Come to the boatyard. We'll chop . . .'

'What Dreamer? They're going to *kill* her! How can you accept that without a fight?' Hari yelled, backing away. In his own pain the stranger did not consider Martin's grief. He did not see Auntie blinking at him, two tears running down her cheeks.

'Superstitious fools!' Hari turned and ran away. He ran to the beach and across the burning sands to the pine tree above Shark Rock.

A black cormorant flew away with swift wingbeats, scudding low over the water.

Hari climbed up into the pine tree with angry pulls. He moved out along a branch, shaking with despair. He was over the sea. Beneath the overhang the incoming tide was swallowing the lower jaw. The waves rippled pleasantly, but they sounded ominous to Hari. The granite rock looked bloodstained. Waves licked the fang. He leant over.

61

He slipped!

He caught a branch, saving himself. A spasm of vertigo shot from his knees into his groin. He snorted. Who would care if he fell to his death? What was he but some stranger found on the beach? Who cared if he lived or died? Life had no meaning. Why should the woman he loved be murdered by some killer Shark? Hari shuddered at the thought of Lina's supple body being slashed by the Shark's jaws. And only this morning, sitting under this pine tree, he had thought it a fairy tale.

Hari saw a fisherman walking down to the beach.

Rolling up his trousers, the man waded to the only boat in the sea. He vaulted over the side, weighed anchor and began rowing towards Shark Rock. A raft floated along in the wake of the boat.

Tonight the Bridal Palanquin, graceful as a black swan, would carry the Bride to her Bridegroom. For the Chosen Virgin was not thrown to the Shark from the top of Shark Rock, as Hari had imagined. She was bestowed upon her divine lord in a dignified ceremony.

The fisherman was rehearsing for the consummation of the wedding, when he had to row the Palanquin out to Shark Rock and leave the Bride for the Great Shark. He was the only man allowed into the sea – to check the currents, which varied from day to day. Tonight no mistake would be tolerated.

The sun danced off the blue, silver-spangled sea onto the hull of the boat. The fisherman turned to look at Shark Rock, letting go of an oar to run his hand through his hair. It was Tao. He had removed the shelter from behind the mast, but Hari felt he should have recognized the fisherman sooner, knowing Tao and his boat as well as he did.

He and Tao would rescue Lina! Hari was just about to shout, 'Tao! Up here!' when he stopped himself. What's the point, he muttered to himself. Tao was one of *them*. His wife was the priest's wife's sister. He was helping to murder Lina.

With two anchors Tao secured the raft in the jaws of Shark Rock, right under Hari. He untied the tow rope and rowed away, looking back at the raft with satisfaction. Tonight it would carry the Palanquin. Tao rowed back to the raft, re-tied the tow rope, weighed the anchors, and began to row back to the shore.

The fisherman was grinning. The Elders had awarded this honour to him because of his recent success. He was in favour with the Dreamer. And he owed this favour to the stranger, who had rescued him from the nadir of using lug-worms for bait.

Tao glanced up. He saw Hari in the pine tree. With a shout of joy he let go of the oars. He jumped forward and prostrated himself so that his forehead touched the bilge. The god was looking after him, literally standing over him. His luck would continue. *Excuse me!* The *grace* would continue!

Hari shook his fist.

He waved! What kindness! The fisherman prostrated again. Then he rowed back to the beach, grinning wildly.

Thoughts of escape flashed into Hari's mind. He would dive off the cliff, rescue Lina from the Palanquin; Tao would row for the horizon, where a tall ship . . . He would ram an oar down the Shark's throat, choking it to death and ridding the village of this yearly menace. In gratitude they would marry him to Lina . . . He would swoop down like a seagull; taking Lina in his arms he would fly over the sea to wherever it was he came from. Yes! That was why fate had brought him here. He would . . .

do nothing.

Lina herself seemed eager to perform the Sacrifice. It was her choice to unite her soul with her mystic lover, the one who knew her before she was born. She would probably reject his rescue, distancing herself from him with a cold look in her soul-deep eyes. That would hurt him more than any punishment the fisherfolk might inflict on him for daring to profane their rite.

The Shark might not come. That was his only hope.

In the water Hari could see the amber and agate of the rocks, the swaying seaweed, the darting fish and even the sea-urchins. He sat so still that a sea-hawk flew up and perched on another branch of the pine tree, its feathers ruffled by the breeze that took the stifling heat out of the afternoon.

Suddenly the sea-hawk – pirate of the skies – swooped. Talons out, it crashed into the sea. Then it flew up again, wings beating, with a sea-bream in its claws. The fish writhed frantically. It was too heavy. The sea-hawk dropped it and lurched in the air, squawking with frustration. It flew away to circle over the bay, soaring on the thermals.

'What an omen!' Hari shouted, catching again at the branch that saved him from falling to his death below. Lina could escape the Shark! That was its meaning. There was no doubt of it. Right here where 'virgin's soul' had cast its spectre of disaster. But how? Somehow! He knew it. From before. *Before?* Who was he? *Not now!* Now the only thing that mattered was to save her. *How?*

The answer would come. He just had to be still. Leave his mind blank. Open like a flower to the sunshine. The answer would come. The answer would float to him like the scent of the desert after rain. *What?* Where did that come from? *Not now!* The answer had to come.

It didn't.

If only he could dream Lina's escape, it would happen. Did anyone have such power? Maybe the Dreamer, whoever he was. But the Seer was too far. Hari could never get to him by midnight.

Only *he* could save Lina. No one else would, not even Martin. But would she be saved? She accepted her fate so blindly. It was unnecessary. She could have married. It didn't have to be to him. Surely that would be better than this hideous slaughter? He punched the tree with his fist until he tore the skin of his knuckles.

64

The bloody sword of the setting sun slashed the ocean, bruising the sky with purple and grey. Night was falling. Alone until the Red Planet joined her, the evening star was shining in the sky.

Then Hari saw the moon rising from the ocean, full, throwing a flame-gold beacon across the sea, calling Lina to die. *No!* To warn him! Anguish stabbed the heart that held no memories. He had to go *there!* Wherever that was. And soon. Within the month. But why? He had to save her.

The answer struck him like a flash of lightning: *others depend on you!* People were waiting for him. *Who?* He couldn't think just of Lina, however great his love for her. Disaster would strike *them,* if he didn't get there in time. *Where?* Only he could save them. *Why?* Who was he? What could he do for anyone? He didn't even know his own name. Others need you. *Who?* Others whose faces were lost in the labyrinth of his memory. He'd got to help them. *Why?*

The moon climbed into the evening sky, turning pale. The tide was coming in. *Oh God!* The moon was beating out the days in the heavens, while the sea was striking out the hours on earth. High, low, high, low. Time to go, time to go. But *where?* Who could tell him where?

The three stars of the summer triangle were twinkling in the night sky when Martin came to fetch Hari.

Standing at the foot of the pine tree, Lina's father called out in an effort to bear up cheerfully, 'Better have something to eat, hunter of the octopus.'

The boatbuilder himself had nothing, however, when they sat down at the table in a silence broken only by Auntie's toothless slurpings. Lina's place was empty.

7

What thoughts went through the mind of the pearl-diver as she awaited her bloody destiny?

Lina sat in the lotus position before the jade statue of the Dreamer. Rice, fruit and vegetables were piled on the polished wooden floor round the altar, which was decorated with sunflowers, gladioli and chrysanthemums.

The villagers knew that however the Chosen Virgin entered the Temple (and the fishermen had to force some of them in, screaming – to the shame of their families), the Bride walked out light of step, her eyes shining.

The fisherfolk thought that drinking the 'Sacred Soup' caused this sea-change. Its principal ingredient (apart from the prayers recited over it by the priest) was the small grey umbrella-shaped plant which grew in the damp ground beyond the bulrushes and was not unknown to Auntie. But Martin's daughter had not touched it.

This rumour buzzed amongst the women – because not even the oath of secrecy, formally administered by her husband, had been able to dam the malice gushing out of Rita's mouth. Indeed the contempt on her face when he muttered the holy words should have caused Lovegod to order Rita out of the Temple. Such exemplary performance of his duties, however, would not have boded well for harmony in the marriage bed.

'Will that hussy do something perverse? Refusing the Sacred Soup! Who does she think she is?' Rita demanded of her sister.

Tao's wife frowned, unable to assist in Rita's quest for

knowledge.

Lina had not refused the Soup.

Entering the Temple, she had walked to the jade statue of the Dreamer and sat down in front of the altar, crossing her shapely legs in the lotus position. And she had not moved.

Watched closely by Rita – for the Bride remained naked apart from her pearl-diving briefs – Lovegod had brought Lina the Sacred Soup, placing the scarlet lacquer artifact that served as both tray and low table in front of her.

'Drink this,' the priest murmured, swallowing as he stared at her breasts.

Lina did not hear him.

The priest's hand seemed to stir with a life of its own. It twitched, then jittered out to touch Lina's shoulder.

Rita cleared her throat.

Lovegod's hand scuttled back to its owner.

Throughout the incense-scented heat of the afternoon, Lina remained meditating, motionless in front of the altar.

From time to time Lovegod came and gazed at Lina's back. The temptation to see her breasts again was proving too much for the divine. He waited until Rita was called away, then he started bumbling about the altar, staring . . .

'What the *hell* do you think you're doing?'

Lovegod spun round, knocking over one of the jade candlesticks. He grabbed and held up the lighted candle before anything caught fire.

'Tidying the altar, my dear.' Hot wax dripped onto the back of his hand. 'Ow!' He put back the candle, and set straight the candlestick. 'It has to be done.' Lovegod rotated the jade vase in which the purple iris flared open before the statue of the Dreamer. He put his hand to his mouth and sucked the burn.

'Serve you right!' Rita's close-set eyes narrowed.

'There. That's it.' The priest scarpered.

'No soup will purify that creature,' Rita snapped, as they walked to their private quarters at the back of the Temple.

'The ungainly wretch will cause trouble.'

'She will bring respect to the Ceremony,' Lovegod answered his wife back for the first time in years. 'She always was a spirited girl.'

'A frivolous hussy. She will bring shame on her ancestors.' Rita gave Lovegod a look that did not encourage further fruitful interchange of ideas. 'More shame, I should say.'

Lovegod sat down and picked up one of the scriptures. His eyes followed the words down the page, but his mind did not absorb the meaning. He sucked his burnt hand. In the face of Lina's holy immobility, he did not know what to do about the Sacred Soup.

Satisfied with his easy job, the priest had no more spiritual aspiration than a donkey carrying a load of religious texts. But even he apprehended that Lina had merged in meditation with the Higher Consciousness, whose 'intermediary' he claimed to be. His eyes looked at the scripture. Glimpses of Lina's back flashed into his mind.

Midnight: the Hour of the Boar.

Torches in brass stands lit the fisherfolk's faces in the Temple courtyard where, only that afternoon, Lina had taken the fated iris. Apart from the 'Waking Dreamers', the whole village had come to the Temple.

The porcelain dragons at the corners of the Temple roof grimaced in the darkness. The frogs in the rice-fields croaked with unusual stridency. Even the insects screeching in the trees sounded tense.

The villagers chatted excitedly. Some lined the winding road down which the Palanquin would charge. All were resigned to the Sacrifice of the girl they knew. The possibility of this Fate had hung over the childhood of all the women of Shark Bay. The grannies champed toothless mouths; grinning with anticipation, they looked at the little girls, guessing who would be the next to go.

The old men, faces worn like antique ivory, had seen victim after victim sacrificed to the Great Shark. 'A beautiful girl, Lina.' 'A shame the Shark has to choose the prettiest.' 'It knows what it's doing.' 'They all digest the same.' 'The girls of today are nothing like the beauties of the past.' 'Lina is gorgeous.' 'Nothing like! When I was a lad . . .'

Martin stood silent, ashen; Ken mulish. Katha was sharp with the children, who sulked. Auntie scowled, pulling at her crystal pendant and looking at Humi, who looked hostile to anything *they* did. Tao glanced at the god, combing his fingers through his hair.

They all started when a night bird shrieked from the forests of the moonlit hillsides.

Boys bent over the water of the Temple pond, trying to catch the carp which hid amongst the water lilies.

In order to catch a glimpse of the Chosen Virgin when the Procession began, older brothers were climbing the camellia trees which stood guard against the typhoons that lashed the Coast. The boys shouted – bagging the best places and daring each other to climb further out along the branches.

Any minute now the drum would boom. The Palanquin would appear, carried on the shoulders of the youths of Shark Bay. The doors of the Temple would open. For a moment the Bride would be visible as she walked across the veranda, down the seven steps and into the Palanquin. Made of black lacquer, the Palanquin, decorated with gold dragons, was the pride of the village.

On the ground the grown-ups jostled for positions to see her. Once the Bride of the Shark entered the Palanquin, no mortal might lay eyes on her ever again.

Children were getting restless. In the camellia tree bigger boys began bullying smaller ones. Near the pond boys were pulling the girls' hair.

As usual the priest was late.

'It's hard work dressing up in all that silk,' the village thatcher bantered. The Dreamer had ordained that people should not wear silk, since it involved the killing of the silk-worm.

69

'Not as hard as filling that pot-belly,' the carpenter retorted.

They all laughed, crow's-feet smiles winging out from within. They knew Lovegod could not delay long – or the Headman would go into the Temple and fetch him. The full moon was high in the sky. The Bride had to be in the jaws of Shark Rock, waiting for her divine lover, before the turning of the tide at midnight.

Lovegod may have learnt the trick of being late from his father, as Martin suggested, but under guidance from his wife he had turned it into an art. Rita judged it finely: she kept the village waiting as long as possible, to emphasize the priest's indispensability, without delaying so long as to incur the humiliation of Big Rama striding up the Temple steps to order Lovegod out.

At last! Seven booms from the Temple drum echoed across the moon-silver bay. Suddenly everyone was shouting, pushing and shoving to make way. The youths of Shark Bay charged round from the rear of the Temple with the Palanquin on their shoulders. The black lacquer and gold dragons gleamed.

The youths were wearing only yellow loincloths. Their muscles rippling copper in the torchlight, they set the Palanquin down in front of the Temple steps and stood to one side, stretching their backs and rubbing their shoulders.

These were the centipede feet of the 'wheel-less carriage' of the god. They had imbibed a full measure of the Sacred Soup. This helped them understand the significance of the heavenly Marriage and throw themselves into the earthly ritual.

The doors of the Temple opened. The priest came to the top of the wooden steps in his orange and silver silk robes. In voice stentorian, he spoke the holy words. Then, in his black clogs, he descended the seven steps and stood at the side of the Palanquin, holding up the bamboo screen door.

So rapidly that many saw only a flash of crimson, Lina

glided out of the Temple, down the steps and into the Palanquin. She was robed only in a garment of hibiscus flowers that concealed her consecrated body from profane gaze. Some did not see her at all, as they complained afterwards.

'Typical of that hussy. What makes the creature think she is superior?' Rita desired to improve her knowledge of human nature.

'Typical!' Tao's wife shook her head.

Even Hari, standing on tip-toe at the back, determined to catch sight of Lina's face, glimpsed only a gold blur in the torchlight, above the crimson robe of hibiscus flowers.

Lovegod let down the bamboo screen and walked round to take his place behind the Palanquin.

The Headman and five Elders were already standing there, waiting with the Father of the Bride. Martin was holding his head high, but looking as if he was at a funeral rather than at a wedding. The five virgins stood as bridesmaids, wearing only their white pearl-diving briefs. Each carried a flaming torch, keeping her other arm across her breasts.

Another boom from the drum!

The youths grasped the massive poles of the Palanquin. With a shout of 'One! Two! Three! Wake –' (echoed with glee from the sagging branches of the camellia trees) they hoisted the Palanquin into the air at full arm's stretch. Then they let it drop onto their naked shoulders, yelling '– Dreamer!' in pain and exultation.

And now the magic of the mystery began to intoxicate the youths! They were bearing the eternal choice of the god. Carrying his Bride to her omnipotent Beloved! They were taken over by the deity – spirit ecstatic! – and the Palanquin would rush down into the village as the Dreamer dictated.

No one knew which lanes the black and gold Palanquin would invade in its turbulent race to the shore. Its will was inscrutable. It was a blessing if it passed your home – but it was also a day of reckoning. The last year's events rushed before the eyes of the god in the same way, it was said, that your whole life can flash before you when you die. And where the Dreamer found fault, disaster struck.

Last year the god – hibiscus-clad virgin swaying inside – visited a family who had not gone to help when another house caught fire. The poles of the Palanquin smashed like twin battering rams through the walls and wooden shutters, wrecking their house.

Torches blazed on the Palanquin. Flames leapt into the air. Sparks scattered, falling on the bare torsos of the youths, who ignored them as if they were possessed.

They were possessed!

'Wake, Dreamer! Wake, Dreamer!' they chanted in unison. 'Wake, Dreamer! Wake, Dreamer!' They no longer cantered. They did not gallop. They flew! Down the hill. Lurching from side to side.

Boys leapt out of the camellia trees, eyes flashing. They raced round, dashing through short cuts. 'This way!' Sprinting ahead. 'Come on!' Then they could see the Palanquin rushing down upon them. They stayed in front of it – daring each other with shouts of frenzy. Screaming, they flung themselves out of its way at the last moment.

Roaring past the stone lanterns brightening the road with candlelight. Through the olive grove. Past the vegetable plots. Hurtling across the bridge and into the village. Racing past the school, where Martin's wife had been the teacher. Past dogs that barked and raced after the Palanquin. Thundering through the lanes.

At the gate of every house stood decorations of freshly cut bamboo, bright with coloured paper folded into the auspicious shapes of cranes and chrysanthemums. Windbells tinkled, for it was a joyous Festival – the Wedding of the Pearl-diver and her Shark Prince.

Next morning at high tide the youngest female in every home (Anna in Martin's, helped by Katha), dressed bright as a tulip, would toss these paper birds and flowers into the waves to bless the happy couple.

This year the Palanquin arrived at the shore without destruction – apart from crashing into a pomegranate tree and ripping it out of the ground.

The beach was alight.

A white paper lantern decorated with scarlet dragons flamed at the prow of each of the fishing boats hauled up on the sand. Every boat owner had cut down a tall bamboo, stripping all but the topmost feathery branches to make a flagpole, then tying flags to it and binding it to the mast of his boat.

'Wake, Dreamer!' The sweating Palanquin bearers all but sizzled as they splashed into the sea and dropped the Palanquin onto the raft, which Tao would row out to Shark Rock.

Tao stood in the centre of his boat, legs astride, hands on hips, regarding them all confidently.

Gradually everyone caught up and stood on the beach, panting and sweating after chasing the virgins, their torches dancing through the night.

The Elders had walked sedately and, with the Headman, Lovegod and Martin, were the last to arrive, apart from Auntie and other old ladies.

Little girls with flowers in their hair fluttered like butterflies in their festival costumes from grown-up to grown-up, asking to be carried.

Waving his fan for silence, the priest stood as erect as his belly allowed. He intoned the words of the Ceremony with solemnity. When he finished, he hitched up his silk robes and the youths rushed forward. They lifted Lovegod shoulder-high with shouts of mirth, carried him into the sea and set him down in Tao's boat.

Big Rama lit fresh torches, thrusting them into the brass sockets on the Palanquin and flinging the old ones hissing into the sea.

Then Tao, rowing with easy pulls, towed the black Palanquin, its gold dragons gleaming in the torchlight, out

73

across the sea to the cheers of the whole village.

'*They* do not swim it, Humi. They tow it,' Auntie pointed out, grasping Hari's arm. '*They* can't swim.'

Tao anchored the raft between the black jaws of Shark Rock. They would gape their widest at midnight, when the tide throbbed to its lowest ebb.

Standing in the centre of the boat, where Tao had previously erected the shelter for Hari, Lovegod intoned the Invocation to the Great Shark loudly enough to be heard on the shore in the still night.

The Invocation completed, the fisherman slipped the tow rope and checked the Palanquin's position. He rowed back.

When the boat's prow struck the sand, the youths raced forward and hoisted the boat out of the water. Waving his arms for balance, then clutching the side of the boat, the priest looked apprehensive.

Tao, arms akimbo, grinned delightedly as the youths carried the boat high up the beach.

They halted and yelled, 'Wake, Dreamer! Wake, Dreamer!' seven times in maniacal crescendo. They lowered the boat to the sand – to the cheering of the rest of the villagers. The youths helped Lovegod out of the boat. He smoothed down his orange robes.

Fireworks rocketed into the night sky. 'Ooohs' and 'Aaahs' greeted the plumes of light, when the fire-flowers (as fireworks were called in the dialect) exploded into blossom. Then there was silence.

It was fifteen minutes to midnight.

A wave of sympathy entered the hearts of the fishermen as they thought of Martin's daughter, whom they all knew. They looked out at the circle of fire created by the torches flaming on the Palanquin, and the reflections on the ocean.

Lina would be kneeling on a black silk cushion, embroidered with gold dragons, waiting for the turning of the tide, for the Shark to knife through the moonbright water, for its jaws to open and sever an arm, a leg.

Babies had fallen asleep in their mothers' arms. The women sang to them, 'How you wax, Grandpa Moon, how you wax!' – rocking them, and handing them to other women to hold when they got too heavy.

Anna played with the sand, but her little cakes were soon destroyed by the boisterous feet of Older Brother.

The sky had been blue all day, but now a beating of clouds like giant wings eclipsed the moon. Frightening in its sudden intensity, darkness covered the bay, making black monsters out of the rocks. A certain force was advancing towards Shark Bay. Women who had lost their men at sea shuddered, terrified of the water at night.

The tide reached its ebb.

The hiss of indrawn breath sounded like the whistle of a line being cast. Tao had seen the Shark. He was pointing.

Boys who had been longing to be the first to shout, 'There he is!' were tongue-tied. They too pointed, stammering.

Hari saw the black triangle of a shark's dorsal fin arrowing towards the flaming Palanquin. It stopped. With the leisurely power of a lord of the ocean, the Shark swam a full circle round his flower-clad Bride. Again he stopped. Now he was motionless, as if consecrating their union.

Now Hari was motionless, terrified, disbelieving, yet seeing the Great Shark with his own eyes.

Now the Shark would devour her. The dorsal fin vanished from sight. The Shark was attacking from below. The great body hurtled into the raft. The Palanquin shot into the air, toppling over and splashing into the sea. The torches fizzled out. The Shark's tail thrashed the ocean.

A wail came from one of the women: it was Auntie.

Danny let out a howl.

Martin himself stooped, turning pale, despair creasing his face.

A spasm convulsed Hari's body.

Then all was silent.

Tao was pointing: the black dorsal fin was speeding out

of the starlit bay towards the open sea. The villagers released their breaths with sighs of relief and terror.

Another flap of the celestial wings revealed the full moon, shining so immaculately that it seemed like a hole in the floor of Heaven, through which light was escaping from another dimension.

Weak-kneed, everyone gazed at the magic carpet of moonlit water, waiting to hear the crying of seagulls as they swooped down to drink human blood.

8

Something had gone wrong.

The villagers looked frightened. They stared out at Shark Rock, unable to detect any blood in the light of the moon. The silhouette of the raft lay across the currents that made elusive patterns in the moon-stippled sea.

Minutes passed. At first the currents might have sucked Lina's blood under, but the ghastly stains should have splattered the surface by now. Even though it was after midnight, the seagulls always woke, scenting the Virgin's blood and screaming with food-crazed clamour. Tonight they were silent.

The fishermen saw others looking at them with alarm. They began to avoid their glances, not realizing that they were looking at the others in the same way.

Yet there was no way the Bride could have escaped.

They had seen the Great Shark cleaving through the bay; they had seen the savage lunge that knocked over the Palanquin and drowned the flaming torches; they had seen the churning of the tail-threshed waters.

They gazed out to sea, where they had seen the dorsal fin powering away from Shark Rock. The flares of the squid fishermen from other villages were glittering on the horizon.

'The Shark is no longer satisfied with a virgin,' ventured one old fisherman, making a frightened guess about what had happened. 'It has tired of young girls.'

'What terror will it now inflict on the village?' asked a woman carrying a baby girl.

'Why?' an old woman queried, her face ravaged with distress. '*How* has the Sacrifice failed?'

For it had failed. That much was certain. The inexplicable had struck like a reef in safe water. The Great Shark had not accepted the Chosen Virgin.

The Shark had not chosen Lina! She had merely taken the last iris. The only time that had happened before, the Shark had miraculously removed the iris head, forcing the Headman to begin the Ceremony again. That had been a sign! Why had they missed it? The Shark would not accept a virgin who took the last iris. He wanted a free choice. They should have started again.

A shudder of horror ran through the fisherfolk when one woman sobbed, 'We will be destroyed. A village extinct!'

Dignified as always, his voice deep, the Headman called the five Elders into a circle.

Despite the heat of the night, the youths shivered in their yellow loincloths. Children began to snivel.

However, one breast glowed with a selfish hope, which the man no one knew tried to keep out of his face. Had that been a true omen, when the sea-hawk dropped the fish it had caught in its claws? Had Lina escaped? Where? How? No one could outswim a shark. But whatever had happened, it was better than the Great Shark ripping her body to pieces.

The Headman clapped his hands twice.

Everyone stopped murmuring and looked towards him.

'No one will enter the sea during the tide of the Sacrifice,' the giant announced, his silver hair in place. He pointed across the moonlit bay. A fringe of white foam curled round the night-black rocks of the cliffs. 'As soon as the tide begins to ebb at dawn, we shall swim out to Shark Rock and try to discover what has happened.'

'Lin-hunh!' Danny burst out.

Some women echoed his cry, prolonging it into a howl that wailed out across the bay and up into the wooded hills.

Wait for dawn, thought the stranger. The dawn of what? A new life. Hari and Lina! They would escape and live happily ever after.

Big Rama clapped his hands twice. 'Until then, no one should discuss this event. Return to your homes now. Reassemble here at the Hour of the Hare.'

As they began trudging back to their homes, one woman, the school teacher, walked across to the Headman and, causing him to bend, asked him something.

Big Rama straightened up and clapped his hands for attention again. 'Let the decorations be left outside your homes, until the Elders direct otherwise.'

Some went rigid. They knew what that meant: the Headman was prepared to go through the whole Ceremony again, starting with the agony of the Betrothal.

The five virgins, who thought they had escaped, ran sobbing into their mothers' arms, sweating with terror.

It was an endless night.

Not a breath of air to relieve the heat. Nothing like this had happened before. Fishermen tossed on their beds, recalling the year of horror when they had sacrificed a goat and the Shark had attacked every week. The Chosen Virgin, who had been 'saved' from the Sacrifice, had been the Great Shark's first victim: it seized her by the leg before she was out of her depth, and sped out of the bay, leaving a wake of blood.

That had been the Year of the Goat. Since then the match-makers had said that girls born in the Year of the Goat made bad wives – until the priest's wife set them right. Rita gave it out that women born in the Year of the Dragonfly made shrewish wives. Lina had been born in the Year of the Dragonfly. When he was told, however, Martin had only laughed: 'That is a subject on which Rita is an authority.'

Even the children were restless. In Martin's home Older Brother, his forehead bathed in sweat, started awake, screaming with nightmares. Anna kept crying.

Ken and Katha retired to their bedroom. The silence was broken by sharp words – followed by a door slamming and an angry man stomping out of the house.

Ken found Tao lying under the jacaranda tree outside Hari's room. Together they watched the stars wheeling and listened to the now poignant tinkling of the wind-bells in the bamboo decoration outside the tea-house.

Tao was the least worried man in Shark Bay. 'The god is here. That is why it didn't happen. How are we to understand his divine plan with our human minds?' he asked nudging his wife, who had at last fallen asleep.

'Rama told us not to discuss it!' Rita's sister snapped. She could not get back to sleep. She started nagging. Tao left their bed and walked to Martin's to be near the god.

From the hills the sound of an axe against wood echoed out eerily. In the moonlight Martin was felling the cypress tree he would need for the mast of the next boat he built. Despite his gentleness, no one dared go and warn the big man that he might do himself an injury, chopping trees down in the dark. If the tea-house owner did not release his feelings on the tree, he might go out of control. Fathers had gone berserk when their daughters were seized by the Shark. If Martin ran amok through the village with an axe in his hands, they might not stop him until . . . they might not stop him.

In their private quarters behind the Temple, the priest asked, 'Are you tired, dear?' This had become the accepted prelude to his conjugal rights.

'Not particularly. Why?' This was the affirmative response. Tonight Rita felt a rare need for physical comfort.

Their flabby bodies joined. The lover of God was more aroused than usual. He kissed her neck. His hand pawed her sweating back – preserving the religious silence in which their sex was consummated. Then Lovegod broke the silence. One word escaped his lips. It was a name – and it was not the name of his wife.

With a toss of her body so agile that neither of them would have dreamed her capable of it, Rita threw the priest off. 'How dare you? That hussy!' she screeched, coupling the two of them with insults. She began sobbing. 'Get out!'

The tears frightened Lovegod. He was inured to scoldings. This was new. He hurried to the Temple. He knelt before the altar and prayed, rubbing his hand.

In his room at Martin's house Hari turned on his bed, sweltering in the heat, unable to sleep – only a few paces from the room where *she* had slept for as much of his life as he could remember. Could she have escaped? No. Lina was drowned under the upturned Palanquin. Or bloodlessly slaughtered by the Shark.

A night insect was squeaking in the jacaranda tree. A tomcat started yowling. Dogs barked. A catfight began. A mosquito buzzed near his face, then landed on his forehead. He slapped it. Silence. Got it! Bzzz! He slapped his cheek. Silence. Good. Bzzz! He swatted his hands everywhere. Bzzzzzz! He had to get away! He groped his way out of the house.

The scent of dawn hung in the air though it was still dark. No light came from the moon, which had dived into the ocean after the Red Planet.

Only when he saw Danny, kneeling at the foot of the pine tree, moaning, did Hari realize he had walked to Shark Rock.

'Hu-hunhhh!' Danny's eyes were like a frightened dog's.

Hari replied with the customary, 'Wake, Dreamer.'

'No Lina! Weh Dream-hunh!' Danny slobbered. He tripped over a pine root and went sprawling.

Hari started hurrying across to help him up.

'Weh-huunh! Danny-Dan go go.' Facing Hari, Danny staggered backwards towards the village, falling and lurching to his feet.

Hari looked down over the cliff at the raft, dark as a dead cormorant in the water. No sign of Lina. What had happened to his love? She had to be dead. Even if the Shark had carried her away to the undersea palace unharmed, she was dead to him. He could not wait for Lina for seven years. Not even seven weeks. He had to be *there* in one month.

The stars were bright, voyaging through the night sky, whirling their predictions of new dawns. *Oh God!* His body trembled. He had to be there by the new moon. He knew it! *By the new moon!* Only two weeks left! Two weeks to find – he had no idea what. To save *them. Who?* Who from? Where could he begin?

His head ached. He put his hands to his temples and groaned. She was dead. What did it matter where he was in two weeks, in two months, in a year? *She* would not be there. But – it did matter. To *them*. The faces he could not picture. The names he did not know – any more than he knew his own.

A cock crowed. Hari looked up. Dawn was lightening the sky. He could see some fishermen walking onto the beach, looking across at Shark Rock.

9

By sunrise, the Hour of the Hare, all the villagers – apart from the 'Waking Dreamers'– had returned to the beach. The bamboo decorations outside every home they passed were bleak reminders of the night's disaster.

It was already late for the fishermen like Ken, who liked to be out at their fishing grounds while the cliffs were still sunk, black and maroon, into the night-dyed ocean.

The Headman and the Elders stared at Shark Rock. The lower jaw was underwater, as if sated. As the tide receded, it would fang out like a recurring nightmare. The ocean itself took on an aspect of sacrifice as the dawn threw a bloody altar cloth across it.

The fishermen's heads were painful from lack of sleep. A catastrophe had wrecked the most important day in their year. They dreaded the consequences. They stood haggard, huddled in small groups. They rubbed calloused hands against their unshaven chins, muttering and staring at the horizon as the sun rose.

The women sat down on the sand and avoided looking at Shark Rock. They spoke to each other in whispers: it could mean misery for ever; one of the five virgins had got engaged, would the Elders allow that?

Martin was not carrying his axe. All were pleased to see that, though they noticed the bags under the boatbuilder's eyes. His stubbled face looked bruised from the night's ordeal. Martin stood with Ken and Auntie in a morose triangle that not even the Headman cared to approach.

Wearing a black cassock the priest was sitting down on

the sand; he was picking up shells and letting them drop. Rita stood behind him, pursing her thin lips.

Big Rama, the only man who had trimmed his beard that morning, looked at the old fisherman who was able to 'see' the turning of the tide. His skill had never been needed more. He nodded to the Headman the instant the ebb began.

The giant clapped his hands twice.

Everyone looked at him expectantly.

'Get up!' Rita kicked Lovegod in the kidneys.

With a cry of pain, the priest got to his feet.

'Let us remember that we are all creatures of a power greater than ourselves and that whatever happens is the will of that supreme intelligence,' Big Rama said in the formal language he used when speaking in his capacity as Headman.

'Say something!' Rita hissed.

Rubbing his back, Lovegod frowned: he could find no ecclesiastical formula to add to the Headman's concept.

The youths (the legs of the Palanquin in last night's Procession) shifted from foot to foot, waiting for the Headman to give the word. They wanted to race into the sea and swim to Shark Rock to seek the glory of getting there first and finding out what had happened.

'Therefore let us humbly try to discern the Dreamer's will in these perplexing circumstances,' the Headman's deep voice continued. 'Before we enter the ocean, let us pray in silence for guidance, knowing that we can accomplish nothing with our own limited personalities.'

Rita was resentful that the Headman had not called on her husband to say a few words. She glowered at Lovegod, still rubbing his back, throughout the silent prayer. She was angry with Lovegod again, because he had not insisted on praying aloud – or added something (she didn't care what, so long as it emphasized his importance) in his sonorous voice.

The villagers stood in silence on the beach – heads

bowed and hands clasped – until Big Rama clapped his hands twice. His voice rang out, 'Heaven be with you. Go!'

'Still the wretch says nothing!' Rita jabbed her finger into Lovegod's well-covered ribs.

The youths sprinted into the waves, splashing and striking out for Shark Rock, to swim there first and see . . . whatever there was to be seen. Then race back with the news.

The pearl-divers and mature men followed the youths, swimming to the Rock with troubled faces, fearing that the Shark might still be lurking.

When the youths reached the 'jaws' of Shark Rock, they dived. With full tide and the sun barely rising above the horizon, it was dark where the Shark had attacked. The Palanquin hung over them, belly up like a dead animal. Once they had swum down past rock and seaweed, the youths recalled how the pearl-divers refused to dive in the jaws because it gave them nightmares. Black fissures underwater terrified the youths.

Martin and Ken did not join the swimmers. Lina's father stood still, legs apart, hands on his hips, watching them swim out and dive. He did not want to be the one to find his darling's body bloated, her lungs filled with sea-water, rocking on the ocean bed in a malicious lullaby. Martin imagined that something had cracked Lina's head, knocking her unconscious when the Palanquin overturned – and that the Shark, with the nobility that marks the most powerful of beasts, had disdained the offering that was no longer perfect.

Nor did Lovegod join the swimmers. He could not swim. He smoothed down his black cassock and tried to look as if he was praying, while Rita cast venomous glances at him.

The stranger did not join the swimmers. Although Hari had walked from the pine tree down to the beach when he saw the villagers assembling, he felt obliged to stand aside. Yet it was his love they were searching for!

Hari stared at Shark Rock, listening to the whistles of the pearl-divers fetching breath. Lina had whistled like that. He wished he could swim to the Rock. He felt sure he would find her. He had something to do, on which the future of Shark Bay depended. That was why fate had brought him here. That was why the Bride of the Shark had found him on this very beach. That was why he thought of her all the time. Lina was his soul-mate. Or would be if this infernal Shark had not snatched her away from him.

The swimmers returned one by one, shaking their heads and spreading their hands in bewilderment. Their eyes were red. They had found nothing. There was no body. They had seen some of the hibiscus flowers that had clothed Lina – but no flesh or bones.

Seagulls were wheeling through the blue sky, occasionally plunging into the sea and snatching something up in their beaks; sometimes alighting on the water. None of them took any interest in Shark Rock.

Lovegod had tied a towel round his shaven head to prevent it burning in the sun. He was talking with his wife. At least, he was listening to her with a sullen look.

'*You!*' An elbow had jabbed him in the solar plexus. Lovegod had doubled up, spluttering.

Patting his back, his wife appeared to be consoling the priest in his choking fit. 'If the blame falls on you, they will drive us out of Shark Bay,' Rita was hissing – and the sketch she drew of life in the mountains was not idyllic.

Lovegod, still in pain, opened his mouth, 'But . . .' Rita told him they must set the blame on someone else. 'But . . .' Rita rebuked him for failing to assert himself, when the Headman made his prayer. 'But . . .' Rita threatened that she would never let him touch her body again if he did not prove himself to be a Man. 'But . . .' Rita alluded to his touch: 'You make my flesh crawl.'

'Reverence!' Big Rama called out, beckoning the priest over to where the Elders had formed a circle.

'You have no more finesse than a pigeon.'

'Be so good as to join the Elders, please.'

'I've told you before and I'll tell you again . . .'

'Sorry to interrupt you, dear. Duty calls.' Lovegod sloped off to the Headman, a smile wincing across his face.

Everyone else drew aside, awaiting the decision of the Council of Elders.

Looking up at Big Rama, the Elders put suggestions in urgent voices.

The Headman was sweating. Whatever he decided would affect the future of the village. A wrong decision might result in destroying it.

Hari sensed a man standing beside him. He turned.

Tao caught Hari's eye. 'Excuse me,' he said, dropping his eyes at once. 'Excuse me, but . . .' He stood there, saying no more. The god could read his mind: would he deign to use his powers to rescue Shark Bay from the danger it stood in?

Hari gave Tao a friendly look, which the fisherman interpreted in a satisfactory manner. Yes, he would intervene. Tao grinned. 'Excuse me.'

They looked across as one of the old women shuffled down to the water's edge. She peered at the shine on the sand left by the last wave, as if to read some secret in the patterns left by the crab-holes. Then she turned, staring haughtily at the people of Shark Bay.

Martin and Ken frowned. Hari felt alarmed.

Auntie slipped off her clothes, letting them fall to her feet. She stepped out of them with a proud toss of her head, as much as to say, 'You've all tried and you've failed. A swimmer from the island – I won't say the island is better: judge for yourselves – a *swimmer* will show you.' She would show *them* once and for all.

A flap of her withered breasts answered that toss of her head, presenting an argument more persuasive than any of Lovegod's sermons against the temptations of the flesh. They knew Auntie had been a beauty. 'She's told us so enough times,' Rita snapped, whenever anyone mentioned it.

Auntie stepped into the waves which, gentle as they were, knocked her off balance. The frail old lady stumbled and fell down in the sea. She got to her feet awkwardly, then paused to re-consider, staring out to judge the distance she had to swim to Shark Rock.

The boys stifled giggles. They put their hands over their mouths and looked down at their feet, frightened to catch the eye of a friend who might set them off.

Auntie put on her clothes and shuffled across to Martin. Crooking her finger to make him incline his head – and subdue a look of annoyance – she whispered in his ear.

'What?' the expression on the face of the Bride's father changed to astonishment.

Auntie whispered again, pointing a twig-like finger towards Shark Rock.

'Are you sure? How do you know?'

Auntie nodded eagerly.

Martin's eyebrows rose with hope. 'Tell them!' He gestured at the Headman and Elders. He bounded across the sand, flinging off his clothes. He dived into the waves and started churning out to Shark Rock.

Some of the youths began running to the waves to swim after the boatbuilder, whom they all admired – until the Headman called out, 'Wait! All of you! We'll see what Martin does.'

Tao walked across to his wife's side. 'The god is working through her, like calling the fish,' he explained, pointing at Auntie. 'No sooner than I asked him. He favours me.' Tao's lips parted in a happy smile. 'Excuse me.'

Tao's wife sniffed. She was not convinced, but she said nothing. She knew the meaning of the word hunger – and since the stranger had been going fishing with her husband, they had eaten well. Further, she had not had to spend the day scratching under rocks for lug-worms to use as bait.

The Headman, followed by the Elders (and Lovegod,

after a finger screwed into his back), walked up to Auntie. With his height and colossal chest, Big Rama stood twice the size of the old lady.

However, grinning at Martin swimming out to Shark Rock, Auntie ignored him.

The Elders looked at Lina's older brother.

Ken curtly shook his head. He had not heard Auntie's whisper and he had no intention of using his influence, if any, to make her reveal what she had said to his father.

'The old goat has taken leave of what senses she had. Martin has gone on a fool's errand,' said Rita. 'Once again that *foreigner* has made a doting imbecile of herself.'

Stroking his well-trimmed beard, Big Rama gave up looking at Auntie and stared out to Shark Rock.

The lower jaw was jabbing out of the sea. Martin caught hold of it, staring down into the depths until he got his breath back. His head disappeared as he dived underwater.

The older pearl-divers shook their heads. 'There's nothing.' 'We've looked.' 'He's wasting his time.'

'As usual,' Rita observed.

After more than a minute Martin's head shot up out of the water. He shook it, sweeping the hair out of his eyes with his hand. He got his breath back, gulping in the air. Then he dived again.

With the sun rising, the sea was now dazzling. Blades of light splintered into their eyes.

The pearl-divers were frowning. Martin was staying down by sheer will power. No one should stay under that long.

Just as they were thinking something had gone wrong, Martin's leonine head broke the surface. He gave a triumphant wave towards the shore, gasping for air.

Auntie nodded, winking at anyone who caught her eye. 'I told you! I told you!'

Martin dived again. This time his head did not bob back above the waves. Minutes passed.

The fisherfolk stared across the ocean with the dread of a victim fascinated by a snake. No one could hold their breath that long. It was impossible. Your lungs would burst.

No one spoke.

Finally the Headman, after looking at the five Elders, who shook their heads, broke the awful silence, 'Martin must have drowned.'

The villagers looked aghast. What was going on? The Sacrifice had failed. Now the Bride's father had been killed. Or had supernatural forces seized them both? Had occult powers tempted Martin to swim to the Rock, using the old woman as their medium? *When all the others had returned!*

'What did that *foreigner* say to make Martin lose his life?' Rita demanded.

'Much that so-called priest's wife cares about Martin,' the old lady retorted. Auntie received some hard stares, which she ignored, although her jaw stuck out.

Creases wrinkled the Headman's brow. He felt the full burden of responsibility. He was not concerned with avoiding blame, but with saving the village. Was the Shark going to destroy everyone who entered the sea alone? Was the whole of Shark Bay in danger? What had they done wrong?

The village thatcher suggested ordering the fishing boats into the sea. This was legitimate. The tide had begun to ebb. Normally at this time they would be towing the black and gold Palanquin back to the shore, washing it with fresh water and carrying it back into the Dream Hall.

With boats they could search better, but the Headman did not want to see any more lives lost. The Great Shark could overturn a boat as easily as smash the Palanquin. Big Rama knew that most of the men and women would be prepared to die for the village, if necessary, but there was no merit in risking lives unnecessarily. And this was the least satisfactory kind of death: a killing in which the body vanished, so that no black and gold memorial tablet could be placed on the family altar.

Tao looked at Hari. 'First, Lina in all her loveliness. Excuse me, the god would be indifferent to her physical beauty – *Excuse me!* But now, Martin . . .' Tao did not dare express it aloud. He knew even the thought was presumptious, but was it not time the god . . . ?

In his own anxiety Hari did not notice the fisherman. Staring at Shark Rock, the stranger raised his hand to shield his eyes from the glare of the sun.

Tao backed away. He had offended the god, who no longer cast his benign gaze upon him. How dare a fisherman question the Dreamer? He could form no conception of what fate He had in mind for their bodies, let alone their spirits. Preventing human death meant no more to the god than the death of lug-worms to him, Tao. Excuse me!

'Look!' cried one of the pearl-divers.

A head angled up out of the sea at Shark Rock.

'Martin!' the fishermen shouted. 'He's safe! He's alive!'

But it was not the boatbuilder's head.

Hari went rigid.

The fishermen, their eyes used to scanning the surface of the ocean, stared and blinked. *It could not be!* They looked again, rubbing their tired eyes.

Another head rose up out of the sea: it shook the water out of its hair. They saw the wave of a massive arm.

They could not believe it!

Tao stared at Hari, running both hands through his unkempt hair, his eyes wide with wonder. The god had done it! Excuse me! Grinning at his wife, who turned away to look at Rita, Tao did a mime of catching a huge seabream and throwing it into the bilge of his boat.

The first head to emerge had been Lina's.

10

The fisherfolk gaped at Shark Rock. The man they thought dead was swimming side-stroke back to the shore, clasping the Virgin whom they had last seen entering the Palanquin as a human sacrifice.

One old woman put her hands over her eyes, muttering that no one might behold the Bride of the Shark after she entered the Palanquin.

'Ghosts!' Rita cried, looking across the bay.

Danny screamed. Some women groaned, their faces puffy and tired. Pearl-divers clutched one another.

These were not living bodies! How could Martin be alive after so long underwater? And his daughter – drowned, even if the Shark had not touched her. And where? *Nowhere!* They had all searched. Some wanted to run, but they all stood gawking.

Again Hari's heart clashed with the others. He could feel their vibrations of dread, but he smiled. A miracle had saved her! Now he and Lina would fulfil their destined love. What did it matter who he was? Martin had said he'd be glad to see him marry Lina. They would live happily together!

Ken walked forward to be at Martin's side, as he waded out of the sea with Lina in his arms, her legs dangling.

The fisherfolk sighed with relief. Fears of the supernatural vanished, since they knew that ghosts have no feet. But some still felt the horror. Friends stood still, who would otherwise have run across to help, as Martin carried Lina to where his clothes lay strewn.

The man in a black cassock took a step forward. 'If you go near that naked hussy . . .' a voice threatened in his ear, while a finger and thumb pinched the flesh of his arm. Lovegod bent down, adjusted his sandal, then took two steps backward.

'She's alive!' Martin called to the Headman, laying Lina down on the sand.

Auntie bustled forward to help. She pulled Martin's white shirt over Lina's body, for the Bride had worn nothing under her crimson hibiscus flowers.

Martin held his daughter in his arms. 'She was inside the cave,' he explained, looking up at Big Rama, who was walking towards him, having waited until Lina's body was covered.

'What cave?' the Headman asked.

Lovegod received so sharp a jab in the back that it jolted him forward. 'She can't still be alive!' he yelped.

'Well, she is!' Auntie snapped, looking across at him. 'The Dreamer, whom so-called priests are supposed to worship, saved her. There is a cave inside the lower jaw. It never gets wet. She was safe in there.'

'You!' Still holding Lina, Martin put one arm round Auntie and gave her a hug. 'How did you know?'

Auntie looked round at the *sprats* of Shark Bay, casting glances of contempt at *them*, while Martin held her.

'How did you know?' the Headman repeated.

The old lady laughed silently, revealing her toothless gums. This was one secret she was not going to tell.

Rita's close-set eyes knitted together. She sidled forward, pushing before her the priest.

Hari too tried to edge through the crush of people to get a glimpse of the girl he adored. What had she gone through? Was she all right?

Lina lay inert in Martin's arms, breathing but unconscious. Her eyes were open, but they were seeing nothing.

The Headman called over one of the older pearl-divers. She was Shark Bay's expert in resuscitation. She told

Martin to turn Lina over and lay her face down on the sand. Straddling the Bride of the Shark, the pearl-diver struck a point between Lina's shoulder blades with her elbow. Then she jumped up quickly.

Lina came to, gulping for breath. She rolled over, her arms flailing.

Martin bounded to Lina's side, going down on one knee. Ignoring the hands hitting his head, Martin gathered his daughter into his arms and raised her into a sitting position, trying to calm her with soothing words.

Lina's hand caught his hair. Martin did nothing as she pulled it savagely. Suddenly she went limp. Her eyes wandered. She stared at Martin, as if she didn't know who he was.

'Lina, you're all right now. What happened, my darling?'

Her gaze roamed from face to face. Her eyes met those of the anxious stranger. 'The Dreamer!' A husky voice unlike her own issued from her throat, 'Go to the Dreamer.'

'Possessed!' Rita screeched.

The old pearl-diver leapt back, knocking Lovegod over.

'By the forces of evil!' Rita screeched again, looking round for support.

'The hussy was not pure,' Lovegod added manfully, getting to his feet. 'She . . .'

'The "hussy"? Not pure?' Martin sprang up. Veins stood out on his forehead. 'What in the name of Heaven do you mean, you hypocritical paunch?' He advanced on Lovegod with his hands outstretched.

What would have happened if Martin's powerful hands had closed round the priest's throat?

The Headman might not have prized them apart before Lovegod joined his ancestors on the family altar.

Big Rama darted between Martin and Lovegod, who was paralysed with fear. The Headman put his hand on Martin's shoulder, 'Calmly, my friend. Calmly.'

Fishermen moved forward to keep Martin and Lovegod apart.

'The Elders will confer,' the Headman announced, his silver hair still in place.

Everyone drew back. At least the danger of a fight was past. They were sure of that. The owner of the tea-house and chandler's shop had recovered his self-possession; he would not disgrace himself by attacking the priest.

Martin knelt beside Lina, who was sitting, staring at the sand. He put his arm around her shoulders.

The priest was retiring, when he yelped again, feeling a stab in his belly. Rita desired him to join the circle of the Elders.

'The *Elders* will confer,' the Headman said pointedly, when he saw Lovegod sloping towards them.

The man of God was free to put aside the call of duty and enjoy the company of his chosen life partner.

Lovegod ignored being called a hypocrite. However, Martin's thrust at his pot-belly upset him. Much as he wanted to shed the mound of flesh, he could not. He feared it as a sign of age. Despite his sermons on the brevity of this life of suffering and the eternal bliss of the next, Lovegod did not greet the heralds of the future with serenity. And Rita's abuse had left him feeling insecure.

Martin had been hurt by the priest's insulting words, coming after the night of anguish. He did not know that Lovegod had intended adding, 'She did not drink the Sacred Soup.' If Martin had realized that the priest had calling Lina 'not pure' was solely because she had not imbibed some magic mushroom soup over which he had pronounced words of unction, he would have ignored it.

The next two hours were more painful to Martin than any in his life. It had not occurred to the big man that the others would not be delighted by the return of his daughter, that they now thought of her as the Bride of the Shark.

'Madam, come here, please,' the Headman called Lina, using the linguistic construction proper to a married woman.

Lina made no attempt to move. She sat, staring at the sand between her feet, as she had done ever since her first husky 'Go to the Dreamer.'

Martin put his arm under her shoulders, raising her to her feet and supporting her as, like a sleepwalker, she approached the silver-haired Headman.

'Tell us what happened please, madam,' Big Rama said.

Silence.

Hari could see that Lina, leaning against her father, would collapse if Martin did not continue to hold her up.

'Madam, tell us what happened, please.'

Another silence. Then Hari heard a hiss from the priest's wife, 'Possessed by the forces of evil.'

Just as the Headman began for the third time, 'Madam . . .'

'Go to the Dreamer,' the husky voice spoke. 'You'll understand all.'

'What did you say?' Big Rama frowned, forgetting to use the formal address.

'Go to Dreamhunh!' Danny explained, his mouth frothing.

'Go to the Dreamer,' Lina replied after a long pause. 'You'll understand all.'

'For what reason, madam?'

'Go to the Dreamer. And find your own soul.'

One man felt a knife in his ribs. 'Who is the Dreamer?' he asked gamely – then cringed, as Rita snarled, 'Idiot!' She screwed her finger into his back, shouting, 'She is possessed!'

'Possessed,' echoed Lovegod.

The veins in Martin's neck stood out like snakes.

'It was like a dream,' said the husky voice. 'No sooner did she enter his Palanquin than she found herself alone on the ocean, waiting for her beloved at the Rock. She knew he was coming for her, as he did at the Swim, before this birth. She had felt his presence when she chose his angel iris. At last they would come together. Her soul-mate would not carry her away as the Great Shark, but marry her as the Dreamer.' Lina spoke as though she was back in the Palanquin at Shark Rock, kneeling on the black silk cushion, waiting. 'She heard his call, as he dived off the cliff.'

Hari started. This was one of the fantasies he'd had for rescuing Lina. Shivers ran up his spine. He felt that he alone was able to comprehend the inner meaning of what she was saying. If only he could understand it!

'He swam towards her, slicing through the water like the blade of a hunter's knife. It was the echo of her own joy. She loved him before this world . . .'

'Before this world!' Rita cried. 'She's lying. What is she trying to hide?'

'Nothing!' Hari turned on Rita. 'She's on a higher plane. Can't you understand that?'

The villagers ignored the outsider as completely as if he had not said a word. They looked at each other confusedly.

The Great Shark had struck the Palanquin with unprecedented force – damaging it. With a shock some of the divers had noticed this, but none of them had dared mention it. Maybe a splinter had pierced the Shark's eye. They had seen how furiously its tail had threshed the water. Perhaps Lina, superb swimmer that she was, had taken advantage of the Shark being blinded, diving underwater and racing to the cave with its air bubble.

'That's why she was always lurking round Shark Rock, searching for a hideaway. The wretch found the cave and told no one except that foreigner,' Rita gestured at Auntie.

Muscles clenched in Martin's shoulders. He turned his great back on the priest's wife. He wasn't getting into a cat-fight with her. He clasped Lina.

'As soon as the Shark hit the Palanquin, the hussy swam like a rat for safety. She was such a . . . ' Rita searched for an insult.

'She took the Shark by surprise,' Tao's wife cried. 'It is used to the Virgin being drugged and passive.'

'That is why she refused the Sacred Soup!' Rita screamed. 'The scheming hussy! The Shark is going to take a terrible revenge. It will slaughter . . .'

'Madam! Silence!' the Headman ordered.

Rita's eyebrows drew angrily together.

Martin's shoulders, hunched with suppressed rage, relaxed as the husky voice began speaking again: 'He threw a veil across the moon and drowned the torches. In liquid darkness he swam straight for her. He lifted her from the cushion. They embraced and he carried her into the moonlight. They soared above Shark Bay, over the mountains, beyond the clouds. The planet glistened below them like a pearl in the oyster of space. Then she was falling, falling through an ocean of consciousness, where this world is but one grain of sand on the shore of the Light. The cosmic mask . . .'

'*Lies!*' Rita spurned the Headman's order.

'. . . fell away. He was Time. She was Space. They were Beyond, Within. Her heart sang!' The husky voice faded away. 'She woke in *his* dimension, the world of Love. She was the Bride of the Shark.'

The fishermen whispered together, exchanging glances. Clouds had eclipsed the moon, but in the light of the flares on the Palanquin their keen eyes had seen the dorsal fin cleaving through the bay. The Shark did *not* swim straight for her. It stopped, then circled the Palanquin, then stopped again. And no one could call the savage lunge that smashed into the Palanquin an embrace.

The Elders did not think Lina was trying to deceive them. They could detect no guile in that otherworldly voice. The ordeal in the cave – underwater all night – had made the Bride of the Shark see visions.

But no hallucination could account for one simple fact: the Shark had not killed her.

'The startling events must have an explanation,' said the Headman with an edge to his voice. He tried to question Lina further, but 'Go to the Dreamer' was the only reply the entranced girl made.

The lower jaw of Shark Rock was now jagging out of the waves – like a nightmare haunting the man with no memory. Hari was observing everything with the closest attention, sure that Lina would be set free if he (and only he) could – *do what?* He had just seen how they would ignore anything he said.

Seagulls were flying in the blue sky, crying.

The villagers were not concerned with Lina. She was dead. She had sacrificed her life the moment she took the iris. They were worried about the vengeance of the Shark. It had rejected the Chosen Virgin, even though they had sacrificed her in the time-honoured manner. The Shark might attack everyone who entered the ocean, until Shark Bay was deserted.

'I said that hussy would desecrate the Sacrifice,' Rita hissed. 'I knew it as soon as she refused the Sacred Soup.'

Martin stiffened. A pulse in his temple hammered.

'Then the priest is at fault,' Auntie retorted, 'For not making the Chosen Bride drink it.'

'I would have asked her to drink the Sacred Soup, if Rita hadn't . . .' Lovegod broke off, going red as he realized he was saying the wrong thing.

'What has it got to do with you, worthless foreigner?' Rita's voice was vicious. 'That creature is perverse. Who else would spend their time swimming round Shark Rock? She sold her soul to the devil. I've always thought it.'

'Then why did your *worthless* brother want her as the wife for his *worthless* son?' Auntie shouted.

Choking with indignation, Rita spluttered, 'That hussy made a contract with the devil and drove off the Shark.'

'How else could she have escaped?' her sister demanded.

The fishwives murmured. Much as they disliked Rita's tone, many feared she was right. That voice! A spirit possessed the Bride's body. *It* was going to reinstate the pearl-diver in the village. Then *it* would use her to destroy them.

Scratching his neck and glancing at the god, Tao pointed out, 'If Lina was afraid of the Shark, she could have married long ago.'

Many offers had come in, as the match-makers had watched Martin's daughter growing in beauty. Rita's nephew had not been the most attractive suitor, and Rita's insistence had been offensive: she had ignored all hints, persisting until Martin had had to say 'No' bluntly.

Lina had offered herself five times at the Betrothal Ceremony. And yesterday they had seen how willingly she had embraced the fate that finally enveloped her.

That was because she knew she could escape!

She was the only Bride to survive! Ever! They would have a demon living amongst them. Martin was influential. *It* might put a curse on the boats he built, on the goods sold in the chandler's shop, on the people who visited his tea-house! *It* had already desecrated the Sacrifice. The village was in danger – lives of terror for them all and deathless shame on the ancestors.

'Someone must die,' Rita screeched as she pointed at Shark Rock. 'Or the village will be destroyed. The Shark must have its victim.'

'The stomach in that black cassock!' Auntie pointed at the priest.

The huddle of Elders opened and the Headman stepped forward; he clapped his hands for attention.

Rita turned her back on the giant, while he announced: 'The Elders ask if you have any suggestions for appeasing the Great Shark.'

The fishermen stuttered out various ideas: from praying and starting the whole Ceremony again, to banishing the Bride like the pearl-diver in the legend.

Tao's wife suggested rowing Lina out to the horizon, then throwing her overboard, bound hand and foot.

'We agree. That is the solution.' 'Yes indeed.' Her proposal found favour with Rita and her husband – not surprisingly, since it was Rita's idea, only she got her sister to voice it.

'Hunhh! Go to Dreamhunh!' To the stare of the angular man was added a sawing motion of the chin, as though it was being moved by some Unseen Carpenter. Saliva trickled down Danny's chin. 'Go to Dreamhunh. Go go Danny-Dan.' Danny's awkward movements brought him to Hari, whose arm he clutched. 'Danny-Dan go Dreamhunh. Danny-Dan good messenghunh.'

The Elders may not have been convinced by Danny's estimate of his own ability as a messenger; certainly they did not accept his proposal to do as Lina's husky voice demanded: to go to the Dreamer.

The Sage was too remote for them to contemplate a journey that might take months. They did not know where he lived, or even if he lived. Although they spoke of the Dreamer often enough, they did not truly believe in him as a man of flesh and blood. *The* Dreamer was always with them, of course, as they were with the creations of their own dreams. But they were not ready for *a* Dreamer, a living man who had found himself and realized he was illimitable consciousness.

The Headman and the Elders drew apart again. They conferred in the full glare of the sun.

Finally the giant delivered their judgment in formal language: 'The Bride of the Shark will be returned to the ocean.' Big Rama glanced sternly at Martin to warn him against defying authority – an action he instantly regretted. 'She will be bound to the lower jaw of Shark Rock.'

Hari's knees gave way under him. He found himself sitting on the sand, trembling. *The incoming tide would drown her!* Lina had not escaped. That false omen! The fish had not escaped: wounded by the sea-hawk's claws, the first predator would kill it. The agony of the woman he loved had merely been protracted. Lina must die. Murdered by the Shark, or drowned by the sea.

Rita said nothing; her eyes narrowed at Lina.

'If the Bride is still alive when the tide ebbs after sunset,' the Headman continued, 'the Elders will release her. She may return to the village without stain.'

A trial by ordeal. The fishermen murmured their approval. The Shark could kill the Chosen Virgin. Or he could leave her to die in the waves. Or, if in his omnipotent wisdom he saw that she was immaculate, he could send a wind to turn the tide, saving her before the sea covered her head.

Martin folded his arms and looked the Headman in the eyes. The expression on Martin's face showed that he would do nothing that might compromise his own self-respect, the honour of his family, or the best interests of the village.

Lovegod looked sadly at Lina. Then he caught his wife's eye, and stiffened.

The smug look on Rita's face indicated how highly she rated the chances of a miraculous intervention.

Her smirk vanished as Auntie pointed her skinny finger at Lovegod: 'When Lina escapes Death again, the so-called priest must take her place. As the thin-lipped woman said, "The Shark must have its victim." '

No one took any notice of the old lady, except Rita: her scowl indicated her intention to revenge that 'thin-lipped' insult in a manner the *foreigner* would never forget. And Lovegod: his stomach heaved, fearing that Martin would tear him apart one dark night after Lina's death.

Danny was not satisfied: 'Hunnyh! Danny-Dan go. Not Lin-hunh. Tide tide high high. Danny-Dan go high tide. Go go hunh?' He swung his head from side to side, dribbling.

Hari put his hand to his mouth, feeling sick. The high tide would drown her. Convulsions of the earth's breath. In, out, in, out. High, low, high, low. Time to go. By the new moon. *Not now!* She was here, now. Where to go? *Not again!* He'd got to rescue her. *How?*

In his deep voice the Headman decreed: 'No one will lay eyes on the Bride of the Shark again. No one is to enter the sea, or even set foot on the shore, until the Hour of the

Dragon, high tide at sunset, when the Great Shark will have made clear its will. Leave the beach now.'

Martin gazed at his daughter for the last time, knowing within himself that he would never see her again in this life. He turned and patted Ken on the shoulder, inclining his head to signify that they should go. Forcing a smile, he took Auntie's arm. Together they began walking home.

Big Rama ordered two fishermen to hew a stake from the pomegranate tree the Palanquin had knocked down.

High above, sea-hawks circled, gliding on the thermals.

When the tide completed its ebb at midday, Tao rowed the Bride of the Shark, with the Headman and the two fishermen, out to Shark Rock. The two fishermen kept glancing into the clear sea below them, fearing the Shark might be lurking and overturn the boat.

'There's a stingray!' one of them cried, seeing an ominous black shape stealing over the sea bed.

'It won't hurt you.' Confident in the overseeing power of the god, Tao had no anxiety. He grinned at Big Rama.

The two fishermen drove the stake into a fissure in the lower jaw, lashing it in place with ropes, which they tied to the Rock itself. Then they bound Lina to the stake with knots she could never untie, their eyes gauging precisely how far the high tide would reach: one handbreadth above her head.

The Bride was wearing a cotton shroud, such as they put on corpses. Although the Headman had told them to make another hibiscus garment, and several women had hurried to the Temple to sew one together, Rita had informed them that there were not enough flowers left. 'This will have to do,' she had said, handing them the white shroud.

'It signifies that Martin's daughter is dead to the temptations of the flesh,' Lovegod had explained.

Lina offered no resistance to anything the two fishermen did. Her eyes were blank. She seemed as indifferent to her trial by ordeal, as if she already experienced a higher

103

consciousness, in which the dreams of this world of dew are interpreted in the light of a different sun.

The sun was at its zenith, the heat oppressive.

The Headman gave an order to one of the fishermen, making a gesture towards the victim.

The fisherman took off his conical straw hat and tied it on Lina's head to shield her face from the sun.

Years ago the giant had dandled Lina on his knee and called her 'Sunbeam'. He said gently, 'Heaven be with you.'

'Go to the Dreamer,' the husky voice replied.

Frowning sadly, Big Rama said, 'Return to the shore.'

Tao ran his hand through his hair, weighed anchor, then began to row back to the beach, gazing at Shark Rock.

Lina was left to the waves of the incoming tide.

11

Hari could not face returning to Martin's home.

He walked out of the village and along the paths between the rice-fields, heady with the smells of summer, kicking stones. Occasionally a startled frog leapt into the water, which reflected the blue of the sky.

The heat drove Hari to look for shade. He walked to the pine tree at Shark Rock, ignoring the Headman's decree. There he could at least see Lina, even though she was bound to the stake. Maybe he could find a way to save her. How could they kill her? His heart ached. How would he live without her?

Hari found Danny again, on his knees before the pine tree. 'Huynh. Pleasunh Dream-hunh. Shark Danny-Dan take. Not Lina. Danny-Dan good meal.' Danny's head sawed from side to side; his mouth was wide open. His swivelling head brought his eyes into contact with the stranger. 'Hunnuyhh!' Danny howled and stumbled away at right angles to the path. Correcting his aim and strug-gling to his feet whenever he fell, Danny staggered back towards the village.

Hari walked to the pine tree. Two cormorants scudded away from the cliff, flying low and fast across the bay.

Hari sat down on the gnarled root of the tree, where the day before he had picked up the dead butterfly. This was the day Tao had planned to go swordfish hunting in the open sea 'where the dolphin play', taking his brothers.

The beach was deserted.

In the afternoon sun the shimmering sea was beginning

to swallow Shark Rock.

Tied to the stake, Lina's head was upright; after high tide it would hang down lifelessly. The woman Hari loved was being murdered. Slowly.

Hari hoped they would take her body away before the seagulls pecked out her eyes. If they didn't, he would cut her loose himself, assuming the Shark had not mutilated her body beyond recognition. At this moment the Great Shark might be swimming into the bay to attack her. Could Hari save her now? He could take a sea-knife from the chandler's shop, cut her ropes – and flee for freedom? No, the Headman was bound to come and inspect.

The sun danced on the sea – mirror wings of a million butterflies, flitting against the rocks, bursting into foam. Hari listened to the sound of the waves. His eyes kept returning, horrified, to Lina at the stake.

Banks of clouds frothed on the horizon like waves from another dimension. A dark cloud puffed out, like some monster growling its way into the sky. A sea breeze sprang up. Hari stood and stretched out his arms, welcoming its touch.

A pair of white herons flying overhead swerved in unison as they caught sight of the human at Shark Rock. They flew on over the mountains beyond the Temple.

The dazzling waves were turning choppy. On the horizon the dark cloud reared up like an ogre. Its horns and ears were wreathed in smoke; black brutes issued out of them, groping for life. A gust of wind shook the pine tree. A swell moved through the bay, striking the beach with ponderous force.

Hari had never seen one before – so far as he knew – but suddenly he was sure of it. A typhoon! Hurtling towards the Coast to throw itself on Shark Bay like a furious beast. The village could be washed away if waves stampeded over the beach at high tide.

Martin had told Hari that after the last typhoon they had taken fish off the yellow tiles of the Temple roof and pulled seaweed wrapped like beards away from the dragons' snarling faces. The typhoon had picked up people's homes, hurling them at other houses and smashing both.

Hari realized with a shock that Lina would be battered to death by the waves that would ride in on the whirlwind. He scrambled down the cliff and sprinted towards the village. They had to release her. No one had expected a typhoon. It was no longer a fair trial. The Headman had to put a stop to it.

In the village the tension was aggravated by the second day of idleness. Fishermen had gone to weed the rice-fields in the scorching heat. Returning home in foul moods, backs in pain, they shouted at their wives.

Women clustered round the well, muttering about hunger and death, faces narrowed with anxiety for their children.

The children were playing up, especially the little girls. Their mothers had promised them they could put on their best clothes again and wave the bamboo decorations over the sea like wands, blessing the happy couple on their journey to the undersea palace.

'Now mummy says we can't!' Tantrums!

Older Brother had been rebuffed by the other boys when they went hunting for red-bellied newts. 'Get away, you. It's all your aunt's fault.'

He picked up his own newt and kept dropping it, trying to ascertain its pain threshold.

Anna's piercing scream for help, after Older Brother shoved his dead newt down her blouse, brought Katha running. When she threatened to call Father, both children burst into tears.

The click of balls had been heard at the hard ground between the palm trees. But it had not been counterpointed by the jests and laughter of the old men at their bowls. After a while they gave up playing and stood grumbling in the shade: 'The Great Shark no longer accepts a virgin sacrifice.' 'It wants the whole village!' 'I wish I had not lived to see this day,' sighed one old man, his chest heaving painfully. 'The Elders will disgrace the ancestors.' Another old man shook with rage: 'The shame of it!'

When they saw the stranger running by, yelling, 'Typhoon! There's a typhoon coming!' it was just one improbable event too many.

The fisherfolk barely troubled to look up at the blue sky. Even if there was a typhoon, how would the stranger know and not them? He did not even know his own name. They could expect more from Danny.

'If there was a typhoon, that would be the verdict of the Great Shark,' one of the ancients wheezed. 'Who are we to oppose it?'

Amazed by their reaction, Hari raced to the tea-house, shouting breathlessly, 'Typhoon! Martin! There's a typhoon coming. No one believes me. Martin!'

At first, rushing in from the sunlight, Hari saw only Auntie. She was demanding an apology from Anna.

Anna was, equally earnestly, grasping a rice cake in Auntie's hand.

'Where's Martin?' Hari panted.

'*Humi!* What's the matter?'

'*Where's Martin?*'

'Over there!'

Martin was sitting on a pile of sails in the chandler's shop, staring at the floor.

'Typhoon, Martin! There's a typhoon coming! We've got to save Lina!'

At first the boatbuilder did not move. Then he got to his feet like a man with back pain. He listened to Hari's agitated words, looking closely into his face. Then he lumbered outside.

Black clouds were looming over the sea.

'He's right,' Martin muttered, like a man rising out of sleep. His back straightened. He squared his shoulders. '*Ken!* Come here! Quick!' he shouted into the tea-house.

Then he ran out into the lane and, cupping his hands to his mouth, roared, 'Typhoon! Typhoon!'

Ken, followed by Tao, then Katha, ran into the lane.

'Typhoon!' Martin bellowed. 'Tao! Run to the Temple! As fast as you can! Ring the bell!'

Tao looked to the god for confirmation of this order.

'Run!' Hari exclaimed, waving his arm at the Temple.

Tao ran.

'Katha! Close the shutters!' Martin called. If the blast entered the house, it could blow off the roof, spinning it into the hills.

'Ken, you go that way. I'll go this,' Martin and his son turned and ran through the village, yelling out warnings.

Within moments people were outside their homes, staring at the sky. Men began throwing ropes over thatched roofs and knotting them round boulders, like anchors. Women put out their kitchen fires, then brought inside anything that could be blown away. They had plenty of experience. The threat of a typhoon hung as menacingly over the village as the Shark Sacrifice.

And now they heard otherworldly peals, clanging out alarm from the Temple, as Tao rang the bronze bell.

The noise of hammering rang out, as Martin and the village carpenter went round the houses, nailing down boards and doors which the typhoon might wrench off and fling over the mountains.

Frowning and champing with determination, Auntie helped Katha pull across the shutters. 'How stiff they are! Why do they have to stick now? *Ouch!* Break my nail, would you? What have I done to harm you?'

Anna burst into tears.

'Look after Anna, Auntie,' Katha gave Auntie a little push. 'That's the most important job. You can do it best.'

Auntie nodded in agreement. She took Anna into her arms. Katha continued pulling across the shutters, a smile on her face.

Defying the Headman's decree, first one, then another,

then eventually all the fishermen ran down to the beach, where they anchored their boats and filled them with sand.

At least the fishing boats were ashore. No lives from their village would be lost at sea. Women spared the time to kneel before their family altar and pray for the fishermen of other villages, but their faces shone with relief that their own men were not out in the open sea.

Ken hurried past Hari, carrying planks from the boat-yard into the workshop. Everyone was trained for such an emergency. They worked tight-lipped, taking all the precautions they knew against the death-bringing storm.

Hari had nothing to do. He would only get in the way if he tried to help. But he was not there to help! He had come to get a reprieve for Lina. They seemed to have forgotten her. Well, he hadn't! He must save her. He ran into the chandler's shop.

A minute later one of the sea-knives was missing from its sheath on the rack on the wall and Hari was hurrying out of the shop. He would cut her loose. They would escape while everyone else was busy.

Hari found the doorway of the tea-house blocked by Auntie; in her arms she was carrying Anna, who was crying. The old lady stared at him. Hari's hands broke out in a sweat. Auntie had seen him take the knife. She would call Ken. Hari grimaced. He could not push the old lady out of his way. She was carrying Anna, but . . .

Auntie thrust Anna into his arms, letting go so that Hari had to catch the baby girl. Auntie winked at him. 'Think ahead, Humi,' she urged as she shuffled off towards the family room.

Hari cuddled the crying Anna. He felt desperate. He laughed, ready to scream. What can Auntie be up to? Whatever it was, it didn't matter. I'll put Anna down and run . . .

'Trust me, you silly boy!' Auntie turned and glared at Humi, tapping her crystal neck pendant.

Hari rocked Anna, the sea-knife hidden up his sleeve.

110

Auntie shuffled back. She shoved a bundle into Hari's arms, as he set Anna down. When Hari opened the bundle, he saw with a shock that Auntie had wrapped up a shirt, trousers and a pair of sandals for Lina.

A small leather bag rolled out off the bundle.

'Pearls,' Auntie whispered. 'You'll need money where you're going, Humi. I've always told you, you can't live on dreams.'

Hari stood there, astonished. How could she . . . ?

'Hurry. What are you waiting for?' Digging her fingers into his arm, Auntie pulled him to the door. 'I shall be waiting for you. Bring me my grandson, Humi.'

Now grateful to be ignored, Hari ran to the beach.

Storm clouds lowered over the bay, shutting out the horizon. The rough sea was grey; dark islands of seaweed had been wrenched up from the ocean bed. Breakers lunged at the shore, vaulting Shark Rock and hurling spray over the cliff.

The gale buffeted Hari as he made his way to the pine tree. The wind tore back the branches. He grasped the trunk. Spray drenched him as wave after wave surged into the Rock. Panting, he looked down at the lower jaw.

If calm, the sea would have been licking Lina's thighs but, driven by the storm, the waves were slapping her face, the swirling backlashes sinking below her feet.

A wave roughly snatched away the straw hat the fisherman had put on her head.

A band of pressure tightened round his forehead. Hari could feel a change in the air. He shoved Auntie's bundle under one of the writhing pine roots, where the wind could not blow it away unless it tore the whole tree out of the ground.

Hari looked up as something struck him. Hard rain. It began pitting the surface of the ocean. At that moment Hari saw a man shambling towards him.

'Huynnh!' When Danny saw Hari, he fell down, arms flailing, his head sawing. He got up, tripped and fell again

111

then staggered away, wailing.

What had Danny seen? Would he tell the Headman?

Made frantic by the typhoon, the villagers would cut off the stranger's head as ruthlessly as they would stamp on a cockroach, if they saw him helping the Shark's Victim to escape.

Hari stripped off his shirt and trousers and shoved them under the root. He gripped the sea-knife. Then he scrambled down the cliff, running to the waves' edge as the sea raged up the sand.

Close to, the waves were enormous. It was here, Auntie had told him, that two boys had been taunting the waves of a storm: 'You can't catch me. Hee! Hee! Hee!' A wave lashed out at them. Their bodies were not found for three days.

Before plunging into the sea, Hari looked round to make sure no one had come to the beach. Suddenly he threw himself flat on his face so that he was hidden by the seaweed belched up from the sea.

The Headman was running across the sand. Had Danny told the giant he was here? Hari trembled. He grasped the sea-knife, a determined look in his eyes.

Big Rama was running towards a boat, over which – now Hari noticed – Tao was throwing ropes. With the typhoon screaming in his ears Hari could not hear their words, but he saw their gestures: 'Get off the beach!' 'Not till I've tied down my boat!' 'Get off the beach, I tell you.' 'Not until . . . ' 'Now!' The Headman's right arm pointed; his left all but spun Tao off his feet.

Sprawling in the seaweed, Hari turned his head to look at Lina. A wave whacked into her. Her body jerked, straining against the ropes that tied her to the stake.

Hari jerked back in sympathy. If he left it any longer, he might be too late. She could take no more. He jumped to his feet and ran into the sea. The wave charged into his knees like a wild boar, knocking him over. He was upsidedown. On his side. Head over heels. Another world

112

flashed into his mind. *He was seated in the lotus position!* He didn't know where he was . . . He was back on his feet.

The next wave sprang up in ten-foot ferocity. Knowing that his life, and hers, depended on his timing, Hari plunged into the wall of water. The ocean fell like an enraged beast on the spot where he'd been standing the moment before. His feet were seized by its thundering tail. It was dragging him under. His feet touched bottom. He kicked off hard. He broke the surface. He swam as fast as he could at the next wave thundering towards him. He dived deep under the wave.

The knife in his hand impeded him more than he'd anticipated. He wished he'd taken the sheath and strapped it to his leg. Too late now! Clutching the sea-knife sapped his energy, as wave after wave pounded his body.

They smacked his face. Hari shut his eyes. He tried to strike out towards Shark Rock. Arms pulling. Legs beating. Losing strength. He opened his eyes and looked. He was as far away from the Rock as before. In the storm he could not see Lina at the stake.

Something slashed his face! *The Shark!* In his eyes! Shut them! Blinding him. Stinging. *Was it the tail?* No! It wasn't cutting. It was – the waves! Whipping his face with the fury of the tempest!

Hari fought against the gale-lashed ocean. The distance was not decreasing. His strength was giving out. He despaired of closing the gap. He could not keep on swimming much longer. Even if he could, the waves were getting rougher. They would drive him back. Already they were beating him about like the seaweed they had ripped up from the sea bed.

It was like fighting a swift-flowing river which was hurling everything before it as it swept down from the mountains. How did he know that? That memory must . . . ? *Not now!* He had to get to Lina.

Every time he looked, Shark Rock seemed as far away as ever. He had misjudged the power of the typhoon – and it had yet to unleash its full violence. Hari felt helpless. He could not save Lina. He could not reach her. If he let go of the knife, maybe he could swim to her. But then he could not cut her loose.

Am I fighting a current? *Is that it?* Do I have only to slip to the side to swim forward?

Hari swam at right angles away from the Rock. Then he struck out for it again, using all his energy. He looked. He was closer. *I was right!* It had been a current. He swam towards the Rock. Now he could see Lina. At last he reached the stake, out of breath, arms aching, legs exhausted. 'I've come to save you!' he gasped, clinging to the stake. A wave clubbed Lina; it almost swept him away.

Hari had expected Lina's face to be bleak with suffering. To his amazement, she was smiling. He started slashing the ropes with the sea-knife. 'There's a strong current. Don't fight it. Let it carry you. See where it's going. Then swim diagonally across it.'

'Go to the Dreamer,' her voice croaked, strained by the lashing of the storm. 'You'll understand all.'

Oh no! Hari's stomach churned. Lina had not regained her senses. The waves battered Hari as he struggled to cut the ropes binding her. He felt sick. Somehow he had assumed she would be back to normal. Lina was indifferent to anything he did.

'Go to the Dreamer – you'll find your own soul.'

The husky voice terrified Hari.

Something scratched his back with barbed fingers. *Was it the Shark?* He whirled round, stabbing with the sea-knife. No! Only a clump of seaweed rasping against him. He slashed at her ropes. He cut through the last strand. If he had not then dropped the knife and caught her body, the waves would have smashed Lina against the granite.

They both went sprawling under the water. Hari clawed for life. Lina did nothing and would have drowned if he had not caught her round the waist, heaving her to the surface.

114

'Swim!' Screaming with frustration, Hari swung one arm round her neck, to swim her to the shore. The next wave knocked her body out of his grasp, sucking her down into the jaws. He dived. It was dark. He could see nothing. His arms searched underwater. His hand caught her hair. Hari pulled her to him and threw his arm round her body. Lina was naked. The waves had stripped off her shroud.

The sea now helped, sweeping the couple ashore. Hari pushed from under her, trying to keep Lina's head above water, getting his own head up just long enough to gulp in air.

A wave buried them. Driving them under into the dark. Somersaulting. Bodies entwined. Which way was up? *Air! Where was air?* Trying to break apart. The ocean backlashing, throwing them together. Down. Blackness. Breathless. Another memory stirred in his unconscious. Why? *He was a boy, fighting an animal underwater, battling for breath. His lungs were bursting.* They were now. Lina's must be too.

Murky with seaweed, a wave caught them up. It flung them forward. The swing of Hari's arm with an involuntary kick from Lina – and they caught the next wave as it broke. It hurled them forward, choking, dumping them on the beach.

Spluttering, Hari leapt to his feet, tugging Lina up the sand before the next wave could crash down and drag her back into the sea. Pushing Lina into the piles of seaweed, he threw himself down beside her, coughing.

Now it would happen. Had the Headman seen them? What had Danny told him? Were angry fishermen waiting to hurl harpoons at them? Hari looked up, his eyes stinging from the salt. He saw no one.

'Come on!' He pointed up at the pine tree. 'If we can get there without being seen, we can hide. Out here on the beach anyone might see us.' Hari started to run to the tree.

Half way, he turned. Lina had not moved; she was still lying face down in the seaweed where he had thrown her. He ran back, raised her to her feet, took her hand and

115

pulled, pointing to the pine tree. Lina fell forward onto her face.

'Make an effort!' Hari shouted. He helped her up and set her on her feet. Her legs gave way.

Hari scooped one arm under her knees and lifted her up. Her naked body was dead weight. He struggled up the cliff, stumbling and being blown down repeatedly. By the time he reached the pine tree, knees and elbows bleeding, the hurricane was bending the upper part of the tree horizontal.

Hari set Lina down, her back against the tree trunk. He pulled the bundle out from the tree roots and thrust it into her lap: 'Put on your clothes.'

'Go to the Dreamer – you'll understand all.'

Turning away from her, Hari put on his own shirt and trousers, struggling not to be blown over by the howling wind. When he turned round, Lina had done nothing. She was sitting where he had left her, staring at the bundle, the rain driving into her face. Fighting the gale to get back to her, Hari knelt down beside Lina.

'Go to the Dreamer – you'll find your own soul.'

He put his hand to her cheek. *You poor girl. What have they done to you?* He tried not to look at her wet body, bruised purple where the ropes had been tied. He struggled to pull the shirt down over her head and get her arms into the sleeves. The wind almost tore the damp cloth, whipping it out of his grasp.

Lina put her clenched fists to her mouth.

Moving her over with difficulty, Hari pulled up her trousers, his cold fingers fumbling with the buttonholes.

'Go to the Dreamer – you'll understand all.'

Hari stared at her. He put his mouth to her ear and shouted, 'You've got to do something, or we can never escape. We've got to get away from Shark Bay.' In that gale it had been hard enough bringing her as far as the pine tree. He could never carry her into the mountains.

'Go to the Dreamer – you'll find your own soul.' The

116

husky chant issued like an incantation from between her fists. Lina ignored the rain drenching her face and clothes, sweeping her hair. She was seeing another world. Somewhere in her ordeal she had received this command, and her spirit would not rest until she obeyed. 'Go to the Dreamer – you'll understand all.'

'All right,' said Hari. 'We'll go to the Dreamer.'

Lina stopped chanting. Her eyes closed. When she opened them, they were clear. She took her fists away from her mouth. She rose to her feet. She caught his arm as the typhoon blew her down. Hari grabbed the tree trunk to stay upright. Despite the rain, despite the scream of the wind, she put her face to his and looked him in the eyes as if nothing else in the world mattered. 'Do you agree to go to the Dreamer?' she asked in her own voice.

'By the new moon.' Enthralled by her face, Hari hardly knew what he was saying.

'You agree to go to the Dreamer?' Lina insisted.

He found himself staring into those soul-deep eyes – and no insincerity was possible. He knew the rest of his life depended on the answer he gave now.

One arm clinging to the tree trunk, Hari took Lina by the hand. Their bodies were bent against the ferocious gusts. As if swearing a sacred oath, and even though he had less idea of who the remote prophet was than of who he himself was, he said, gazing into her eyes, 'Yes, Lina. I will go with you and search for the Dreamer until we find him.'

Lightning cracked across the sky. Thunder trumpeted as if an avenging deity was storming through the clouds towards Shark Bay. Soon the full fury of the typhoon would strike the Coast.

Doubling up against the rain, Lina began to run, leading the way up the overgrown track into the mountains. 'There's another path up from the Temple,' she turned to call over her shoulder. 'Hurry. They could cut us off.'

'Slow down!' Hari caught her soaking sleeve, shouting to be heard. 'If you get a stitch, we'll have to stop. They'll catch us easily.'

Hari did not know if the fishermen were chasing them, but he was certain he and Lina would be killed if they were caught. He hoped the fisherfolk would be too busy fighting the typhoon to notice that Lina was no longer tied to the stake. Or that he was missing. *Oh God! Auntie might give us away!*

Whatever the villagers did, Hari and Lina had to flee into the mountains. They could not hide in Shark Bay. Nor clamber round to the next village: the waves would batter them to death against the rocks. Even in the mountains they might not survive the night, exposed to the typhoon.

Screeching, the wind drove the rain into their flesh like icy darts. Creepers whipped the fleeing pair. Bushes tore their clothes as they pushed through. Water gushed down the path.

How far they climbed, they did not know. There was no sunset that night – just a malevolent shutting out of the light. They were cold, wet, hungry, bruised and bleeding.

After her ordeal Lina was barely able to keep going, but it was not until a stone turned under Hari's foot and he stumbled that she said, 'I can't go on.'

'Nor can I,' Hari grunted.

A tremendous gust shook the tree ahead of them; a branch crashed down, blocking the path.

They hauled themselves into the dripping undergrowth, and dropped onto the wet ground under a tree.

'Thank you for rescuing me. I know you risked your life to save me,' Lina looked at Hari with an exhausted smile. 'Whoever you are.'

Hari's heart glowed.

Facing each other, they curled up. Lina fell asleep immediately. Twice that day she had been hauled back from the gates of the next world.

They woke together, staggering to their feet in the dark, as a crash split the heavens. The earth lurched.

The fist of the typhoon struck Shark Bay as if trying to

knock it out of existence. The blast hurled Lina into a bush. Ignoring the thorns that scratched her skin, Martin's daughter clutched her heart. Pain stabbed her from within. She curled up, her body shaking; tears ran down her cheeks.

Hari threw himself over her, trying to protect her from the rage of the typhoon.

Next morning the sky was blue. The death-dealing hooves of heaven had stampeded away, leaving a trail of destruction.

Shark Bay was devastated. The wind had uprooted trees and rocked houses. Beams had crashed down. Walls had fallen in. The storm had ripped off thatched roofs and flung them into the hills. It had blown down two palm trees and stripped the fronds off the rest. It had smashed three fishing boats – and whirled Tao's boat out to sea. No one ever saw it again. The roof of the tea-house lay upside-down in a rice-field.

That first crashing punch of the typhoon had rattled the tea-house as if the gods were playing dice with it. The cedar beam shuddered, terrifying the swallows, whose mud nest began to crumble. The two fledglings looked out, beating their wings and squeaking. In a moment the nest would crash to the floor. Older Brother ran to tell Martin.

The boatbuilder rushed out of the chandler's shop with a ladder, shouting at Older Brother, 'Run to mummy!'

Martin threw the ladder against the juddering beam and started to climb up.

The wind shrieked. The house shook.

'Get out of here!' Martin yelled. But as he spoke, the cedar beam sprang loose, knocking the ladder aside. Older Brother stood below, mouth open in a silent scream of terror.

With agility incredible for his size, Martin leapt from the ladder – in one movement picking Older Brother up and flinging him across the room. The beam crashed down onto Martin's skull. The roof exploded into the air and the

119

birds were swallowed up into the maelstrom.

At dawn Shark Bay was as silent as the incense burning on the family altars, before which men, women and children grouped in tearful silence. It had been the worst typhoon in living memory, killing six people.

Cocks began to crow. Donkeys brayed asthmatically. The cicadas were screaming.

As if rising from a coma, the village came to life. Fishermen emerged from their homes. Men took axes to chop up trees which had been blown down, blocking the lanes. Youths rolled back barrels which had blown away. Boys removed debris. Women set their homes to rights. Children buried the corpses of birds.

A gangling figure hobbled into the confusion of the village, one arm waving to the women at the well, the other clutching something to his chest: 'Huynhh! Lina escape. Over mou-huhntain. Danny-Dan see hunh. Rock from go.' He tripped over a fallen palm tree and fell on his face. He looked up, slobbering. 'Hari go too. With Lina away run. Mou-huhntain over. Go go Danny-Dan? Danny-Dan good messenghunh. Go to Dreamhunh. Danny-Dan run. Lina run gone.'

Danny's words came out so mangled that the women at the well could not make out what he was saying.

Danny tried to get to his feet. He fell down. His head sawed the air. He held up the object he had been clutching, sticking his tongue out as far as it would go.

The women saw that it was the white cotton shroud in which they had dressed the Bride of the Shark.

12

Hari and Lina woke to birdsong. The damp undergrowth was dazzling in the dawn sunshine. Spiders were spinning webs of silver in the gleaming branches.

Hari started. *Spiders! There it was again! Mists swirling in the cobwebs of his memory!* Something to do with spiders. No, he couldn't . . . He rubbed his two-week-old beard. Two weeks! Within two weeks he had to be – *where?*

'We'd better hurry,' said Lina. 'They may send out a search party.'

They started walking uphill. The spiders' webs clung to the fugitives like nets dragging the pair back to the villagers' vengeance. They were both in perfect physical condition. Lina from her daily swimming. And Hari? Not from sitting under the awning in Tao's boat, watching the sun dance on the waves, looking for dolphins and dreaming how he could he burst out of the chrysalis of his lost memory?

The wind had dropped. All day they climbed uphill in oppressive heat. Lina moved with surprising agility. After yesterday's struggle with the waves, every muscle in Hari's body felt wrung out. Here and there they found puddles. They were able to quench their thirst and freshen up their sweating bodies. Their hunger grew.

By twilight they could hardly keep moving.

They came to a wild persimmon tree. Wiping the sweat from their faces, both pulled off raw green fruit thankfully, and bit into the flesh. They ate till their teeth were on edge. A trickling acid rasped their throats. Their stomachs hurt.

They threw up and began retching. Then they were writhing on the ground with stomach cramps.

Agonizingly they crawled into a bamboo grove, its feathery fronds swaying with each quiver of the evening air. With a glance at each other – but without a word, they were so exhausted – they collapsed onto the bed of fallen leaves.

Minutes later they were on their feet, scrambling up the mountain track, their flesh throbbing with pain. Mosquitoes infested the bamboo grove.

Lina saw a cave in the dusk. She started walking towards it.

Hari heard a wolf howling at the moon. He caught her arm: 'Wait. It could be the lair of a wild animal.'

He picked up two stones the size of his fist. Stooping to enter, he advanced into the cave, sniffing, ready to fling a stone at any beast that attacked him.

'There's nothing here,' he called, after rolling one of the stones into the dark. 'Come on in.'

The cave was so low they could not stand erect, and so narrow they kept knocking into each other. They sat down side by side, then lay down wearily, hoping they would not be plagued by mosquitoes.

'If they chase us through the night,' Hari said, 'They could catch up with us tomorrow. We must start early.'

Lina did not reply. From her breathing Hari could tell she had fallen asleep. Suddenly he was very much awake, his mind caressing the girl at his side. He listened to her breath. He imagined the rise and fall of her sleek belly, his hand gliding to her breasts, up to her cheek, her hand clasping his neck and drawing his lips down to her warm mouth.

Somewhere in the mountains the wolf howled at the moon.

Turning over in the cave, his arm brushed against hers. Her breathing changed. He knew she was awake. His heart began thumping. He wondered if Lina could hear the beats

122

pounding through his body. Her breath grew faster.

His arm moved – and touched Lina's. This time it was deliberate. His arm lay against hers. He could feel the warmth of her flesh. Lina did not move, but her body was as tense as a bow string.

Then he did it. In what was supposed to be a natural motion, Hari rolled over towards Lina and placed his arm across her waist.

In the darkness Lina let it lie there for a moment. Then, between thumb and finger, she took his wrist and moved his arm off her body.

Hari rolled back with a moan.

Lina broke the silence: 'If I were free, Hari, you would be my man. I would not think of anyone else. But you know I am promised. I will only marry the one who knew me before I took birth.' She paused. 'Let's find the Dreamer. Then I'm sure it will all fall into place.'

'Who is this Dreamer?' Hari retorted, feeling rejected. 'How can he know?'

Hari could not see the pearl-diver in the night-black cave, but he felt her silent reproach, reminding him of his promise. Somehow he knew that promises made to, or by, Lina were made until Death – and beyond.

'We do not know the relationship between us,' Lina replied after another silence. 'But if it is eternal, no power on earth can separate us.'

They woke before the sun rose. They left the cave, found a puddle, drank and washed, and then began struggling up the path. In places it was so overgrown they had to crawl between creeper-choked trees as if through a tunnel.

They knew that some of the plants were edible, but not which. After yesterday's persimmons, they dared not experiment. Their stomachs growled when they saw wild chestnut and banana trees, even though they had no fruit.

By midday their clothes were soaked in sweat. They saw an orange tree with green globes in the branches. They

123

looked at the hard oranges longingly. Their stomachs growled.

Hari pressed one and said, 'I'm going to risk it. Don't you have one till you see what happens.'

Hari peeled and ate the orange. Then he fell to the ground, doubling up in agony, and groaning.

Lina was at his side in an instant, her hand on his shoulder, 'Oh, no! Not again!'

Hari sat up, grinning, 'Just teasing. They're fine.'

Lina raised her hand as if to give him a playful slap, but she did not touch him.

'Delicious!' she laughed, sitting down beside him and eating one. 'And to think that if Katha had put these on the table at home, Father would have bombarded her with them.' She added in a whisper, 'I wonder how they all are.'

'All right, I'm sure,' Hari said to cheer her up, longing to put his arm round her shoulders. 'You know Martin.'

'I wonder if Father is in the hunt after us.'

He wasn't. At that moment Lovegod was leading the chanting of the funeral rites at the tea-house, prior to the procession that would carry the boatbuilder's body to the cremation ground. Soon Martin would be an ancestor, looking down from his black and gold memorial tablet on the family altar at 'the illusory separative existence' – the Dreamer's term for what mortals call the real world.

Eventually Hari and Lina reached the top of the mountain – to discover it was only a crest. The mountain continued upward. They sat down despondently, wiping the sweat from their faces with their torn sleeves and rubbing their aching legs.

From the top of the mountain they had hoped to see a road, cultivated fields, a town in the distance. Now the journey seemed impossible. Even if they were not attacked by robbers or wild beasts, they would die of starvation – presuming they were not first caught by the furious villagers, who must by now have discovered that the Bride had escaped.

'Go to the Dreamer,' Hari murmured, his head in his hands. 'I've been trying to pluck up the courage to ask . . .'

'Yes?'

'What happened to you at Shark Rock? When you were under the water and received that message, I mean.'

'I don't know,' Lina hesitated. 'It's like remembering you had a dream, but forgetting what it was about.' Her stomach howled like a tom-cat. 'You were having a strange dream last night.'

'Was I?' Hari blushed, fearing he had embarrassed Lina.

Lina laughed, 'You kept going on about the moon:

I've got to be there – and I don't know where.
Before the day of doom – will strike. The new moon!

I didn't know you were such a good poet.'

Hari did not laugh. He stood up, punching one hand into the other. *The new moon!* He hadn't thought of it all day! Less than two weeks to go! He'd got to be *there* – wherever that was – by the new moon. Or calamity would fall on them. *Who? Why me?* He rubbed his beard, trying to catch the memory. He'd got it! The new moon meant . . . No. It slipped away as he was catching it. Time was running out. Not even two weeks. *Twelve days!*

The stranger to Shark Bay sat down; he told Lina as much as he could of the maze in his mind.

'That too will become clear when we find the Dreamer,' Lina said, after hearing him out in silence. She jumped to her feet. 'We must hurry. Come on, nameless man.'

On and on and on.

Somewhere Hari had taken the lead. He stopped. Lina bumped into him. They both laughed.

'We've lost the track.'

'No!' Lina exclaimed. 'Then what's this?'

'It's the bed of a stream.'

'Do we have to turn back?'

'I don't know how far we'd have to go,' said Hari,

125

wiping the sweat from his neck. 'We might have missed the path anywhere – as far back as that bamboo grove. And we might not find it. We missed it once. We might lose a day and run back into . . .'

Lina knew what he meant. 'Then let's carry on.'

'I think that's best,' Hari agreed, but they both sat down on the ground. 'At least they are not trackers like the nomads. If they have kept to the path, they will miss us.'

'Nomads?' Lina's eyebrows rose. 'Who are they?'

'Oh, you know. They migrate – like swallows.'

The pearl-diver did not know.

Another memory exploded in his skull. *Nomads! The desert. Hunters! The Hills of – what?* Hills were trying to burst into the light of day. *It was connected to the new moon!* What could he have to do with nomads?

'Ow!' Lina swatted off flies settling on the blood where spear grass had cut her legs. 'Look!' She pointed to a flat, lichen-covered stone. If they had not been sitting on the ground, she would not have noticed the straight edge.

Hari got up and pulled away the ivy: 'And here's another! It's a flight of steps!' He looked at Lina excitedly.

'They must go somewhere!'

He wanted to hug her. They started going up the steps with renewed energy. Some of them had crumbled away. Occasionally Hari had to search, scrabbling ivy and weeds and earth away with his fingers, to find where the mysterious staircase led.

The sun was setting when the couple struggled out of the undergrowth onto a wide, grassy ledge. Beyond was a sheer drop. Rocky crags soared above them.

Skipping towards them, they saw an old man, wearing a white robe. His long hair and beard were white, but his movements were as light as a child's.

'Oh! What joy to see you in the flesh at last!' he beamed at them, his sky-blue eyes shining. 'Now you can tell him . . . ' he pointed at his own chest 'do you conceive God as a personal deity or as pure consciousness?' He looked at them, as if nothing could be more important to them right now.

Hari turned to Lina. Is he crazy? Has he been expecting us? Or has he confused us with someone else?

'It's the Dreamer!' Lina exclaimed. 'We've found him!'

The old man burst into laughter.

They laughed too. They had found him straightaway! No. He had found them! He had attracted them to him with his occult powers. *That was why they had lost the path!*

'You're the Dreamer!' Lina said, smiling.

'We seek without. We find within,' the old man smiled at them, his skin glowing with vitality. He tapped his ear, 'He knew two humans were coming up the mountain. Not even the wild boars make that much noise crashing through the forest.'

He pointed to the fire, where rice was cooking in a black pot, then cupped his hand to his ear again. 'He put some rice on to boil. He needed no secret powers to hear the call of your stomachs. Yes, you look famished.' His eyes twinkled, as if that was the most delightful condition anyone could hope to be in. 'And you want a wash – ooh! Look at you! Pooh! Go over there to the spring.'

They both laughed. Their hearts throbbed, as if some sleeping part was waking, like the butterfly stirring in the dreams of a caterpillar.

The old man led them to the spring, skipping along the edge of the chasm. They stepped after him, keeping well away from the precipice. They both drank the mountain water. Then they washed the dirt and dried blood off. Some of their cuts reopened.

'Now that's what he thought they'd do,' said the old man, as if nothing could be more charming. He pressed the wounds with some leaves. The cuts stopped bleeding. He handed them other leaves. 'Rub these on your bruises and aching muscles.'

Hari and Lina sat down by the fire – on the side away from the precipice. In the gathering darkness the old man

127

ladled out their meal from the black pot. It was only boiled rice but, with the pickled radish he put out for them, it tasted more delicious than anything they had ever eaten.

'You are the Dreamer,' Lina said, putting down her bowl.

'He is a woodcarver. He comes here for perspiration,' the old man mopped his brow. 'Whew! Whew!' He jumped to his feet and skipped across to a cave, shaded by a mimosa tree – its yellow flowers luminous in the firelight.

'Inspiration!' Hari smiled at Lina.

His white robe flying, the old man skipped back, carrying a camphorwood carving of a boy riding a deer.

'There you are,' he said, handing the carving to Lina touching the deer's antler with his forefinger. 'And there you are,' he added, winking at Hari and tapping the boy on the head.

Yes! His dream of the desert. Hunters were chasing a deer. The boy had to save it . . .

'It is marvellous,' Lina smiled, and wiped her forehead with the back of her hand. 'You have perspired a lot.'

The woodcarver laughed so hilariously he fell down and lay on his back.

'Tell me,' Lina said, when he stopped giggling and sat up. She looked at him as she had looked at Hari when making him promise to seek the Dreamer. 'Are you the Dreamer?'

'He'll tell you,' the old man whispered, giving his white beard a tug. 'Come close. It's a mystery.'

Lina smiled at Hari.

They moved across and sat down beside the old man.

Leaning forward, the woodcarver put his arms round their shoulders, drawing them so close to each other that their hair touched. So quietly that above the pounding of their hearts they could hardly hear, he breathed, 'Your heart contains the answer to any question your mind can ask. Just dive inside – and see.'

He drew back, looking at them so innocently that despite her disappointment Lina began to laugh.

128

'Blessings are smiling down upon you,' the woodcarver waved to the stars, as eagerly as if he expected them to wave back. Taking them both by the hand, he led them to the cave. 'You are sleepy, sleepy. Dream away, but . . .' he put his finger into his mouth like a puzzled child, 'who is it that creates your dreams?'

Hari lay down on the sandy floor, soothed by the scent of the mimosa. Facing the woman he loved, he fell asleep.

'Come here!' a voice called.

Hari got up and went out of the cave. The moon had risen; it shone brightly on the grassy ledge. In the mountains an owl hooted. Its mate screeched back.

The old man's robe, hair and beard gleamed white in the moonlight. He looked like a ghost as he danced from the precipice right up to Hari.

'Look at the stars,' he said, pressing his forefinger between Hari's eyebrows.

The constellation of the Hunter was shining above. *Something to do with hunters! Yes! Like the moon, the stars were telling him – what?* Hari found himself staring into the woodcarver's sky-blue eyes. They fused together and became one, changing to blood-red.

Hari sensed some energy sucking his spirit into an occult vortex. He fought against the power, but he could not resist it. He felt weak. He thought he was going to die. Then he heard a voice within: 'You identify with your senses. Let go, boy hunter, and you will find yourself.'

Hari relaxed.

Suddenly he saw a ruby as big as a watermelon. He caught his breath! Was it the Dragon Pearl?

'Yes, this is your Dragon Pearl. How it grows! It would never fit into an oyster now.' The woodcarver jumped on to the Dragon Pearl. 'You will create it, when you wake to who you are.' He jumped off the giant ruby, then lay down on his back at the edge of the chasm, looking up at the star-filled sky.

'What do you mean?' Hari asked, walking across and

kneeling beside him. 'Who am I?'

'You know yourself. If you want to know what you know, search within. Surrender your mind,' the woodcarver laughed. 'You are not what your senses tell you.' Chuckles echoed round the mountain crags. 'Your mind is the only obstacle. Get out of here, as the butterfly said to the catterpillar.' His words echoed across the chasm. Helpless with laughter, he rolled to the side. He fell over the precipice.

Hari's hand shot out to save him – the old man clutched it. Hari was caught. He was falling!

The man with two weeks' memory woke. It was dawn. Lina was waking too, rising on one elbow. She looked across at him and smiled. 'I dreamt I once lived here.'

'For perspiration?' Hari smiled back, feeling as if the gates of heaven were opening.

After washing in the spring, Lina said, 'I feel so fresh.' Her bruises had vanished. None of their muscles hurt, even though they had been throbbing with fatigue last night.

They walked towards the woodcarver. He had already lit the fire. He stood up to greet them, looking at them with a warmth that made their hearts glow. Water was boiling merrily in the black pot.

The old man gave Hari's bristly cheek a pat. 'I bet you can't remember when you last had a shave.' He stroked his own white beard. 'Nor can I. Listen!' He flung his arms out – his head up to the sky. Birds were singing. 'Stay here today.'

'Thank you,' said Hari. 'But we've got to hurry.'

'You want to search outside. It is easier, but you find outside only what you see within. Please your mind!' The white-robed man tapped his own heart, cocking his head as if expecting it to reply. 'Look into your own heart. What makes it beat? If that's not God, he is not the Dreamer.'

'You are the Dreamer!' they said together.

'We are all the Dreamer,' he giggled. 'We can't all be,

except for him. Can we? That wouldn't be fair.' He put his head on one side like a bird.

Lina laughed.

The woodcarver skipped across to the edge of the chasm; he lay down on his back, as in Hari's dream.

'Come here!' Hari jumped up. 'Please!'

They sat down and began eating. It was only rice and pickled radish again, but it tasted as wonderful as before.

When they had eaten, the old man accompanied them, capering happily, as far as the mountain pass, waving to the butterflies fluttering round the flowers that dotted the path. In the distance they could see the town.

'Goodbye and thank you . . .' Hari began.

'You never answered his question,' the woodcarver interjected. He skipped along, then stopped to wave to an eagle soaring above the mountains. 'Which do you worship?'

They looked at each other.

He stood still, stroking his white beard, his sky-blue eyes shining. 'They are both the same. Like marriage and the wife. You can't have one without the other.' He smiled from Hari to Lina, then put his head on one side again. 'Talking of her, go to the town and ask for a *sword* polisher called Julian. Swordsmen'– (the old man pronounced the 'w') – 'from all over go there to have their *swords* polished. Julian likes to hear their tales of travel, and may have heard of your Dreamer.'

He bent and picked a daisy. 'It's not bye bye, for . . .' he danced 'we are One. You too,' he said to the daisy. 'And you,' as he waved the daisy at a dragonfly landing on the tip of a branch. 'So long as you think you are awake, you are off the point. The daymare is not to realize you are asleep. Wakey, wakey! You will be Dreamers!'

Soon sweat was running down their bodies as they walked downhill. There was no shade on the path. Their tongues were parched by the heat. They walked quickly. Hari thought they must have escaped any pursuit from

131

Shark Bay, but he was not taking any chances. He did not want Lina to face death for the third time.

The slope grew less steep. They found themselves walking between terraced rice-fields. Hari and Lina drank from the shallow water and washed off their sweat. They walked on.

Snakes, which had been basking peacefully on the path ahead of them, slid into the shallow water as the humans approached.

The rice-fields had been emerald green in Shark Bay, but here they were gold. Women in baggy trousers tight at the ankles were weeding for the last time before the back-breaking work of harvest.

Lina began singing.

Temple bells were ringing through the twilight when they eventually reached a town with broad, paved streets lined with plane trees.

'Look!' Lina pointed at the houses. 'Every home has its own well!'

Their pace slowed. They gazed with admiration at the shops in the tree-lined avenues. At the brilliance of the flowers in formal flower beds. At the vermilion humped bridges. They marvelled at the silk dresses of the women.

They stared at the swordsmen, whose faces were concealed by boxwood hats. Their silk robes were handpainted with beasts and thunderbolts. They carried two swords, as subtly curved as the new moon: one for the enemy, the other for their own belly, should honour require. They regarded the sword as their soul. Every day they woke prepared to die.

'Excuse me!' Hari said to catch the attention of one of these men to ask the way. The swordsmen seemed not to hear him.

Hari tried again, speaking louder to the next swordsman. The man's face reflected his iron self-discipline, the first pillar of which was, 'Never lie to yourself.'

The swordsman swished by, quickening his pace.

Hari put out his arm to stop the next swordsman. The man moved so fast Hari did not know what happened – except that he was sprawling on the ground at the foot of a plane tree. 'Insolent!' the swordsman growled, striding on.

'Are you all right?' Lina ran to Hari's side. She put her hand out and stroked his head.

'Not hurt, but surprised,' Hari got to his feet with Lina helping him up. *She touched me!* 'Try asking one of the women.'

'Excuse me,' Lina said, raising her hand towards a woman with an exquisite coiffure.

'How dare you, beggar!' the woman hissed, looking straight ahead.

They understood. Their torn and dirty clothes elicited contempt from the townspeople. Their feet were covered in dust; their sandals had all but worn out. And Hari's two-week-old beard made them look disreputable. Now they felt embarrassed to ask the way to the sword polisher.

In a poor quarter of the town they came across a street vendor selling rice wine, and a group of men sitting on benches under a tree.

'We should receive help from these people,' Hari said. He went up to one of the men, 'Can you please tell me the way to the house of Julian, the polisher of swords?'

The drunks jeered at him, demanding to know what the tattered country bumpkin could possibly want with Julian, before whose house even the swordsmen dismounted so as not to look down on the polisher of their 'souls'.

'Can you please tell me . . .' a hare-lipped thug with only one arm mocked Hari's country accent.

A lout with dark marks round the armpits of his shirt, got to his feet, leering at Lina, his eyes like a rat's. 'Look under those rags. The tramp's a beauty. How her eyes flash!' He staggered towards her, one hand fumbling his crutch.

'Let's get out of here!' Hari pushed Lina away with his

133

hand in the small of her back.

They came to a market square. The market was over and litter lay scattered about. Layabouts lounged around while the stallholders dismantled their stands.

'I don't know if we dare go to the sword polisher,' said Hari, rubbing his beard.

'We've got the pearls,' Lina replied. 'We can buy some clothes.'

'Good idea.' Hari walked across to a seller of watermelons. He asked quietly, 'Can you please tell me the way to Julian, the sword polisher? And where I can buy some clothes? I will give you a pearl.' He took the leather bag out of his pocket, untied it and picked out a pearl.

While Hari was holding it up for the huckster to see, they heard an ugly voice behind them: 'What do *you* want with Julian, tramp?'

They turned to see that the lout with rat eyes had followed them.

Suddenly the lout noticed that Hari was holding a pearl. His eyes went wide – he could see that the leather bag was full of them.

Other ruffians slouched forward. 'What's Rodent found?'

Hari quickly pushed the pearl back into the bag and shoved the bag into his pocket.

'The tramp's got a pearl!'

'He's got a bagful,' said a thin hoodlum, his face like a weasel's.

More ruffians surrounded Hari and Lina. Their voices were ugly: 'They won't do you any good where you're going.' 'The dead don't wear pearls.'

No one noticed the swordsman, his face hidden by his boxwood hat, standing in the shadow of a mulberry tree.

'Give it me, tramp!' Rat-eyes howled. He grabbed at the pocket that contained the bag of pearls.

Hari leapt back, keeping Lina behind him with one arm, the other fist raised. If only he'd kept the sea-knife he'd used to cut Lina's ropes at Shark Rock! He had no weapon. Surely they hadn't gone through all that struggle only to be killed by street villains?

'One of you against all of us!' hissed the weasel-faced hoodlum, drawing a dirty finger across his throat.

Hari inched back, his body shielding Lina. Would they let her go if he gave them the pearls? *No!* Could they be trusted? *No!* Could he open the bag and throw it to the ground – and run with Lina, while the swine fought each other for the pearls? He saw a stone, the size of his fist, beside a water barrel.

Hari bent down, seized the stone and straightened up before Rat-eyes, who leapt back fearing the tramp was attacking, realized that his guard was down. Hari glared, his arm coiled, a lethal weapon.

The ruffians jerked back. Their street cunning saw that the tramp knew how to throw – and they did not want to be the target.

'Touch me and you're dead,' Rat-eyes snarled.

A villain with a knife took a step towards Lina. She cowered back towards the mulberry tree, terrified. Were these human beings?

They were closing in like a pack of dogs.

'Get away!' Hari shouted, taking a step forward.

This time the ruffians did not jerk back. They knew he could not hit all of them. But the stone in his upraised arm kept each of them from being the fool who attacked first.

Out of the corner of his eye Hari noticed the weasel-faced hoodlum slinking round behind them. His dirty hands reached out to seize Lina.

Hari flung the stone.

'Aaaeiegh!' The hoodlum's scream was ear-splitting. He fell to the ground. The stone had smashed his knee-cap.

'Get her!' yelled Rat-eyes, lunging towards Hari to grab the pearls. 'Get her!'

135

13

'Lina go escape!' Danny dribbled. He stood up, withdrawing his tongue. 'Huynhh!' He dropped the shroud, fell to the ground and grasped it, pressing it to his chest.

They all stared at the white shroud which the Bride of the Shark had worn. What had happened?

The priest and his wife were strutting towards the well, looking smug. The Temple, the most solid building in the village, surrounded by its sturdy camellia trees, had suffered no damage at all – divine vindication of the priest's conduct. Lovegod and Rita looked up at the palm trees by the well, which the typhoon had stripped of their fronds. Rita clicked her tongue. Lovegod shook his head, placing both hands on his pot-belly.

'Look what he's found!' Tao's wife pointed to Danny, as he got to his feet.

Rita walked across and put out her hand to take the shroud.

Danny clutched it tighter. 'Go go Danny-Dan. Hunh?' He avoided Rita and stumbled across to Lovegod. With his free hand Danny fumbled the sleeve of the orange silk robes, which the priest was wearing at Rita's behest – officially Lovegod was not allowed to wear them outside divine service.

'Lina escape!' Danny splattered Lovegod with saliva. 'Mou-huhntain over go. Go with huh-Hari. Danny-Dan go go too? Holy hunh?'

Lovegod was always flattered, yet embarrassed, when Danny called him, 'Holy one.' He turned for help to his wife.

'How dare you touch his reverence?' Rita wrenched Danny's hand away from Lovegod's robes. 'You will vomit all over him again!'

'Hoiynnh!' Danny stretched his hand out again to grasp Lovegod, clutching the shroud to his chest. He stuck his tongue out full length.

'Away!' Rita shoved his shoulder. 'Hoiynnh!' Danny went reeling. He tripped over his own feet and fell down, blubbering.

Rita bent over him, grabbed the shroud and pulled.

With both hands Danny clutched it tighter than ever.

'What's the matter?' the Headman called out, bringing the roof of the well back from the school playground with three young men. They were all stripped to the waist and panting. Big Rama's gigantic chest was bathed in sweat, but his silver hair remained in place. 'Put it down, lads.'

Rita let go of the shroud and turned to consult her husband.

The giant walked over and went down on one knee beside Danny. 'Are you all right, Danny-Dan?'

'It's nothing!' Rita snapped. 'The idiot fell over.'

Danny gave her a wounded look and began crawling away.

'It's all right now, Danny,' the Headman put his large hand on Danny's shoulder.

'He found that,' said Rita, pointing to the white shroud Danny was clutching.

Big Rama put out his hand.

Danny placed the shroud on it.

The Headman stared. 'What happened, Danny-Dan?'

'Danny see gone. Lina. Huh-Hari go too. Danny-Dan go too? Hunynh? With Lina go go Danny-Dan.'

'I'll take a look. Danny, show me where you found it.' The Headman stood up, his brow furrowed. 'Come with us, lads. Reverence, would you join us, please? I'm sure your wife can manage without you for a while.'

'Yes, of course. Excuse me, dear. Duty calls.'

Rita shot a glance of contempt at the Headman's sweating back as, supporting Danny, Big Rama led the men to the beach.

Lina's corpse was not tied to the stake at Shark Rock. The stake was not there. Shark Rock itself had vanished. The typhoon had shattered the overhanging upper jaw. Hundreds of tons of granite had crashed down on the lower jaw, which collapsed like a tooth with a cavity.

'Lina escape,' Danny slavered. 'Huhuh-hu-huh!'

'Yes, Danny-Dan,' Big Rama agreed. 'Lina has escaped to a better world.'

'Flee. Fly. Over mou-huhntain.' Danny pointed one hand at the horizon of the ocean, and the other, in line with his wet chin, at the mountains.

'Yes, Danny-Dan,' said the giant, pointing up at the sky. 'Over the clouds too. She's gone to Heaven, where we'll all go one day. You will see her there.'

Danny grinned. His head sawed the air. Suddenly he flung up his hands and fell down. 'Hunehh!' He lay on the ground writhing.

'What is it, Danny-Dan?'

'*All* go Heav-hunh? *ALL*? *Rita* go Heav-hunh? Danny-Dan not escape. Hhuh-hunyhh?'

Big Rama heaved a sigh.

The man of God intervened. 'Of course Rita will go to Heaven, Dan, like all good people, including you and Big Rama, and me, I hope.' He smiled modestly. Privately, Lovegod (whose notion of Heaven was as simple as Danny's – human bodies in a golden palace) doubted the likelihood of the idiot sitting in glory in God's throne room. However, ideally, since it was Paradise, he did hope he would find Lina there, rather than his wife. In public, however, the priest could not appear to lag behind the Headman in sympathy for the unfortunate.

'Holy huynnh!' Danny let out a howl. 'Danny-Dan not go. Danny-Dan stay. Not not *not* go Danny-Dan!' Feebly he scratched the ground with his fingers, frothing at the mouth.

That evening, the villagers were summoned to the Temple. The Headman announced the verdict of the trial by ordeal. It was as unexpected as it was awesome. The god had rejected the impure Bride and sent a typhoon to execute her. Shark Rock, where the pearl-diver had hidden, had come crashing down, simultaneously crushing to death and burying the Sacrificial Victim. No black and gold memorial tablet could be placed on the family altar. She was to be obliterated from their memories. Miraculously, the Great Shark had thrown back the shroud as a sign of satisfaction.

'The creature tried to disgrace the ancestors of the entire village,' Rita denounced.

14

'FIGHT!' With a terrifying roar the swordsman charged out of the shadow of the mulberry tree.

Two feet slammed into the ribs of Rat-eyes, as he lunged at Hari. The lout went crashing into a stall and slumped to the ground. He did not move.

Landing on his feet after the chest-high kick, the swordsman lashed out with his right foot at the head of one of the ruffians. A jaw broke. Spinning, he smashed his left knee into another's solar plexus. The ruffian doubled up in agony.

The swordsman feinted with kicks that came within an inch of three men's faces. They screamed, though he didn't touch them. Now he did. With controlled fury his feet cracked into shoulder, stomach and chest. Three thugs went sprawling.

The villain with the knife ran at his back. The swordsman side-stepped. His foot skidded on a piece of watermelon. He slipped. The knife caught his hand. Blood spurted. He dived to the side. Back on his feet, he sprang towards the man with the knife. The swordsman's right foot struck the villain's wrist with the crack of breaking bone. Before the knife hit the ground, the swordsman pivoted, shooting his right heel into the man's groin and, whirling, his left foot into his throat as he buckled up. A croak came from the villain's chest, his body moving in spasms across the market square, until he collided with a cart.

Six thugs remained, eyeing the swordsman with hate. Running forward, the swordsman dropped on one leg as if he himself had been knocked down. He scythed round with the other leg. One man's knees were shattered. He fell to the ground, screaming with agony.

The rest ran.

Eight bodies lay on the ground, writhing and groaning, or unconscious. The swordsman's boxwood hat was still in place. The fight had lasted one minute.

At the corner of the square the hare-lipped lout and another man turned, glaring at the swordsman who had stolen their pearls and woman. They did not dare fight, but they shook with frustration. They knew that the swordsman would not deign to draw his sword – his soul – to cut down vermin such as themselves, but that even if they came back armed, any swordsman worthy of the name would have techniques for plucking the weapon from an unworthy adversary. They had seen what he'd done to the man with the knife.

The swordsman took a pace towards the two louts. He stamped his foot. They ran away.

'Thank you . . .' Hari began.

'Move – before they come back with others,' the swordsman cut Hari short. 'Follow me. I'm going to Julian.' He strode out of the square, his boxwood hat so low they could not see his face. He was wearing an old silk robe with a pattern of flying cormorants. And he flew. They had to run to keep up.

Hari picked up two stones, glancing round in case the ruffians attacked again.

Lina was trembling.

Hari looked at her, longing to put his arm round her. More! He wanted to throw his arms round her and press her to him so hard that she would cry out laughing for him to stop, then smother him with kisses.

Crowds scurried past, jostling them, as Hari and Lina hurried after the swordsman. They hardly noticed the lanterns lighting the oleander-lined streams, throwing pools of light between the willow shadows.

Two louts barged into Hari, pushing him away from Lina. One was the man with the hare-lip.

Thinking it was another attack, Hari raised his hands to crack their heads with a stone.

'Sorry,' stammered the man with the hare-lip, pointing helplessly to his missing arm.

'Sorry.' The other man looked shifty.

Hari lowered his arm. The two louts slunk off into the crowds.

'Wait!' the swordsman ordered, when they came to a house surrounded by a wall. The main wooden gate with its own roof was shut. A starry web of passion flowers clustered round the side gate, which opened noiselessly as the swordsman pushed it, stooping to go through.

'Watch out!' Hari said to Lina. With their backs to the gate, they waited, peering into the dusk, vigilant against another attack.

The side gate opened. A maid came out and, bowing, asked them to enter. She took them to wash, then showed them into a small room, placing two silk cushions at the low table on the reed-matted floor.

In the alcove, a hanging scroll depicted one sword with the words 'Not two' in exquisite calligraphy. Below, a hibiscus stood in an antique vase, recalling the poem:

'In a vase that has seen a thousand winters,
 a flower that does not last a summer's day.'

Lina knelt and Hari sat down crosslegged on the silk cushions.

The maid brought two bowls of green tea and five bean cakes – and an oil lamp, since it was getting dark.

They knew that politeness expected them to leave the fifth cake, but they had had nothing to eat since leaving the woodcarver at dawn. 'You have it.' 'No, you.' They ate half each.

'How I long for home!' Lina blurted out. 'Maybe they are

all sitting round the table in the family room. If only . . . but I can never return.'

'Maybe you can go back one day?'

'After seven years like the pearl-diver in the legend?' Lina forced a smile. 'Father must be missing me.'

When the maid came in to trim the lamp, she looked at the empty plate and suppressed a smile. She left, then returned with a jug of water, two glasses, and a plate piled with bean cakes.

They ate them all. Then they felt guilty about eating the cakes of the sword polisher who, they feared, would be more arrogant than any swordsman. They had only come to ask the way to the Dreamer – sent by a crazy old man in the mountains. They would offend the famous sword polisher if they offered to pay him a pearl for the cakes.

'The pearls!' Hari cried, feeling his pocket. 'They've gone!'

'Gone?' Lina said, looking at him with a smile. 'Don't look so alarmed, Hari. There are plenty more.'

'Plenty more? Where?' The shifty faces of the louts who had barged into him flashed into Hari's mind.

'Where those came from,' Lina laughed. 'The sea.'

'But . . .' looking at her, Hari started laughing too.

The paper door slid open.

A woman bowed and entered, greeting them both with a smile: 'I do apologize for keeping you so long. It was literally a matter of life or death. At least I see you are enjoying yourselves.'

Hari wondered if Julian had been assaulted. Life or death! But at least his wife was friendly.

'You're Julian!' Lina exclaimed.

'Yes,' Julian smiled, looking at them closely, as they adjusted their minds to this lady being the awesome polisher of swords. Sword polishing was an unusual occupation for a woman to undertake, but the swordsmen respected only one criterion: the excellence with which their 'souls' were polished. Julian put her heart into her craft, making it her 'Way' to bring her spirit into union

143

with the Dreamer.

'You come from the Coast, judging by your accent,' Julian said, then guessed shrewdly: 'You met my husband, Halcyon, in the mountains and he sent you to me?'

'Your husband?' Lina stared.

'Halcyon!' Hari exclaimed. 'The man who came to Shark Bay? Martin said he was the Dreamer.'

'It was *him!*' Lina clapped her hand to her mouth. 'The Dreamer, who told me I could only marry the one who knew me before I took birth. Oh! Why didn't I recognize him? His words have dominated my life.'

'Halcyon did not want you to recognize him,' Julian answered.

'We must go back,' Lina said to Hari. 'He'll tell us everything.'

'He used his powers to throw a veil across your memory,' Julian smiled. 'He reveals himself only as far as you are open. However close you may come to him in the body, you hear only what you are ready to hear.'

The door slid open. Kneeling in the passage, the maid told the sword polisher, 'The water is hot now.'

'Thank you.' Julian turned to her guests. 'You'll want a bath and some fresh clothes. I think those are best discarded as reminders that all mortal things are transient.'

They smiled.

'Then we'll have something to eat. You'll both stay the night of course.'

They nodded gratefully.

'While you take your bath, Hari, I'm going to ask Lina to tell me her story. Then while you are in the bath, Lina, Hari can tell me his version. Oh! I'm not trying to catch you out,' she laughed. 'One story, told by two people, becomes two stories. I find few things more fascinating than seeing different viewpoints.'

Hari bathed, wallowing in the wooden tub. How wonderful that hot water was! He put on the clean clothes Julian had given him. While Lina took her bath, he explained to

144

Julian why he had not shaved off his beard, 'It is always there, reminding me: who am I?'

Hari was amazed by her graciousness. But Julian laughed it off with 'The guest is God, as we say' and 'Good Heavens! Matchless elegance!' when, after her bath, Lina walked back into the room with her hair washed and brushed.

Julian took them into another room for dinner. Its sliding walls had been removed for coolness. Hari could not make out where the house ended and the garden began, since under a wistaria canopy the verandah stepped out over a pond filled with lotus flowers.

They sat down on silk cushions round the low table.

Hari asked, 'Were our stories so different?' hoping the sword polisher would reply: 'No, I can see why you love each other so deeply; it was as if one soul lived in two bodies.'

'Completely!' Julian laughed. 'If I had not known, I would never have guessed it was the same adventure.'

A carp splashed in the lotus pond.

In deference to her guests' country tastes, Julian had served a simple meal, but it was more refined than anything Lina had ever seen. Raw fish, such as she ate in Shark Bay, but sliced so delicately! And served on plates that were works of art.

'I do not think the Dreamer is there now,' Julian told them, helping herself to a sliver of ocean bonito. 'There was a man with that title; he lived with the nomads who migrate to the Hills of Heaven for their summer pastures.'

'The Hills of Heaven!' Hari gasped. His heart seemed to swell till it hurt. 'That's where I've got to go. I know it!'

Lina looked at him, 'You mentioned the nomads before.'

'Yes. They . . .' he shook his head.

'The swordsman who brought you here has just come from the Hills,' Julian smiled. 'He'd heard the Dreamer was no longer with the tribe. He didn't say why he'd left. Missing, or ill, or even dead, I suppose. If only I'd seen you first, I would have asked him.'

145

'He's gone now?' Hari asked, looking out at the stone lanterns throwing light on to stepping stones that led into a moss garden.

'Vanished into the night,' the sword polisher replied. 'The law allows swordsmen to kill. Sometimes one kills an enemy fairly, but he has to remain on guard for the rest of his life against the vendetta of the family. I'll say no more.'

Hari could imagine the swordsman, concealed under his boxwood hat in a tea-house, overhearing someone saying that the Dreamer had left the tribe – but asking nothing.

'That's why it is fortunate you only smashed that man's knee,' Julian went on. 'If you'd hit his head and killed him, that mob would never have let you out of town alive.'

'But they started it,' Hari protested.

'They'd have finished it too.' From her salad Julian took a slice of carrot, cut in the shape of a flower. 'And it's as well those pickpockets stole your pearls. The scoundrels will take no interest in you now. But take care on your journey: street thugs are nothing compared to the bandits who, having relieved travellers of their possessions, assume they have no further wish for life.'

'Thank you for putting it so elegantly,' Hari smiled.

'Please thank the swordsman for us, when you see him again,' said Lina, drinking *miso* soup from a lacquer bowl. 'Why did he help us? The other swordsmen were so unfriendly.'

'Oh, he didn't help *you*,' Julian said. 'He was grateful for the practice.'

'Practice?' they said together.

'Swordsmen fight to the death, so they are glad to get into brawls to refine their skills. Did you notice that he used only his feet?'

'No,' said Hari. 'Why?'

'In case an arm got broken or cut off in a real fight.'

'A real fight!' cried Lina.

'You mean?' Hari exclaimed. 'What was a struggle for life

146

to us was just an opportunity to hone his skills for the swordsman?'

'I told you I found different viewpoints fascinating,' Julian smiled. 'He learnt a valuable lesson. He slipped on a water-melon. If that villain had been trained to fight, the swords-man would be dead. You too probably.' The sword polisher laughed, as if this was a charming joke. Hari thought of Hal-cyon. ' "That warned me to look out for anything," he said. "The watermelon was a hidden enemy, ready to stab me in the back." '

'The best swordsmen spend as much time meditating as in sword practice. That gives them the concentration that brings timing and speed,' Julian added, taking a sliver of sea-bream. 'Theirs is the most testing of all the "Ways" that lead to union with the Divine. If you make one mistake, you lose your life.'

'That would help your concentration,' Hari murmured. He helped himself to a tiny piece of shredded jellyfish.

'If you are determined to search for this Dreamer of the nomads . . .' the sword polisher looked at them. They turned to each other and nodded. 'You have a harsh journey ahead of you. Before you come to the Hills of Heaven, you have to cross a desert where no birds fly. And where, they say, the only signposts are the bones of the camels that have gone ahead of you. You will have to buy a camel.'

Day after day Hari and Lina travelled towards the Hills of Heaven and, they hoped, the Dreamer. The language changed into another tongue, and they had to communicate by gestures. Only the dogs were the same everywhere: always running out to bark at the strangers.

In the rice-fields, peasants, blackened by the sun, rested from the labour of cutting and stacking the harvest. They sat back against sheaves of rice with as much ease as any potentate.

Julian had given Hari some money. At first the man whose name no one knew had refused it, saying he would find work, but the sword polisher had laughed, 'Pass it on to someone else, when you are able. That way it may come back to me in another incarnation when I need it more.'

At night they lay side by side in fields, never touching each other. Yet coming to know – and love and respect – each other with an intimacy closer than physical union. Daily they grew more comfortable together, feeling it was only the other's company that made them whole.

Sometimes Hari found Lina expressing the thought in his mind. Occasionally he heard her repeating his idea. Often their conversation skipped happily over ellipses no one else could have followed. Now and then they did not need to say a thing: a glance could convey whole sentences.

They stopped in front of a wayside shrine beside a fig tree. Fresh flowers stood in an old vase before a statue of the Dreamer, represented as a carpenter making a sickle, the dying and rising god associated with the rice harvest.

Lina used the brush of twigs, kept at the side, to sweep the shrine clean. Then they bowed their heads, steepling their hands before this conception of the Illimitable.

Both stopped praying at the same moment.

Hari brought Lina a bunch of forget-me-nots, sitting down beside her under the fig tree and handing them to her without a word.

'I never will,' said the woman he loved, pressing the sky-blue flowers to her heart. Their eyes spoke smiling joy. 'Even if you vanish into thin air at the new moon.'

'*They* depend on me. If only I knew why.' Hari held her eyes with his own. 'I've promised to go with you until we find the Dreamer – and I'll never go back on my word – but if I'm not there by the new moon . . .'

'I release you from your promise with all my heart.'

'First tell me where . . .' Hari broke off. 'You come into it! Lina, something connects your Dreamer with my new moon. By saving them, we will find who knew you before birth. That's why I went to Shark Bay. The Dreamer sent me to bring you to him by the new moon. Could that be it?'

'What for? Another sacrifice?' Lina murmured, putting her nose into the bouquet of forget-me-nots. 'You knew me before I took birth.' She looked at him. Their eyes locked. 'I feel it.'

A dreamtime later, Hari said, 'Maybe he's dying. He has foreseen his death at the new moon. We have to reach him and receive some secret teaching before he leaves the body.'

'I believe in you.'

Hari stood up. 'Come on. Let's walk until nightfall.'

'Let's hope it's the right direction,' Lina laughed. She laid a stone in the shrine before the Dreamer, then knelt, holding the sky-blue flowers against her heart: 'Bless you for bringing me this man. Even if I did not know him before birth, I will treasure his memory in my heart as long as the blue sky stands over the mountains.' She placed the forget-me-nots upon the stone.

Lina prayed silently, so Hari would not hear. But the man she had found on the beach did hear – inwardly. A lump formed in his throat. Who was he? How could he ever be worthy of this woman?

15

They bought the camel using sign language. It could carry Lina and the water. Hari would walk.

With his head bent over and resting on his hands to suggest sleep, Hari asked the number of nights they would need to spend in the desert.

The caravanserai keeper winked: of course the attractive couple – so delighted with each other's company they couldn't possibly be married – wanted to sleep together.

Hari ignored the wink.

The caravanserai keeper held up four fingers.

'Four,' Hari murmured to Lina. 'That will bring us to the new moon.'

The caravanserai keeper presented Lina with a white burnous. He could not take his eyes off her. His hand reached out to pat down the burnous, which did not hide the swell of Lina's breasts. He stopped dead at the look she gave him. He turned to busy himself with the halter – and did not come within three paces of her again.

Hari paid for the burnous, holding his hands out, full of money. The caravanserai keeper helped himself with a smile. Raising his eyes to heaven, he put one hand on his heart: God was his witness he was not cheating the trusting foreigner.

The camel was a cantankerous beast. It turned on Hari while he held the rein as Lina mounted. It would have bitten him if he had not whipped his arm back so fast.

The camel began walking into the wilderness. The landscape was utterly barren, except for a few camel-thorn bushes, and an occasional camel, front and rear leg hobbled, browsing.

Hari could see that Lina was apprehensive. She looked ahead with a furrowed brow. All her life she had lived within the sound of the waves. She had swum and played in the sea every day. She loved the smell of low tide. Now the pearl-diver had gone ten days without even seeing the ocean. She had to face this stony desert, where nothing grew, inhabited only by snakes and deadly insects.

The heat was appalling. The camel plodded over the desolate ground with the supercilious smile on its face that signified, so the poet said, that it knew the 108 names of the Dreamer (cosmic, immanent, transcendent, and so on).

Apart from the heat and the constant thirst – her tongue was swollen and her throat rasping – the journey across the desert was not as bad as Lina had anticipated, once she got used to the swaying motion of the camel.

Looking into her eyes, when they stopped to drink their water ration, Hari pointed out that the desert had something of the infinity of the ocean. His tongue running round his parched mouth was the only sign that he was affected by the waves of heat thrown off the desolate ground. The man Lina had found on the beach kept sniffing the air, as if he could not drink in enough of the boiling elixir.

And all the time in the distance they could see the magenta mountains of the Hills of Heaven.

They were not prepared for the nights. They were freezing. In the moonless dark Hari and Lina huddled together for warmth against the camel.

The third morning, as Lina mounted, the camel reared up on its hind legs with a roar of pain, throwing her off. It galloped away, screaming and crazed with agony.

Hari ran to Lina's side: 'Are you all right?' He took her hand, putting his arm round her shoulders.

'Yes, I'm fine,' she said, looking across. The camel fell down. It was bleating for a full minute before its movements ceased. 'Poor camel.'

Getting up, Lina almost put her other hand on something. Hari saw it raise its lethal stinger: black, malevolent.

'Lina!' He pulled her away. The tiger-scorpion was huge. It scuttled under a rock.

They drank deeply, then walked on, carrying as much water as they could – and looking with regret at what they had to leave behind. Stomachs bloated, they could not stop thinking of the dead camel, whose bones would soon be a signpost for future travellers.

They reached the oasis at the edge of the desert by nightfall, though they had been sold rations and water for four days and nights. A donkey and two camels were tethered to the date palms by the well.

Lina was glad to have made such good time. 'I'm looking forward to a night under a roof,' she said, as they entered the caravanserai, made of sun-baked mud bricks built against a ruined fort.

'And I want a hot meal!' said Hari.

'Me too!'

Smiling at each other, they pointed, ignoring a gecko, to the most expensive item on the menu hanging on the wall.

'I hope it's substantial,' said Hari.

'And hot!'

To the amazement of the caravanserai keeper, when he brought them the speciality of the house, they looked at each other, then burst out laughing. It was salad on a bed of crushed ice, which he stored in a cave underground.

By the time the sun rose next morning they were already walking into the foothills, where the nomads spent the winter. In the spring, Julian had told them, the tribe migrated to the Hills of Heaven for their summer pastures.

They walked all day, passing two ruined villages.

By evening, their legs and backs were aching. As the couple were trudging up a ravine, Hari thought wearily: tomorrow is the new moon.

He had thought of it often enough, well aware that the present moon was slipping away. The moon did not rise now until the stars had vanished. Each morning the dwindling crescent of the moon glimmered less brightly in the dawn sky and disappeared more rapidly in the glare of the desert sun.

That morning Hari had seen no moon at all. And *they* depended on him. *Who?* The nomads? *Why?* He looked up at the duskblue sky. Soon it would be dark; they would have to start looking for somewhere to sleep.

'Do you think we will find the Dreamer amongst the nomads?' Lina asked.

'We have to. It's our only hope.'

'Then let's walk through the night. If we reach the nomads and the Dreamer is with them, he will explain everything,' said Lina. 'We can sleep as much as we like tomorrow.'

'There's not much time,' Hari agreed. Then he groaned. Not much time! No time! It was no longer weeks, or even days – it was *hours* before the birth of the new moon. And . . .

AAAIIEEEGYH! A shriek ripped through the twilight. Stones shot past their heads. Figures stood silhouetted on the rocks above.

They turned. Other figures were threatening them from behind. On the left a precipice dropped sheer. They had been ambushed. The shrill yells in the gloom terrified them.

A bitter jest by fate, Hari scowled. They had come all this way safely. Now, within hailing distance of the nomads and their Dreamer, bandits were going to rob them. Can we show them we've got nothing? No. They will kill us anyway.

Not without a fight! Hari stooped and grabbed two stones. Two of the bandits would die.

Stones whizzed past their heads. Whoops screamed out. A clatter of stones landed at their feet. Then the silhouettes vanished. What were they doing?

Hari looked down into the abyss. Push Lina over first. He would not imagine what the bandits might do to her body. *No!* I'll take you in my arms. We'll jump over the precipice together. Embracing death, united eternally.

'We can't escape,' said Lina. 'Let's die together.'

Hari put his arm round her. He dropped the stones. He would not kill. The bandits were not worthy to share their death. 'Let's jump.'

Lina nodded. Smiling into his eyes, she put out her arms to embrace him.

Laughter rang out. It was a jest. Not by fate, but by the boys of the tribe, posturing in attitudes of intimidation. The nomad boys did not push it too far, however, knowing with what blinding speed a swordsman could kill. The stranger did not walk like a swordsman, but they sometimes wore disguises.

'Wake, Dreamer!' The boys shouted the greeting loudly to disarm suspicion. At least, from the words' rhythm, that was what Hari supposed them to mean.

'Wake, Dreamer!' Hari called back in the language of Shark Bay. However, he and Lina stood with their arms round each other at the edge of the precipice, ready for anything.

The boys scrambled towards them, shouting triumphantly – they had scared the travellers out of their wits!

Hari looked straight at the leader, as he ran up to him.

The leader caught Hari's eye. The boy stopped. He uttered a few words as if shocked. They all stared. Then the whole pack turned and fled, screaming, 'Neru! Neru! Neru!'

'Those are the nomads' children,' Hari grinned at Lina. He wanted to hug her. 'We've found the tribe!'

'You'll have to shave, if your beard has that effect on them.'

They smiled into each other's eyes.

Now they would find out who the Dreamer was. They

154

would kneel hand in hand before the great sage. Looking deep into Hari's eyes, he would penetrate Hari's mind, and *reveal* who he was. Using his awesome powers the Dreamer would restore Hari's memory. Hari would learn whom he must save, why and how. The Dreamer would explain how their destinies were linked. He would *show* Lina who it was who had known her before she was born. It was him, Hari! It had to be!

And the new moon would be born minutes after Hari saved the unknown faces waiting for him.

They hurried after the boys, who had run out of sight behind the hill. Hari and Lina climbed to the crest. Ahead they saw a plain. Smoke was rising from numerous camp fires amidst a sea of fawn-coloured tents; the nomad women were cooking their evening meal.

Hari and Lina would have walked past the encampment if the boys had not played their prank! They looked at each other, smiled, then started walking towards the tents.

The men of the tribe were coming out of their tents and walking forward to greet the strangers, with the easy strides of those used to covering long distances on foot. The boys were cavorting round them, shouting excitedly.

Even in those countries where 'The guest is God,' the nomads were famous for their hospitality; but this, the welcome of the whole tribe, showed such generosity of spirit that Hari felt embarrassed. Of course the nomads would have few visitors in these hills, but Hari was surprised at them giving this treatment to two such ordinary strangers as himself and Lina – unless it was to make up for the boys' prank.

The nomads poured water from skin containers into wooden cups. The couple drank thirstily, while the nomads surrounded them in a friendly warmth. No one said a word, until a little girl came and put her hand into Hari's, murmuring something happily.

'We are friends,' Hari said slowly, laying his free hand on his heart and nodding towards Lina. 'We have come to see

155

the Dreamer. Is he here amongst you?'

The nomads gave him puzzled looks.

A plump and jolly woman, looking younger than Hari, ran up to the two travellers, and threw her arms round Hari in a loving embrace.

Some of the nomads laughed, as Hari started back, looking in confusion at Lina. Her face had gone pale. Hari could see what she was thinking: *Is this woman your wife?* He looked as dismayed as Lina.

The plump woman started chattering. She took Hari's hand and led him forward, beckoning Lina to follow.

Lina did so, though hardly able to move one foot in front of the other. Hari looked at her. *Is she your wife?* The little girl was still holding Hari's hand. *Is she your daughter?* Hari shrugged with anguish.

The nomads parted before the strangers. Led by the woman, Hari and Lina came to a circular area in the middle of the encampment, where the tribal fire was ready to be lit. Outside the largest tent stood an imposing man with arms folded: undoubtedly the Chief.

'Wake, Dreamer.' The Chief spoke in the nomadic tongue, steepling his hands together and bowing to Hari.

Hari removed his hand from the little girl's. 'Wake, Dreamer,' he replied in the language of Shark Bay, steepling his hands too and making sure his bow was lower than that of the Chief.

The Chief said something that sounded like a welcome.

'Thank you,' Hari responded. 'We have made a long journey to find the Dreamer. Is that the name of your holy man?'

The nomads laughed, as if out of politeness at a feeble joke.

With his regal bearing the Chief walked right up to Hari. He put out his hand, stroking Hari's four-week-old beard and staring into his eyes. That straight look bewildered the man with no memory. It said welcome and well done but, above all, I believe in you, my most valued friend.

'You are very kind,' Hari murmured.

The Chief stood back and said some words loudly enough for the nomads to hear. They stared at Hari with worried faces.

'I'm sorry. We can't understand what you are saying.' Hari looked at Lina, who nodded. She could not understand the words, nor guess at their sense. And she didn't want to!

With a courteous gesture the Chief invited Hari to go with him, indicating that the plump woman should take Lina away.

With a delighted smile the woman took Lina by the hand, patting it. Lina snatched her hand away. She was close to tears. The little girl took Lina's other hand. The woman led them into the maze of tents.

The Chief preceded Hari to another tent in the central circle. He called out and waited for a reply. A middle-aged woman came to the entrance and held back the tent flap.

The Chief, beckoning to Hari to follow, walked into the tent, stooping to pass under the deerskin flap.

Hari bowed when he entered. He steepled his hands and bowed again when, in the darkness lit by one lamp, he saw an old man lying on deerskin blankets on the ground.

The Chief knelt down beside the old man.

Hari did the same. *This must be the Dreamer!* Hari's spine tingled. *They had found him!* Before the new moon! This explained the rumour that he was no longer with the tribe. He was sick. Now he would answer everything! *If only Lina was here!*

The woman brought Hari a cup of water. Then she knelt at the old man's side and mopped his sweating face.

The Chief began to speak in an earnest tone.

When he stopped, the sick man answered with difficulty, gasping for breath with every word he uttered.

Then they spoke to Hari, in turn, with long pauses so that the guest might reply.

Hari did not reply. His body slumped with despair. He

157

had never imagined the Dreamer could not speak his language. The Dreamer knew everything. That's what raised him above ordinary men. How could the Dreamer have acquired such an exalted reputation if he was not master of the languages of those who came to him for help?

Maybe he went into trance, revealing truths as an oracle – like those rhymes long ago for Shark Bay. What if he gave no explanations – just some riddle, which they could interpret only when it was too late?

Maybe he could not even go into a trance. Hari's lower lip pouted. The Dreamer was only a nomad. A good man, doubtless, and very wise so far as nomads went, but incapable of telling Hari who he was – or of telling Lina who had known her before she was born. They *called* him the Dreamer because, simple nomads, they knew no better. This was not a true Dreamer: one who knows God. His reputation had been grossly inflated on its journey through caravanserais and tea-houses to the Coast.

The sick man's eyes glittered at Hari.

'I'm sorry. I can't understand a word you are saying,' said Hari, breaking into the silence, trying to keep the petulance out of his voice. 'I . . . can . . . not . . . understand.' Seeing the expression on the Chief's face and appreciating that it was not their fault that they did not speak the language of Shark Bay, the man called Hari added, 'I'm sorry. Excuse me.'

The invalid was seized by a cough that left him helpless. An awkward silence followed, disturbed only by the retching of the old man. *If he had all that wisdom, he would not get ill like ordinary human beings.* Summoning up all his strength, the sick man wheezed out some words, choking. His head fell back; he lost consciousness.

The Chief nodded. He took the cloth from the woman's hand and dabbed the sweat off the old man's face. Then the Chief turned and indicated with a courtly gesture that Hari should leave the tent.

Hari straightened up as they came out of the tent, trying

to not to show his disappointment.

The Chief was smiling, however. It was now dark. Some older boys were lighting the tribal fire. The Chief's eyes shone in the flames as the fire crackled into life.

His smile gave Hari hope. In his wisdom the Dreamer had solved the problem! Maybe with one of his holy verses pregnant with meaning? We'll stay with the nomads till we've learnt enough of their language to speak to the Dreamer. He will tell us . . . Hari's shoulders sagged. He knew there was no time. The old man was dying.

The men of the tribe stood back, making way for the stranger as the Chief led Hari to a tent on the other side of the Circle. It was directly opposite his own tent: not so large, but decorated with coloured beads in swirling patterns.

In his gracious way the Chief motioned Hari to enter. He stood aside, as much as to say: you are the guest; this is your home for as long as you wish.

Hari raised the decorated flap and walked into the tent. It was dark. The Chief did not follow him.

This, Hari supposed, was where he was to sleep: the male guest tent. Where was Lina? They must have given her a tent with the women. This would be the first time they had slept apart since they left Shark Bay, except for the night at Julian's. Hari groaned: he was never going to marry her.

He lay down on the deerskin carpeted floor, resting his aching body. Were the nomads going to give them something to eat? He might see Lina then. He would wait a while. If no one called him, he would ask to see Lina. He was not a prisoner, so far as he knew.

The Dreamer had failed them. And he, Hari, whoever he was, had failed *them*. Failed even to find them. He put his hands to his head. And Lina – he had done nothing for her. He had brought her to the Dreamer. At least he had kept his promise.

Hari heard the voice of the Chief outside the tent.

159

'Come in, please,' he said, getting to his feet.

Light from the blazing camp fire flickered through the opening, as the Chief raised the tent flap. He walked in and set a lamp on the floor. He looked at Hari: 'Wake, Dreamer.'

'Wake, Dreamer,' the man with only one month's memory replied, trying to pronounce the nomadic tongue.

Smiling, the Chief left the tent.

Hari looked round the tent, his eyes beginning to distinguish shapes in the gloom. They seemed familiar.

It came to him in a flash! *The boys had recognized him!* They had not run away because of his beard, as Lina had joked. The boys were not scared of strangers. This was their world. At first they had not realized who he was because of his one-month-old beard. They were used to him without it. *They knew who he was!* They knew his name, where he fitted in. That's why the whole tribe had come forward to greet him. *They remember me! They know who I am!*

If Lina had been there, he would have flung his arms around her, lifting her off her feet and whirling her round the tent. He had found himself!

They are the ones I have to save, the nomads. *How?* What have I got to do? *Who am I?* He stood up and started towards the opening of the tent.

He stopped, rigid with astonishment.

Something glowed in the lamplight, throwing out rays of blood from mysterious depths. A thrill of recognition erupted in the base of his spine. It shot up to the crown of his head. Spasms shook his body.

Halcyon's stone! On a wooden pedestal was a ruby like the one he had seen in his dream by the precipice. It was as big as a watermelon and dominated the tent. The Dragon Pearl!

Hari could feel the ruby pulling him into its occult vortex. A psychic force dragged him down before the Stone. It wanted him to surrender, to plunge into the abyss.

160

No! He fought against it, but he fell to his knees on the deerskin carpet. He was exhausted. Not just tired from the journey, the endless walking, not knowing where they would stay at night, the hunger and thirst. This was fatigue of the spirit, caused by four weeks of waking up every morning not knowing who he was: aggravated by the reminder of his growing beard; intensified by the time-beat of the moon, ringing out in the heavens.

The moon. *The new moon!* Hari struggled to stand up. His body would not obey. The Dreamer was going to die at the new moon. That was it! That was why he had had to get here in time. He must speak to him now – or he'd never find out. Now!

He fought to get to his feet. He struggled to move his legs towards the opening of the tent. Heavy, so heavy. Dizzy. Hari reeled round in the gloom. He was facing the wrong way. He could not pull himself away from the mysterious power. Falling. He had to surrender. He could not resist it. His legs collapsed. His body dropped towards the ruby Stone. He fell to the floor of the tent. His head landed on the Dragon Pearl – with the gentle flutter of an autumn leaf.

His mind leapt. He shed the personality of Hari and soared on wings of the soul. The Stone was a grain of sand on the shore of the ocean of bliss. It was waiting for him. He was its oyster. A smile transformed his face. He had come home. In less time than it takes to say 'Wake, Dreamer,' he was asleep.

The desert sky was full of stars. The constellation of the Hunter was shining brightly overhead. The Milky Way spiralled like the body of a dragonfly from horizon to horizon, from consciousness to consciousness.

He was dreaming.

16

When they were 13, the boys of the tribe took part in their Initiation hunt.

The great deer would come trotting up from the plains, swimming across the river and climbing into the Hills of Heaven, their summer pastures. Every year the herd took the same trail for the spring migration.

About a thousand nomadic deer would wade into the water. Bucks, does and fawns would swim across.

Not all of them would succeed in reaching the other shore. The river, turbulent with blocks of ice and melted snow, would carry away those weakened by age, sickness or injury.

Neru had waited for this for years. He had reached the age of manhood – 13 – only the week before. On that very day the tribe scouts had seen the cloud of dust, and heard a rumbling like thunder across the plain.

Each year, eyes wide with admiration, Neru had watched the older boys on the cliff: they dived into the freezing water, seized a deer and let it carry them to the shore.

Then they killed it with their antler-handled hunter's knife. The Chief had invested them with the new blade the night before in the firelit Ceremony that commenced the Initiation. The kill was the climax. Then the boys were men.

There was no second chance. If they failed, the Initiates could not climb back up the cliff and dive into the river again, to strike at a second deer. They could not return next year to repeat the test. If they made one mistake, they could never be hunters. They would have to stay with the women of the tribe, cooking, mending tents and looking after the children, while the men went out to hunt. Very few could endure this; they preferred to walk out into the desert and die.

The false dawn gleamed. Soon a grey shadow would fall across the desert; then the sun would rise, lighting the Hills of Heaven in gold and magenta.

Wrapped in his deerskin coat, Neru gazed out at the vast open sky, then down at the river, rushing down from the mountains. His turn had come. He stood alone on the cliff, high above the water they had to dive into.

Throughout the winter Neru had leapt into the icy water, swimming hard against the current till he was numb, his hands and feet white from lack of circulation – toughening his body for today's rite of passage.

He withdrew his horn-handled knife from its sheath. He shivered. Not from the cold, and not from fear that he would fail. He had mastered the hunting skills better than most of the boys who would swim today; he was a stronger swimmer than any of them. No, he would not fail. But something inside him – a voice he had already learnt to trust – told him that this year would not see a 'Swim' like any before. He licked his finger, then ran it along the shining blade of his knife.

'Do you swim?'

The Initiate spun round. He saw an old crone, fixing him with a stare. She was dressed in a black 'tent', as they called the women's shapeless clothing. Round her neck she wore a silver chain with a shark-tooth pendant shaped like a crescent moon.

Neru was surprised he had not heard her approach over the stony ground. 'Yes, Auntie,' he replied, sheathing his new knife and pinching his arm with irritation at himself. His father had told him often enough: 'Sounds do not escape the hunter.'

163

' "Woman", you should say.'

The Initiate reddened, 'Yes, woman.'

Boys called women 'Auntie', but after receiving the hunter's knife, they addressed the women in the tribe as 'woman', even their own mother.

'It will not be your Swim.'

Neru went cold. Sometimes these old women had magic powers, the boys whispered. They could strike you lame with a look.

'What do you mean?' He held up his hand to shield his eyes from hers.

'It will not be your Swim.' The crone snatched his hand away. Cackling with laughter, she clutched his wrist.

Neru shuddered. The cold from her hand seemed to snake through his body. She could only mean he would fail. Fail to catch a deer after diving into the swollen river. Or fail to kill it. Sometimes in that moment of truth when the hunter, barely more than a child, looked into the soft eyes of the deer, he could not bring himself to take its life.

The new hunter's knife would fall away from his hand; he would slide down from the deer's neck. The animal would bound away, unaware that the nomads would condemn the boy to a life of humiliation; unaware too of how close it had come to death – and reincarnation in human form, since its last thought, which governs the next birth, would have been of the man-child it was fighting.

Each year the Dreamer assured the Initiates that all the deer killed in the Swim would progress to a human birth. They were ready to leave the animal level and rise in being. 'And this year is auspicious for them,' the Dreamer had told them last night in the Initiation Ceremony. 'As you know.'

They did. This was the Year of the Dragonfly. In the tribal mythology a dragonfly had saved the deer from being exterminated.

Similarly, any Initiate who failed to make his kill – the proof of manhood – was certain to sink to a lower birth,

164

after he had dragged out his life amongst the tents. Maybe he would be reborn as a deer, maybe something lower: a jackal, a scorpion, a spider.

Neru looked away.

The old woman caught his ear, pulling his head round to face her: 'Look into my eyes!'

The Initiate shut his eyes tightly.

'Open your eyes, Neru, son of Narad.'

Something clutched his heart. How did she know his name? He had never seen her before. Neru found himself forced to obey. Her eyes went opaque. He felt she was looking right into him: she could see all his secret thoughts.

'No. The Swim is not for you.' She prodded his shoulder with her forefinger. 'Tomorrow you will awake.'

The Initiate stared at her like a frog petrified by a snake. Pointing to her shark-tooth pendant, she added the words he was dreading: 'She has dreamed the Swim.'

Not even the Dreamer was able to dream the Swim. For many years the Dreamer had had no power. The results in the Dream Contest were hardly adequate to justify the winner assuming the ornate Cloak of the Dreamer.

The boys whispered that some of the old crones could reveal dreams of power. Because they were women, however, they were not allowed to enter the annual Dream Contest, which decided who would be the Dreamer for the coming year.

Could this crone, wrapped in her dusty black 'tent', have been the real Dreamer all these years?

'Yes, Neru, son of Narad, she can reveal dreams of power,' the old woman cackled. 'When she was a girl, the Dreamer was the sublime Halcyon, 30 years in succession. She learnt from him. True, he would not teach her . . .' She anticipated his protest that women were not initiated into the Way of the Dreamer. 'But she lived for nothing else. She entered the Beyond Within, as a caterpillar flies into the sky after its sleep in the chrysalis. Halcyon knew it immediately. That night he disappeared. The tribe never saw him again.'

Neru remembered: Yes, his father had told him about Halcyon. Halcyon's mastery of the art had been 'sublime'. The Chief had only to ask for, say, rain and Halcyon would put on the Dreamer's Cloak and retire to the Dreamer's Tent, decorated with swirling patterns of beads. He would sit down crosslegged on the Stone that was his seat in the day and his pillow at night. Clouds would form in the sky. The rain would begin to fall within minutes of him entering the Trance.

Some said that he had used up all the psychic energy for years to come, because no Dreamer since Halcyon had been able to control the elements, the animals or even the birth of children.

This old woman had been the Dreamer!

'The deer will not swim today.' She stared into him, jerking her head at the dust cloud raised by the herd.

The boy hunter's shoulders relaxed; he smiled. She was wrong. The herd was only three miles from the river, and thundering towards it. The deer would be stepping into the river before the sun began to beat down in all its fury. And if she was mistaken about the deer, she must be wrong in saying, 'It will not be your Swim.'

The other Initiates were starting to line the top of the cliff, wearing their deerskin coats. Some of the youths of the tribe were climbing along the bank, looking for the best places to watch from.

'Tonight she will enter your dreams.' The old woman prodded him between the eyes with her forefinger. 'Be aware.' Munching toothlessly, she turned and shuffled away.

'Wait!' Neru grabbed at her black 'tent'. He missed. He ran after her, but she hobbled away more swiftly than he could run. She seemed to glide over the ground, bent forward at the waist, her arms stuck out weirdly behind her.

Neru could not catch up with her. He stopped; he trembled. She had the Dreamer's Walk: the ability to move over any surface. She could 'walk' like that for hours if she wished. No Dreamer had had that power since . . . Halcyon. She had convinced him.

The Initiate ran down from the cliff, looking at the deer. They were still trotting forward, but Neru's inner sense told him to believe the old woman. The deer would not swim across the river today; and he would not . . . He returned to the encampment, looking at the ground as he walked between the brown tents made from the hides of the deer.

Squatting by the fire, his little sister looked up, greeting Neru with laughing eyes. 'Soon the deer will be swimming. Then you will be a man!' Maya giggled, as if this was the most improbable thing under Heaven, but her eyes shone.

'The deer will not swim today,' Neru muttered.

'But . . .' Maya looked at him, her puzzled frown reflecting his worried look. 'What has happened?'

'I don't know.' The boy took off his new belt with the sheath and hunter's knife and handed it to her. 'Look after this, Maya.'

' "Woman," you must call me now,' Maya corrected, but she flushed with pleasure, clasping the antler handle to her chest.

'You are too young.'

Maya's shining eyes followed her brother, as he walked away.

Neru stopped outside the tent of the Dreamer. After a moment's hesitation he called out, asking permission to enter.

When he sat down in the gloom, the Initiate asked, 'When will the deer swim?'

'Soon,' the Dreamer replied, looking down at the deerskin carpeted floor of his tent. The old man had the habit of holding his head still, while moving his eyes to look at something. This gave even his most innocent glance a furtive aspect.

'Did you dream the Swim?' Neru asked.

The Dreamer looked across with his eyes and, as if by mistake, into Neru's eyes. That eye contact told Neru more than anything the Dreamer might say. The old woman's words were true.

'What is it to you, boy? Are you afraid? Be on your way,' the old man retorted with a wave of his hand. 'Do you not understand that I am busy on this day?'

Neru did not point out the Dreamer's solecism in calling an Initiate 'Boy'. He rose to his feet: 'The deer will not swim today.' Bending his head at the flap of the opening, Neru stepped out of the tent.

Some of the nomads, who had taken their places on the cliff to watch the Swim, were returning to the camp.

'The herd has stopped!' said one bearded hunter, his deerskin coat open, walking rapidly across the stony ground.

Women put their hands to their mouths in dismay.

'The deer must cross the river today,' another hunter retorted, gripping the handle of his knife.

'The Initiates must blood their knives by midday,' said a young thin-faced hunter. 'The Initiation was last night.'

With confused looks they all hurried to the Circle. The sun had now risen. Dawn shadows slanted from tent to tent.

The Marshal of the Hunters despatched two scouts. They soon ran back, confirming that the herd had stopped advancing; the deer were settling down, as they did for the night.

Except for the Initiates, remaining on the cliff in their deer-skin coats, and the women with babies, the whole tribe assembled in the Circle, the central area of the encampment.

The Circle was formed when the Dreamer selected a site for his tent; then the Chief set his tent 41 paces due east. The camp fire was placed in the middle, and the hunters pitched their tents round it.

The Chief – a powerfully built man who could run very

fast – sat down on his haunches. The hunters, all with beards, who had been standing, waiting, squatted down like the Chief.

The Chief told the young thin-faced hunter, who had been an Initiate last year, to summon the Dreamer.

The old man came out of his tent, blinking in the sunlight, which glittered on the embroidered Dreamer's Cloak he was wearing. His encounter with the son of Narad – and the Initiate's assurance – had shaken the Dreamer. His shifty eyes picked out the boy standing outside the Circle of Hunters: Neru had not rejoined the other Initiates on the cliff.

The Dreamer squatted down on his heels.

'The Initiation was last night. Today must see the Swim,' said the Chief. 'Dreamer, cause the deer to swim across the river and begin the ascent of the Hills of Heaven before the sun reaches its zenith.'

'The deer will not swim today,' the Dreamer answered. Although facing the Chief, his eyes looked at the ground.

Wearing his Cloak, the Dreamer had spoken. He could not go back on his words, even if he wished to.

The Chief sent the Marshal of the Hunters himself to ascertain what the herd was doing. Six hunters attended him.

The nomads remained silent until the Marshal returned.

'The deer are now sitting, their antlered heads erect, as dignified as so many realized sages,' the Marshal reported, loping back with the six hunters. None of them was out of breath. 'The deer show no sign of moving today. I think they will begin the Swim at sunrise tomorrow.'

The Dreamer was right.

Some of the greybeards shook their heads. This flaunted tradition. No good would come of it, that was certain. Better for the youngsters to swim across the river and kill the deer on the wrong bank than to leave the new blades unblooded.

'None of the Initiates should take part in the Swim this year,' the thin-faced hunter declared, looking fiercely at the Marshal. 'The Chief should banish them to the tents – to

169

reflect on the shame that deprived them of becoming full male members of the tribe.'

The Marshal said nothing, but the Chief pointed out: 'In the ordinary hunt it is sometimes necessary to delay. Where Nature leads, Man should not hesitate to follow.'

Most of the hunters nodded.

The Chief ordained, 'Tomorrow will see the Swim.' He looked at the Dreamer, whose eyes darted at the ashes of last night's fire. The Chief called the Initiates back.

The tribe settled down to wait till the next dawn.

To a nomad the waiting of a day is nothing. His life is not subject to the hurry that, the Dreamer says, robs all actions of their dignity. However, this delay caused uneasiness, particularly amongst the 13-year-old boys and their fathers. No one had ever heard of a boy receiving his hunter's knife at the midnight Initiation and not using it to establish his manhood before the sun reached its zenith. That was the climax of the Initiation: to blood the knife.

That night Neru dreamed of the old woman.

He was standing on the cliff above the river, ready to fling his arms forward and spring out. The Initiates needed a good leap to clear the rocks jutting out below.

She jabbed him on the shoulder. Neru whipped round as if stung by a hornet. Again he had not heard her approach. He pinched himself angrily. Her mouth was champing, but closed; the words seemed to echo out of her shark-tooth pendant:

> 'The dear deer's name is now Anil.
> So if you dare, use all your skill.
> With clothes and pearls and fishing knife
> She'll save the girl from death-in-life.'

Grinning toothlessly, the crone gave him a push. 'Hurry, hurry, hurry!'

Neru toppled over the edge of the cliff, arms flailing. He

heard her words echoing across the desert: 'Hari, Hari, Hari!' He was falling onto a rock. It was already crimson with the sticky wetness of his blood.

He flinched as his shoulder hit the rock.

'*Change!*' chanted the crone.

The rock turned into her black 'tent', which was billowing out in the wind.

Neru found himself flying across the river.

The old woman was riding a firefly!

'*Change!*' she chanted. She was riding a Phoenix.

'*Change!*' It became a Desert Lion.

'*Change!*' chanted Neru. He was riding the Dragon, which had dreamed the world into creation.

'*Change!*' he chanted. The Dragon turned into a Shark, which threw the boy off. Neru was swimming in the river. The Shark turned to attack him.

'*Change!*' Neru chanted. The Shark did not change.

'*Change!*' Neru screamed. The Shark raced forward to tear him to pieces, its tail threshing the water.

'*Fight!*' shrieked the crone.

Neru drew back his fist, as the Shark swam at him. It dived. It was attacking from below! Its jaws opened.

'*Change!*' Neru chanted. He changed – into a dolphin. He leapt forward to butt the Shark then, laughing, blew it a kiss. '*Change!*' The Shark changed into a female dolphin.

The dolphins played in the water together.

'Clever,' the old woman cackled. 'You learn fast. *Change!*'

Neru changed into a Great Shark. The female dolphin fled. The crone began riding him like a succubus.

'*Change!*' Neru chanted. The old woman changed into a girl of 17, riding him in white pearl-diving briefs. He seized her in his jaws, and swam for the underwater palace.

'*Change,*' she whispered, as he swam through the golden gates. They changed together into something so incredible . . .

17

Before the sun rose the Initiates climbed the cliff. The wind was bone-chilling. They pulled their deerskin coats tightly about them. At the last moment each of them would fling off his coat and dive from the cliff into the freezing river, naked except for his new hunter's belt and knife.

Some boys drowned in the Swim. The nomads did not mourn them, although the Initiate's mother often fell ill. One of the purposes of the Initiation was to weed out the weaklings. Only thus could the tribe remain tough enough to survive in the wilderness.

At dawn the deer were on the move, as the Marshal of the Hunters had predicted, raising a cloud of dust as they trotted towards the river.

The boys lined the top of the cliff, facing the test of their lives. Most looked eager. They gazed across at the approaching herd, gripping the handles of their knives. One thin boy with a frail chest looked down at the river; he was shivering.

Neru's shoulders stooped. He seemed different from the Initiate who had gazed out across the river yesterday morning. His world had turned upside-down. The Dreamer, a man with occult powers, had been exposed as a sham. And an old auntie, lost amongst the brown tents – he had no idea who she was – had shown him that she was controlling the tribe as a puppeteer her puppets. She had said it would not be his Swim. Why? What had she got against him? Or had she come to all the Initiates? Neru glanced at the boy nearest him. Too late to worry about that now.

The stag that dominated the herd was stepping into the river, testing its force. Not for itself, but for the weaker members of his herd. If it judged that too many would be carried away by the fast-flowing waters, the leader might cause the deer to wait another day.

Usually the boys, like leopards chasing their prey, would seek out a weak deer. They dived in and swam for it. They grasped it round the neck and let it carry them out of the river. This needed judgement, because if the deer was too strong, the boy might not succeed in killing it; if the deer was too weak, it might not be able to swim, with the extra weight of the boy, across the swirling current. If it did not reach the other shore, the Initiate failed.

When they were safely on dry ground, the boys killed the deer. Then they were no longer Initiates; they were Hunters. And any boyish desire to shout with exultation had to be quelled by a sense of manly dignity. They never forgot that deer. It was said they would meet it in their next birth.

Returning to the camp, naked but grinning with triumph, they would put on their new hunters' clothes. They never wore again the clothes they had worn in their boyhood.

That evening the Chief would bestow the title of 'Hunter' on each of the Initiates in a Ceremony before the blazing tribal fire. But that was only the tribe's formal acknowledgement of the boys' new status. They became Hunters the moment they killed the deer.

Neru's back stiffened. He was not looking for an animal weaker than its fellows. He was staring at the leader of the herd. A smile spread across his face, as if he recognized a long-lost friend. The dream words of the old woman echoed in his mind: 'The dear deer's name is now Anil.' What did she mean?

The leader, sniffing all the time, had tested the water long enough. It turned round to look at its herd. Then it walked forward until the current swept it off its feet. The stag began to swim.

The herd would wait till the leader swam across, till it clambered out of the river, till it turned to face them, till it bellowed its full-throated roar.

Then a thousand animals would trot forward, step into the rushing waters and follow the stag across to the other side.

This was the Swim.

Neru let the deerskin coat fall from his shoulders. Some inner force, like that leading the unborn bird to crack out of its shell, caused him to lean forward, craning his neck to see the great deer. He had to see its face.

The old woman pushed him! So he thought! He was falling! He had no spring away from the cliff. He saw his body crashing against the side, jagged rocks gouging out his flesh – worse than in his dream.

Neru shouted, 'Change!' Nothing happened. One rock grazed his thigh, but he managed to fling himself clear of the rest. He turned his fall into a dive, and called, 'Wake, Dreamer!'

His head hit the water. He clenched his body against the cold. He slid through what only days before had been snow frozen on the mountains.

Neru reached the bottom of his dive. His hand grasped the handle of the knife the Chief had given him. He started to swim up. He saw a light. Was it the sun? No, it was the crescent-moon pendant at the old woman's neck. He heard her cackle: 'The dear deer's name is now Anil.' In the shark-tooth he saw the girl of his dream. Her face sparkled! She looked into his eyes.

Thrills surged up his spine, as his head came up out of the water. Was this because of the girl? He panted for breath. Or was this the ecstasy of the hunt? No one had ever taken the leader. And with good reason! No animal became the leader of a thousand others without amazing strength and intelligence.

Even if Neru managed to cling to the stag until it swam out of the river – and it would try a dozen tricks to throw him off – the Initiate might fail to kill the huge animal, victor of innumerable fights.

Neru did not hear the gasp from the nomads when he dived. All were astounded: the 13-year-olds on the cliff, the hunters in the best positions along the bank, the old men and the women and children. One of the young boys cheered with admiration. Last year's Initiates scowled; the thin-faced hunter glowered with hostility at Neru's egotism. Some women, including Neru's mother, looked shocked by his foolhardiness.

With alarm the Chief looked at the Marshal of the Hunters, whose face had gone ashen. The Chief feared he might have to order the Marshal to kill the Initiate.

The Chief looked ahead, seeing ghastly consequences. If Neru did catch the stag, it might fail to bellow to the herd when it crossed the whirling river. Would the rest of the deer then stay on the other bank, waiting for the command that never came? If so, they would fail to reach their summer pastures. Then the deer would die. Because one boy dived off the cliff too soon. And if the herd perished, the tribe would be dispersed – the one thing the nomads were taught to dread. They depended on the deer for their food, their clothing, their tents. They even used the dung of the deer as fuel for their fires.

'Stone the Initiate if he draws his knife!' the Chief ordered the Marshal of the Hunters. 'The stag must bellow to the herd.'

'You, you, you and you!' the Marshal pointed to four hunters. 'Go there!' His arm swept across to indicate a stony beach downstream where the stag could wade out of the river.

Four of the tribe's best hunters began to run to the spot.

'First, we will see if he catches the stag,' the Chief said to the Marshal. 'That itself is far from certain.'

'A lord of beasts,' the Marshal replied grimly. 'But that Initiate has a will of iron.'

Another danger heightened the uncertainty.

While the herd was swimming across, the Initiates would dive off the cliff two hundred paces upriver. The current would fling them forward so fast that as soon as they came out of their dives the boys were on top of the deer.

All the hunters saw the risk Neru was taking: if he misjudged the dive, he would have no other deer to catch. The river would spiral him past the leader of the herd. The current was far too strong to swim against.

Neru would clamber out of the river somewhere, quivering with cold and shame, and stumble back to his tent. He would have to hand his knife back to the Marshal. The rash boy would be confined to the tents. He would be unable to hunt, unable to choose a mate. He would be the shame of his family – and the scorn of the tribe.

Neru did not misjudge the dive. He swam up to the surface, shuddering with cold. The current hurled him towards the stag. The boy froze. Close to, he saw this was an enormous buck, its face carved with the scars of a hundred fights. Its antlers were awesome weapons.

The deer looked at Neru, while the river threw the Initiate forward. They looked into each other's eyes.

And the son of Narad was afraid. It was not the fear of being killed, or even of failing to kill his chosen victim. Neru was afraid of doing wrong. What force was driving him to attack the leader of the herd? Who was he to separate this king from its subjects, to sever this being from its life?

I can't hurt this magnificent stag, Neru thought, trying to turn across the current. He would not go through with it. He would swim down and climb out of the river. Better to be scorned by others than to hate yourself.

The raging waters threw the boy against the deer.

He grabbed the muscular neck and clung to it.

The stag bucked in the river. It flung him off – or tried to. But behind those terrible antlers the Initiate was invulnerable. As long as he could hold onto its neck, the stag could do nothing to hurt him. The icy torrent impeded the tossing that might have maimed the boy hunter on land.

Neru sensed what the stag was going to do. He took a gulp of air as the deer dived under. His shivering hands did not release the stag. The current was hurtling them downriver all the time. The pressure on his lungs mounted. Neru felt intense pain. His heart thundered. He had to let go or he would drown.

Darkness invaded Neru's mind. Was this the approach of Death? He swore that his lungs would burst, but he would not let go. Desperately he opened his eyes. Under the water the black fog remained, smothering. Yet he had fought this battle before! *Where?* His arms were weakening. He was losing his hold. His lungs were exploding. His head was splitting. He felt a warm numbness seeping into his blood.

Neru felt faint. Still grasping the deer, he began to choke, unable to hold his breath any longer. Water went into his mouth. The stag twisted and bucked. Water rushed down Neru's throat. The stag kicked to come up to the surface. They were both spluttering; both gulped in the air.

Neru was choking, but he had won! He had beaten the stag in this contest of will. However, the son of Narad felt no triumph, but a curious loss, as he clutched the deer – as though he had won the Annual Stone Throwing Contest, then been told that the enemies of the tribe demanded the winner's sister as a hostage.

The stag struck out for the Hills of Heaven. Neru realized it could have swum back to its own shore, where the herd could have gored the boy to death. The stag swam diagonally across the current to the opposite bank and clambered up, tossing its head and kicking up its hind legs.

Neru twisted his legs round the stag's neck, locking his ankles. He grasped its antlers in the crook of his arm, turning the deer's weapon to his own advantage.

The stag galloped away from the river.

177

They raced towards the Hills. How deftly the stag avoided the rocks on the ground and the occasional camel-thorn bush! It was a wonderful sensation! The wind whistled in Neru's face. It blew through his hair. It coursed over his bare back. He wanted to shout with delight as the deer moved under him. Suddenly the stag swerved to the side, throwing its head back angrily.

Neru shot forward. The jolt broke the lock of his ankles. His legs swung out wide. His arms slid up till they were caught, the flesh tearing against the antlers. His weight pulled the deer's head down. Neru's feet hit the ground. He bounced back from it, spinning his legs round the stag's neck again. His hands clawed for a hold, pulling out fistfuls of russet fur. He caught the deer as before, and clung to it, gasping for breath.

The lord of the herd stood still, as if thinking. It looked up at the vault of blue sky. Then it turned and cantered back to the bank. The stag bellowed to the deer on the other side of the river.

The four hunters looked at each other, then at the Chief. If Neru had drawn his knife, they would have stoned him to death. The Chief signalled them to stay with the stag and the Initiate.

The stag waited while the herd began to rumble forward, till the bucks in front walked into the river and began to swim, till the first buck reached shallow water and clambered out, till the does, protecting their fawns, began to swim.

Neru heard the other Initiates shouting, 'Wake, Dreamer!' He saw them diving off the cliff. Suddenly his teeth began chattering. With the exertion he had not noticed the cold till now, but on his wet body the wind, whistling down from the snow-capped peaks of the Hills of Heaven . . .

The stag threw itself on the ground.

Neru loosed his ankle hold. Flinging his leg back, he saved it from being crushed under the deer's shoulder.

178

With a leap Neru regained his position. He twined his legs like a creeper round a tree as the stag rose to its feet. Suddenly it reared up. It fell right over onto its back, trying to crush the rider. Neru was ready. He jumped aside. As the stag got to its feet, he leapt back on.

With a startled look in its eyes the stag began to canter, then gallop towards the Hills of Heaven, rapidly out-distancing the four hunters.

Again it was a heart-thrilling experience. Neru no longer felt as if he and the deer were enemies. Had he ever felt that? No, they were united on some plane. They had been fused into one by the river. The wind blew in his face – into his soul! The stag bounded forward with the energy that made it a king of animals. They raced over the boulder strewn ground towards the mountains.

Neru thought they would fly over the summits, beyond the clouds! Sometimes he had dreamed he was a winged horse, mounting into the blue sky. He felt like that now. At full gallop he and the deer were transformed. They were One!

The stag put its head between its knees and bucked. Its hind quarters went straight up. With nothing in front to hold onto, Neru flew over its head. This time he came right off. Somehow his right hand still clung to one great antler. The stag veered off at right angles. Neru's arm was wrenched out of its socket. He knew it was dislocated. His feet left the ground. He did not know how he held on. His grasp was slipping. In a second he would let go. The stag shook its head with triumph, ripping its antler away from the boy's hand.

Neru had lost.

As he fell to the ground, a memory flashed in his mind: *'The dear deer's name is now Anil.'* Everything Neru had ever felt went into his scream: all his hopes and fears: 'ANIL!'

The leader of the herd went rigid. For a moment it remained motionless.

Neru used that instant, leaping up from the ground to

179

swing his leg over and lock his ankles, clasping his hands round the stag's neck. Agony tore through his dislocated shoulder, but he was back in position. He had won. He had only to stab his knife into the deer's throat. Then he would be a Hunter.

Again Neru did not drink the nectar of victory. He felt as if he had cheated. Till then it had been a fair fight. The stag had not swum back to the other bank, where he would have had the boy gored to death by the herd. Neru had lost. Then by a witch's trick he had cast a spell on his opponent, who flew through the air like a god.

The stag snorted. Neru saw flames bursting from its nostrils! It charged at a brown outcrop of rock which reared up vertical before them. The stag was going to lower its head, as it did in its battles for mastery of the herd, and hurtle headfirst into the cliff, breaking its own neck. It obviously intended suicide rather than death at the hands of this man-whelp.

No! Neru retched. *No!* The stag must not gallop into the rock and kill itself.

No, it would swing round at the last moment and crush Neru's leg against the cliff. The sweat of relief broke out on his face, even though he knew that if this happened he might never walk again. He would lose his leg. He would fail to kill the deer. He could never keep clinging to it without his legs. Already his right arm was useless.

He could save his leg by swivelling to one side before the stag hit the rock – provided he chose the right side, for the stag could swerve either way. If Neru chose the wrong side, his body would be maimed. He might be killed. Even if he did choose the right side, he would have no grip with his ankles. The stag would shake him off his back as easily as a dog shedding water when it bounds out of a river.

Neru had not won. Whatever made him think he had? Just because he knew the 'name'of the deer. The stag was going to fight back with the will that had made it the leader of a thousand animals. It was not going to lose to a man-whelp a tenth of its size. Neru was sweating, yet smarting from the freezing wind whistling down from the Hills of Heaven.

It will not be your Swim!

That was why he had felt bad when he thought he had won. It had not been compassion. His inner vision had seen his leg mutilated, which would have meant spending the rest of his life as a burden on the tribe, not even capable of doing women's work.

The son of Narad could not face that. He would walk out into the desert one night and starve to death rather than endure the contempt of the men, the condescension of the women, the ridicule of the children. But he might not even be able to walk!

Neru kept clinging to the galloping deer. The cliff loomed nearer. The stag had won too many fights. It did not know how to give in. It was determined to conquer.

Neru perceived things as if he had never seen them before. The stony ground was so precious. The sky so blue. The deer was so warm, its fur so soft, its smell so sweet.

The cliff was on top of them. In a second it would be over. The hunters would come and collect his body. If he was alive, they would despise him – and he would be a cripple. He could let go. Jump now! He would lose the stag, but save his limbs.

Neru held on, the agony in his dislocated shoulder stabbing right into his heart. He closed his eyes and grasped the warm neck even tighter. His short life flashed before him as, the Dreamer said, it did when you die.

The stag charged at the cliff as if it was going to knock it down.

'Neru.'

He heard a voice. The Angel of Death had come for his soul. It was calling his name as he passed through the invisible gates.

The stag had crashed into the cliff with such force that he had been killed instantly. Neru's spine was in agony, but he did not feel dead. However, the Dreamer had said that when death was sudden and violent, the soul often failed to realize it had parted from the body.

'I seek the Light,' Neru said, making the response they were taught to give on entering the next world. Now I will find out what life is all about. I will see the Light. It will tell me who I am, where I am to go.

18

When they saw Neru dive off the cliff, the nomads gasped. This would be no ordinary Swim. And no Swim was ordinary.

The hunters of the tribe watched with worried faces, until the stag bellowed to its herd. Their brows cleared when they saw the deer begin swimming across the fierce current and the first bucks wading out on their side of the river. The Swim had not been disrupted.

The Chief's eyes were bloodshot from lack of sleep. He put his hand to his forehead. He took it away immediately and placed both hands on his hips. He did not like to show signs of stress to his tribe, but he looked drawn. From yesterday at dawn when the herd stopped rumbling towards the river – with the failure to blood the new hunters' knives – a vertical frown had creased the Chief's forehead.

When the stag galloped away with the boy on its back, the Dreamer had said, head facing the hills, eyes turned to the Chief, 'The stag is an embodiment of evil. It enticed that boy into the river alone, where it could subdue his will. Now it has snatched his body.'

The Marshal of the Hunters said nothing. He glowered as the Dreamer continued, his eyes darting from one to another of the hunters: 'The stag will take revenge on us for killing the deer. By exercising its evil powers on the spirit of that boy and using his knowledge to attack the tribe, the herd may gore the strong and trample the weak to death.'

One moonless night, within living memory, the deer had

gone berserk. The thunder of hooves stampeding towards the encampment – terrifying in the dark – had awakened the nomads from sleep.

The Dreamer had been ill, shivering with malaria on his deerskin blankets on the ground. The hunters had lifted Halcyon, put his Dreamer's Cloak around him, and laid his head on the Dreamer's Stone. Halcyon's body went hot; he began to sweat, shaking more than before.

Suddenly a cloud of fireflies flared above the galloping herd, dazzling them with green-gold fire, as they alighted on the antlers of the deer.

The herd slowed down with delight, neighing in deerlike laughter. They came to a stop and began to dance together in the light of the fireflies.

The nomads walked forward, hand in hand, to watch this miracle from the land of dreams. And one little girl's eyes were sparkling with wonder as she gazed at the Dreamer's tent.

Halcyon's power had saved the tribe.

But no one had any confidence in the Dreamer now. Some even spoke of abandoning the Annual Dream Contest. However, that was impossible. The most hallowed Tradition of the tribe said that if they were without their Dreamer for one month, Heaven would visit upon the nomads the ultimate catastrophe: the tribe would be dispersed.

If the Dreamer possessed power, the hunters wanted to ask, how was it that the herd had delayed for one day? Why had the stag run off with the Initiate? Neru had not even drawn the knife he was supposed to be blooding. For some of the hunters that seemed proof that the Dreamer was right: the stag had bewitched the boy.

Should not the Initiate have blooded the knife by now?

There was no law for that, except the law of common sense. Delay meant danger: anything could happen when fighting a wild beast. Having ridden out of the river, the young hunters usually killed at once, except when a weakling failed the test.

But they all knew the son of Narad. He was no weakling. He was deadly with the sling; though still a boy, he had come 18th in the last Stone Throwing Contest. And he was fearless. Indeed, if his manhood matched the promise of his early years, Neru looked strong enough to lead the tribe.

He was riding the great stag as the tribesmen of the East rode their camels. Why? Neru was no different from the others. He had a mother and a sister. His father was Narad.

'It is because of the knives,' the Dreamer muttered.

That must be it. The hunters frowned. Women groaned. The Chief had invested the boys with their antler-handled knives in the firelit Initiation Ceremony – new blades shining and tears sparkling in the eyes of their mothers – but the boys had not blooded them before the midday sun. It mocked Tradition.

'*Majumma*,' said the Dreamer, his head still, eyes shifting to the stag. The word meant 'accursed and banished'.

The Marshal of the Hunters looked away from him.

With tormented faces the women looked at the galloping stag. Hunters clasped the handles of the knives they had blooded at their own Initiation and watched the stag charging towards the cliff with Neru on its back.

The Dreamer should have foreseen that the herd would not cross the river on that first day; he should have ordered the Presentation of the Knives to be delayed. Foreseen! He should have had the power to make the deer swim. He should have sent a swarm of hornets to sting them into galloping into the river, if he could dream up nothing better.

The Chief ordered the Marshal: 'Kill the stag and seize the Initiate. Do not return to the encampment without him.'

The hunters noted that the Chief had not stated that the boy had to be taken alive.

While the Marshal was pointing to various hunters, indicating who should accompany him, the Dreamer hissed again, '*Majumma!*'

185

The Marshal and 25 hunters left, running in the manner of the nomads. They would be able to keep up that pace until sunset.

19

'Your name is Neru.'

Neru thought the words came from the deer. Yet its mouth could not pronounce human speech. Had the Angel of Death assumed the stag's form to take him into the next world? Neru heard the words as clearly as he had heard, 'The dear deer's name is now Anil.' He opened his eyes.

The stag's front legs had gone straight as tree trunks, its hind legs right under its stomach. Almost as if sitting down, it had skidded to a violent halt, churning up the dust. To prevent Neru going straight over its head, it had slewed round. Neru fell sideways, his back cracking into the rock with a shock that sent acute pain right up his spine.

The stag got to its feet. It remained motionless, panting. Its flanks were sweating. With his good arm the boy pulled on the fur of the deer's neck, swivelling himself up so that he was again on top of the stag. He realized it was waiting for his command like a trained camel.

Neru understood that he was not dead – though he had been hurtling into the next world. He felt as if he had fallen off a precipice, closed his eyes, and landed lightly on his toes in the ravine below.

'Who are you?'

On hearing the words, Neru spun round, expecting to see the old woman. Pain stabbed through his back. Suddenly he knew they were words of the spirit – and they came from Anil.

Neru heard words spoken in reply: 'I am the Dreamer.'

With a shock he realized the words came from himself.

'You did not enter the Contest.'

'I was too young.'

'Then you cannot be the Dreamer.'

'I have assumed the Mantle.' Neru became aware that the Dreamer's Cloak – he had never heard it called a Mantle before – was draped over his shoulders. Although it was on his back, Neru could see the design as clearly as if it lay on the ground before him. It was the Dreamer's Cloak, with its complex markings said to have been embroidered long ago when the Hills of Heaven were still covered in green trees.

Neru had seen it often enough before, at the annual Dream Contests and whenever the Dreamer appeared at ceremonies. He had worn it yesterday morning and the night before. It was said that the Cloak gave its wearer occult powers.

Previously, however, the Cloak's markings had been only an abstract pattern of whirling beauty. Now Neru could read the Mantle, as a scribe reads a manuscript – and it radiated an aura of timeless wisdom.

The design embraced the 'mounts' of all the Dreamers: from the Cloud of the first Dreamer and the Dragon who dreamed the world into creation, to other potent and more familiar vehicles, such as the Eagle, the Desert Lion, and the Phoenix of the sublime Halcyon, who had been Dreamer for 30 years before disappearing like the morning dew.

Then came confusion. From a Tree that shed its leaves in an endless gale, reptiles slithered – the mounts of false Dreamers. A Spider was spinning webs of deception, from which a Firefly was trying to escape. Neru saw that this Firefly was the mount of the old woman.

Even as he looked, the Mantle changed: the Spider scurried from the centre of its web, and lurked out of sight. A Stag cantered forward to dominate the Mantle, its hooves trampling the ensnaring webs. The Firefly escaped, flying up to perch on the Stag's antlers. In the eye of the Stag

Neru saw a Great Shark, flickering as though lit by lightning. In its eye Neru saw another eye, then another, and another, and he knew they were the mounts of Dreamers yet to come.

He was the Dreamer. He knew things no man had ever been told. He saw things other eyes could not see.

The Dreamers had never spoken of the symbols of the Cloak. Neru understood that this was the secret confirmation of his calling: the Transmission handed down from Dreamer to Dreamer. They, the real Dreamers, inherited the Mantle on becoming aware of its significance. The other Dreamers merely wore the Cloak.

'And you are my mount,' the Neru that was not Neru told the deer.

'How shall I know?'

'You know already. You spared my life.'

'It is true,' Anil replied. 'And you have not drawn your hunter's knife.'

That too was true, Neru realized with a jolt. Only once since his hand slid to the antler-handled knife, to make sure he had not lost it when diving into the icy river, had he thought of using the weapon. After leaving the river he could have pulled the knife out of its sheath at any time and cut the stag's throat.

They were very still, as this understanding spread through their consciousness. The Dreamer and his mount thrilled. Joy washed against their souls like waves from the sea of Bliss. They were eternally One, dancing on the shore of the Infinite . . .

'There!' A shout brought them back to earth.

Neru almost fell off the deer. He looked round and saw a group of hunters running towards them.

It was past midday.

Neru knew that even the best throwers were not accurate at over 70 paces but, if he and Anil stood still, the hunters would soon have them within range.

The Initiate could see they were treating this as a hunt to

189

the death. The Marshal might have sent other hunters round to outflank the stag, cutting it off. Neru assumed that he himself was in no danger. But a stone might shoot down from the cliff, striking Anil between the eyes. They wanted to kill the stag! Why? What had Anil done?

Neru had to protect the deer. He imagined his Dreamer's Mantle there like a shield, for he knew the hunters could hit Anil time and again without touching Neru himself. The sparse vegetation of the Hills of Heaven did not afford trees, so the nomads were not expert with bow and arrow. But there was no shortage of stones, and with their slings they were lethal.

Neru would rather die than let them kill Anil. He felt so close to the deer that he could no more contemplate the murder of Anil than the rape of his sister, Maya.

The stag turned to face the hunters. With its springing step it began to trot towards them.

Neru would put his arms in front of the stag's head, protecting its eyes. He would call out to the hunters that Anil was his friend. He would tell them about the old woman. Would they believe him if he told them he was now the Dreamer, a real Dreamer? Or would they dismiss him with 'He's only a boy'? And not just any boy, but an Initiate who had failed to blood the knife. They would never acknowledge that he was a man, and not just any man, but their Sage: 'Equal to Heaven'. As for the supposed Dreamer – how would the old spider react?

Neru looked at the Marshal of the Hunters anxiously. Would he accept . . . ?

'Majumma!' yelled the young thin-faced hunter who had wanted to banish the Initiates to the tents.

The terrible word rang out on the desert air, fanged like a snake. Others picked it up. It gathered venom as they hurled it at the boy. If the Chief said that word to anyone, he was banished from the tribe.

So far as Neru could see, the Chief was not there. The word had no formal meaning of banishment when used by

190

others, but it worked on the minds of the nomads. Skilled in hunting, they knew the meaning of every marking in the desert; they did not need a second glance to see where a doe had urinated and a buck had pawed the ground, or to tell from its tracks if a buck was in must. But in other ways superstition rode them like a genie.

At that first hysterical scream, the hunters trembled more than if they had trodden on a scorpion in the wilderness.

'Majumma!' Each time the cry rang out, more voices added their bewildered fury.

'Majumma! Majumma! Majumma!' Apart from the Marshal of the Hunters, they were all screaming it now. It was like a death threat.

A shiver of fear ran up the son of Narad's neck. He was afraid because his tribe had turned against him.

A nomad does not have a house he can call home. All he has is the tribe. If he is banished, he is like a bird that has lost its migrating instinct. He can skulk off to the towns, but he never joins the people. His eyes mark him out: they seek the horizon, the vault of blue day and the starlit sky at night. Town life is a cage to the nomad. The dust clogs the nostrils that long for desert air. Banishment was the one thing nomad children were brought up to dread. They feared it as the tribe feared dispersion – more than Death.

The stag was a majestic creature. It was now taking them towards the tribe's hunters. In a moment it would be within range. The hunters would draw back their slings. First one stone, possibly flung by the Marshal of the Hunters himself, then others, would smash Anil's head.

Neru could sense no fear in the stag. It could not be unaware of the danger. Anil needed sensitivity as much as strength to lead such a mighty herd. The air was heavy with vibrations of hostility. And the cries of 'Majumma!' were cruel threats.

Neru saw that the hunters were determined to destroy the stag. Placing himself in front of Anil would not shield

191

the deer. They might stone him too. Even if they left him untouched when they killed Anil, he was as good as dead since they were certain to banish him. The shouts of 'Majumma' showed they were convinced that he was possessed.

Neru did feel possessed – but with the power of love. He loved Anil, as he loved his own sister. He knew Anil. On the plane of choice before birth, Neru and Anil had chosen to meet in these forms. He saw two steps in the dance of Destiny fluttering like cloud shadows over the earth.

'You are the Dreamer.'

The words came, reminding Neru who he was. Yet they were not words; no one standing beside the deer could have heard them. Again Neru saw the Mantle, invisibly covering him and draped over the stag's back.

As easily as if he had done it countless times before, Neru went inside. He knew immediately that this was the divine trance, in which the Dreamer rose in consciousness to see the visions that gave him power.

In this state nothing could have been easier than to raise an invisible shield between the stag and the hunters, which their stones would beat against in vain.

This might save Anil now, but the Dreamer knew it would set a barrier between himself and the nomads. To them, it would prove that he was working to exterminate the tribe.

Even to cause one of the sudden storms of the desert, which could turn a dry river bed into a raging torrent within minutes, would only confirm that hostile forces had seized his spirit. He would be *majumma*, accursed and banished.

'The wings of dream are poetry and purity,' Halcyon had said. Now Neru understood what he meant: purity gave power, but poetry captured the heart. He had to do something that only a true Dreamer could imagine.

One of the starlit myths of the tribe, handed down from generation to generation round the camp fire, told how the

192

nomads had been attacked by ferocious warriors.

The Dreamer had walked out alone to meet the enemy. The warriors greeted him with a hail of arrows – which turned into roses in the air, so that the Dreamer was buried under a cloud of pink. And the warriors fell to their knees as the Dreamer made his way out of the rose petals and continued to walk towards them in his Cloak of many colours. The warriors joined the tribe, doubling its numbers and bringing new fire to its blood, while the nomads gave a reed-like flexibility to the men of war.

But Neru could not repeat the shape-change of the ancient Dreamer. That would be imitation. It indicated power, but it lacked poetry. It would convince the tribe that he was bewitched by the stag.

'Majumma! Majumma! Majumma!'

Anil was walking towards the hunters as confidently as the Dreamer in the legend.

Neru had to think of something at once.

They could turn and gallop away. But other hunters might already have cut off a retreat and be hidden, ready to stone them. Even if they were not, the nomads with their tireless jog could hunt the stag down within the day. And running away was hardly the intuitive solution of a true Dreamer.

Neru's consciousness dreamed immortality. He slipped out of Time and entered a Dimension beyond. He could remain there for seven years – then return to find that the stag had not placed one foot further forward, that the hunters had not drawn breath again to shout that word of horror.

Now Neru had all the time he needed. Not to think – for the answer would never come on the level of mind – but to be. To open like a flower to the sunshine. To let the answer float to him like the scent of the desert after rain.

And he saw it. His nerves tingled with joy.

It was a round, ruby stone, as big as a watermelon, sparkling on the dun ground of the desert. It was a

Dreamer's Stone.

Tradition said that every Dreamer would discover a Dreamer's Stone on the day of his Assumption of the Cloak of the Dreamer. The nomads had lost sight of this Tradition as Dreamer after Dreamer failed to find a Stone. No Dreamer had found a Stone since the sky-blue 'egg' of Halcyon.

On the plane of the Dreamer, Neru saw the ruby Stone with startling clarity. For a timeless moment he trembled, wondering if he would be able to materialize it when he returned to the world of the senses. At once he understood: he had dreamed it into existence. It was already lying on the desert floor: as soon as he returned to waking consciousness he would see it. The Stone was the first manifestation of any true Dreamer's power.

Neru was inspired to wonder if the old woman had a Stone. She flashed, munching, into his vision. Her crescent-moon neck pendant twinkled with the light of a hundred fireflies. The shark-tooth was her Stone – and she had worn it for all to see! At the same time the nomads had been giving the place of honour to 'The Beyond Within', as they called Halcyon's Stone.

Now Neru knew what to do. He looked for Halcyon; he found him sitting on the edge of a chasm, swinging his legs.

'I will not see you again in this lifetime,' Neru whispered to the deer. 'After leading the herd to the Hills of Heaven, leave them. Go to this precipice.' He visualized Halcyon's grassy ledge and flashed it into Anil's mind. 'There you will leave your body. Where you will be reborn, I do not see, but Halcyon will guide you.'

He slid down from the neck of the stag. 'The time will come when you need me. Call me – and I will be with you.'

His hand stroked Anil's forehead. He gazed into those soul-deep eyes. He would not see them again until 17 years later, when he would wake up after an extraordinary

194

sleep, not knowing who he was in a village by the sea. He would find them staring into his own eyes, smiling like a long-lost friend.

'You are always with me,'replied Anil. 'We are One.' The stag cantered away with the dignity of a born leader.

The first stone hit the deer's hindquarters.

Neru spun round with anguish in his face.

Except for the Marshal, the hunters were all flinging stones at the deer.

'They will not touch you,' the Dreamer said, using the voice-mode of command. His right arm hung limp at his side. He picked up the ruby Stone with his good arm. It would have been impossible without the affinity between the Dreamer and his creation. He began to walk towards the bearded hunters.

'Stop!' the thin-faced hunter yelled officiously. 'You are *majumma!'*

'I am not. Where is the Chief?' Neru retorted without breaking his step. 'Without his mace and his proper oath, your cries of *majumma* have no more meaning than the screaming of children. I am the Dreamer.'

'You failed,' the Marshal of the Hunters said in a voice colder than the desert nights. A hard light that Neru had never seen before glinted from his eyes. Something in the boy's heart whimpered.

'Weakling!' the thin-faced hunter taunted.

'I did not fail,' the son of Narad answered with an assurance that revealed none of the uncertainty he felt in standing up to the Marshal. 'Old ways change. I am not a hunter. I am the Dreamer.' The Stone was in his left arm. He raised it slightly. 'Here is my Stone.'

'Stop!' the thin-faced hunter ordered, raising his sling threateningly. 'You are *majumma!'*

'Stop!' 'Coward!' *'Majumma!'* 'Beardless boy!' others shouted. No one seemed to hear him declare he was the Dreamer.

Neru was only 20 paces from them now. He stopped.

195

'Look!' He used the voice-mode of command. He lifted the Stone above his head with both hands. In his face none of them saw the agony it cost him to raise his injured arm.

The sun shone down on the Stone. It radiated a ruby light, as if energy was flowing out from its depths.

They all looked at the Stone with excitement. Several of the hunters let the stones in their hands drop. Two walked forward, then suddenly halted, remembering that they had been calling the Initiate *majumma*. Even the thin-faced hunter's eyes opened wide.

With no vegetation on the barren ground, an interest in stones becomes part of a nomad's life, as inevitably as an eye for cloth develops in the carders and spinners of the towns. The nomads considered rocks in the desert to exceed in beauty any sculpture made by man.

They could not doubt it. This was an exceptional stone. Its full-moon shape and its ruby colour indicated a rare spirit.

But that did not mean it was a Dreamer's Stone. Neru had won no Dream Contest; he was too young to enter. And no Dreamer had found a Stone since Halcyon. His Stone was egg-shaped, sky-blue and the size of a baby's head. However, they knew it was said that every Dreamer found a different Stone, suited to his own destiny.

On the night of the Ceremony of the Assumption the new Dreamer would throw his new Stone, and the old Dreamer his old Stone, into the tribal fire. In the morning the new Stone would have absorbed the old. The tribe would stare at it, gleaming phoenix-like in the ashes.

This had last happened when Halcyon became Dreamer and threw in his 'egg', as he called it, laughing. When Halcyon disappeared, however, the tribe worshipped his Stone as 'The Beyond Within'.

Whatever this ruby Stone was, the nomads perceived its Finder to be one out of the ordinary. Normally they would have looked at him with respect.

'Return with us to the camp,' the Marshal of the Hunters

said tersely. 'You will stand before the Chief.'

The Marshal sent one of the hunters to run ahead and give the news to the Chief.

The sun was low in the sky as they walked back towards the tents. The Marshal of the Hunters walked in front, alone.

The corners of Neru's mouth turned down with distress when he saw that the Marshal, whose face had always lit up on seeing him, would not look in his direction.

None of the hunters came close to him. Neru was wearing the Dreamer's Mantle, but he knew they could not see it.

The hunters did see that the boy, still naked apart from his hunter's belt and knife and who that morning had been but one of the Initiates of the tribe, walked with a straight back, bearing himself with as much poise as the Marshal.

They walked straight to the Circle, with the Chief's Tent at one end, the Dreamer's at the other, and the tribal fire in the middle. The fire had been laid with brushwood and deer dung.

Hearing the hunters return, the Chief came out of his tent. Carrying his silver mace, he sat down in his place – and the hunters squatted round the fire, forming a circle and positioning themselves in order of seniority.

The Dreamer always sat directly opposite the Chief on the other side of the fire. His place was empty.

The Chief looked across. 'Call the Dreamer.'

20

He was not in his tent. Young boys were hanging round the edge of the Circle. They were not allowed to sit with the men until they became hunters. They ran off in different directions, hoping to be the one to find the Dreamer and give him the Chief's message.

With a kindly gesture the Chief indicated that Neru should sit down between him and the unlit fire.

Only now did the Chief see the ruby Stone. He blinked his bloodshot eyes. He was a good man. He had been a hard-working hunter who could run very fast. The nomads had elected him to be their Chief because he was brave and generous, rather than resourceful or far-sighted.

While Neru walked to the place indicated, the Chief beckoned to Neru's mother, who was standing with the other women outside the Circle. 'Bring a coat to cover the nakedness of the Initiate, your son.'

Neru placed the Stone on the ground in front of him. He stood waiting.

Maya suddenly ran through the Circle of Hunters, and threw her arms round her brother, crying, 'I believe in you.'

The thin-faced hunter got up and grabbed Maya. He carried her, struggling under his arm, to her mother, as she returned with Neru's deerskin coat. With a stern look the young hunter told the mother to hold on to her daughter. She took Maya's hand and led her back to join the women outside the Circle.

The hunter took the coat to Neru and pushed it at him.

Two boys had found the Dreamer. Grinning, they skipped ahead of him as he made his way to his place.

The old man did not say where he had been; he sat down without a word. He had been looking for the Dreamer's Cloak, wanting to appear in his regalia. It had vanished.

That boy must have stolen it yesterday morning, when he came into my tent: the spider had thought. Glancing about furtively, he had gone to Narad's tent. He called softly, then casting a look over his shoulder, slunk into the tent. He looked in every corner. He found nothing. He sneaked out and started walking to the cliff. Maybe that brat had hidden it up there. Suddenly he remembered he had worn the Cloak since the Initiate came to his tent. How could he have forgotten? Had that brat put a spell on him? He had sensed some threat ever since the Initiate asked, 'Did you dream the Swim?'

'In the presence of the Dreamer,' the Chief announced, holding up his mace, 'The tribe is assembled.'

'In the power of the Dreamer,' the hunters responded, 'The tribe is assembled.'

Where was the Cloak? Without turning his head, the Dreamer's eyes darted from hunter to hunter.

The morning's Initiates grinned at each other, wearing their adult clothes and waiting to be seated in the Circle with the men for the first time.

Each of the new hunters went red when the Marshal led him to his new place. Standing before the 13-year-old, and laying his right hand on the boy's left shoulder, he said, 'Sit here, Gautam. Be a pillar of your tribe.' The Marshal called the new hunters by their boyhood names for the last time. In the firelit evening Ceremony later, the Chief, one hand on each shoulder, would bestow upon the Man his adult name: 'Remain here, Muni. Be a pillar of your tribe.'

Outside the Circle the young boys' faces were eager with suppressed excitement. They knew they would be sent to their tent if they made themselves conspicuous. They pushed each other in the ribs, peering, pointing and

199

whispering. They watched with the women. They could not speak.

The greybeards sat in the Circle of Hunters but, once they had ceased to hunt, they could speak only if the Chief asked them to.

'Speak!' the Chief looked at the Marshal.

The Marshal of the Hunters told the Chief how they had caught up with the Initiate, apparently bewitched, astride the stag, unable to draw his knife; how the stag had cantered away 'with the grace of the dawn and the splendour of the noonday', so that they had lowered the arms they had raised to stone it; how Neru had walked towards them, carrying a Stone 'glowing like the third eye of the Heavenly Dragon'; how the Initiate began claiming that it was a Dreamer's Stone and he was the Dreamer.

'What do you say, Dreamer?' the Chief asked.

The Dreamer shifted on his haunches. 'How can it be a Dreamer's Stone?' he queried, looking down. 'The Dreamer's Stone is in the Dreamer's Tent. "The Beyond Within" was discovered by Halcyon, my sublime predecessor. Does the accused seek to destroy our traditions?'

'What of the Tradition that every Dreamer must find his own Stone?' asked the Chief.

'It is an ancient Tradition,' the Dreamer said with a sly smile. Facing the fire, his eyes shifted to the hills, his finger pointing. 'It derives from the time when these bald hills were covered in green trees, when men were giants and their hair was golden. It is no longer a truth for our modern world.'

The hunters nodded in agreement. The mountains were dying. The Tradition of the Dreamer's Stone belonged to those far-off days when the world was young.

The Dreamer noticed this swing in his favour. He sat back on his haunches more firmly, steepling the tips of his fingers together and resting his chin on them. 'Restore the trees and I will find you a new Dreamer's Stone.'

The Marshal of the Hunters said nothing. He looked intently at the Dreamer.

200

The meeting continued in its stately manner. Once a hunter began to speak, no one except the Chief might interrupt him. Whatever his idiosyncrasies of expression, he too embodied the Dreamer, the divine conscious force that pervades all existence.

The Chief heard the hunters of the tribe. Gradually their opinions were revealed.

The son of Narad had failed in the Swim. They did not know why, because he was brave and strong. All the other Initiates had killed their deer, except one thin boy whose frail chest had seized up when he hit the water. The current had hurled his body down-river and tossed it up onto a rock.

Maybe, confronted with the reality of Death, Neru had lost his nerve. It happened. That was the purpose of the Initiation: to establish whether a boy was worthy to be called a Man.

Neru had found a Stone, a Stone of wonder, no doubt about that. He was using this lucky chance to cover up his disgrace – and the humiliation of his father, Narad. With shameless audacity he was attacking the Dreamer, a challenge which the old man rightly repudiated.

Neru was guilty.

He sat in front of the Chief, motionless on his haunches, apparently paying no heed to what they were saying. Typical of a boy, some hunters thought. Even if it had been a Dreamer's Stone, he was far too young to be the Dreamer.

The Chief did not make his views known or try to lead their thoughts. He wished to elicit the feelings of the tribe. And this he had done. Neru had failed. He would have to surrender his antler-handled knife. The Marshal would destroy that weapon of dishonour.

The Chief would relegate Neru to the tents. The tribe would watch him. After one month they would decide whether or not to banish him. Appearances were against him, but not sufficiently to justify branding the son of Narad *majumma*.

Now it was Neru's turn to reply.

The Chief looked at him. He was struck by the Initiate's posture. He sat with a self-possession that matched the dignity of the Marshal. This was no adolescent receiving the censure of the tribe and awaiting judgment. This was the Finder of a Stone – and truly his spirit must possess unusual grace for such a Stone to attract him.

'Do you have anything you wish to say, son of Narad? This will be your last chance before I pass judgement.'

'Yes.' Neru spoke for the first time, his voice cutting crisply into the heavier air of the older men.

There was a rustle as all turned to stare at the boy.

Women carrying babies changed arms.

The Initiates fidgeted and shifted on their haunches, trying to look solemn as befitted their status as Hunters, sitting for the first time in the Circle.

Their fathers glared at Neru: this meeting threatened to interfere with the Celebration of Manhood, due to take place before the tribal fire when the moon rose. Fathers wanted to go to their tents and be with their sons on this auspicious day, which was in danger of being ruined by the son of Narad, who had behaved so rashly.

When he spoke, Neru made no plea or excuse. He gave a command: 'Ask the man you call the Dreamer to state the shape, colour or size of this Stone.'

The Chief realized that the Dreamer could not see the giant ruby. He had gone to his place on the opposite side of the Circle. The unlit fire hid the Stone.

The Chief stood up so that he could see the Dreamer. He looked at the old man with the question on his face.

The Dreamer's eyes revealed his uncertainty. He was weighing up the chances of jumping up to catch sight of the Stone, then using his cunning to argue his way out of the trap. His eyes glanced here and there. But the nomads would see through the subtlest argument he could spin. And he might fall into a trap: the Stone might not be there. Rushing round to see it would make him a laughing-stock.

The Marshal of the Hunters was staring at him.

His head facing the unlit fire, the old spider looked at the Chief's mace. He made a desperate attempt: 'It is less than spherical and of a colour that is not quite brown.'

'To put it even more precisely,' Neru said, without turning round, 'It is nearly its own shape and almost its own colour. And its size is just right.'

Except for the Chief and the Marshal, they all laughed.

The Dreamer blanched. He had lost the sympathy that had been his by this evasion. He would have routed Neru's challenge if he had said he didn't know and he didn't care. It was not a Dreamer's Stone. Who should know if not him? The accused's demand had no validity.

By answering the question he himself had given it validity. What a mistake! How could he have been so stupid? Him of all people! That boy had put a spell on him. He put both hands to his forehead.

Neru did not move.

There was something so certain in his demeanour – so much in contrast with the shifty glances of Dreamer – that this alone might have convinced the nomads.

The interchange of words was conclusive. For an hour the hunters had been establishing Neru's guilt. With one breath he had blown it all away – like one shout waking you from a dream. And that, some of them recalled, was contained in the Song of the Dreamer:

'With a laugh he scatters the clouds in the sky
As one stone shatters the moon in the lake.'

They had forgotten its meaning and relegated it to 'the time when men were giants'. Now they had seen it happen.

Silence followed. The Chief sat down. He knew the value of waiting. He would give them time to digest this new information, time to adjust. Eventually he asked, 'Do you have anything to add, Dreamer?'

'Only this: tonight I do not sleep on the Stone,' Neru said, before the old spider could begin the defence he had been weaving in his mind. 'I shall throw it into the fire of the phoenix. You will do the same with the Stone of Halcyon.'

The nomads caught their breath, marvelling at the way Neru had assumed as his own the question addressed to the old man. Neru had taken Hakim's title.

Throwing his Stone into the fire was the first duty of a new Dreamer, the hunters remembered with a shudder of awe. No one had mentioned 'the fire of the phoenix' for years.

The man they called the Dreamer slumped as though he had been hit in the stomach.

The Chief stood up and took a couple of steps towards him. Ever fair, he repeated his question without words, giving Hakim his last chance. The Chief could not call him Dreamer but, having called him 'Dreamer' for so long, he would not call him by his name.

After a time the man they called the Dreamer said in a voice that cracked, 'I shall remove my things from the Dreamer's Tent.'

The Chief could feel the delight of the tribe. So could Neru. And had he been merely a boy, he would have shouted with triumph. If he had been only a man, he would have smiled at his victory. He was the Dreamer.

Maya pulled her hand away from her mother's. She dashed forward to run into her brother's arms. As she scampered through the Circle, the thin-faced hunter caught her again. He tucked the girl under his arm; unsmiling, despite the laughter of the tribe, he carried Maya, squealing, back to her mother.

Neru remained seated on his haunches.

Hakim got to his feet, straightening his back with difficulty. His eyes on the unlit fire, he uttered the verse normally kept for the moment of leaving the body:

'The sun sparkles in the rain drop,
Even when it drowns in the ocean.'

Neru rose lightly to his feet. Turning to face the old Dreamer for the first time, he replied:

'The moon dances in the waves,
Even when they break.'

The old man stared at the boy.

The nomads looked at each other with wonder. This was the first time they had heard someone spontaneously adding to the scripture.

The sun was sinking below the horizon, but they all saw clearly as Neru stepped onto his ruby Stone. The Dreamer's Stone! This was sacrilege! The nomads gaped.

'Let the fire of the phoenix be lit!' Neru called out in a ringing voice.

The young boys, who had been silent outside the Circle, looked at the Chief. He nodded. They rushed forward to do the bidding of the new Dreamer. Maya, her dark eyes laughing, scrambled out with them, avoiding the thin-faced hunter. She began rubbing the fire sticks.

His mother stared at him. This was not Neru!

'Let it be acknowledged how properly the former Dreamer has relinquished his position,' the son of Narad continued, while the boys lit the fire. 'A Dream Contest will be held at the new moon. The new Dreamer trusts he will step down as graciously, if he fails to win the Contest.'

The women laughed. They could hardly grasp the idea of having a boy as their Sage, but they were sure Neru was a true Dreamer. He would go on winning the Dream Contest year after year like Halcyon.

The Chief noticed how Neru spoke of himself in the third person. That was another Tradition that the Dreamers had not observed since Halcyon. He glanced at the Marshal of the Hunters, who did not return the look.

Narad was squatting on his heels, gazing at the ground between his feet. On concluding his report he had looked down, and had only glanced up twice, to stare at the old Dreamer. Yet the Chief knew that Narad had been listening to every word with the keen insight that had led to him being appointed Marshal of the Hunters.

'The right arm of the Dreamer was damaged after the Swim,' Neru went on, pointing to his damaged arm. The hunters had observed it hanging feebly. 'It is well known that Hakim's art in healing ascends to the heights of mystery. The Dreamer asks him to use his skill to reset the arm.'

Above the crackles of the fire there was a gasp. Everyone in the tribe stared. Narad grimaced. Women clasped their hands to their mouths. They all knew Hakim was adept at replacing joints. However, manipulating the arm was a delicate business: a twist one way could replace the limb in its socket; a different twist might maim the boy for life. After the humiliation of losing his position as Dreamer, Hakim might seize this chance of revenge.

Neru was placing himself at the old man's mercy.

A dangerous glint came into Hakim's eyes. His head facing the Marshal, his eyes on the boy, he walked stiffly across to the Initiate who had ousted him. Neru was still standing on his Stone, as if to bring himself up to the right height.

The fire began to blaze. It lit the twilight, as wood sputtered and burst into flame.

Neru looked the former Dreamer in the eyes, but Hakim would not meet the boy's gaze. He looked down at Neru's hand.

'Step down.'

Neru stepped off the stone.

The old man put out his left hand and placed it on the boy's shoulder – as if to feel the vibrations, like the ripples of a stone thrown into a pool – while he took Neru's right hand and waggled it. Still not looking at Neru's face, Hakim swung the arm to left and right a little.

206

With alarm the nomads saw a smile playing round the old spider's lips. They looked at the pair, lit by the flames, in the same way they sometimes watched two of the red-brown stags fighting for supremacy.

Frowns furrowed many foreheads. The Chief rubbed his bloodshot eyes. The hunters rose to their feet. Why was Neru putting himself into Hakim's power like this? The women feared that Hakim could jerk the arm in such a way as to choke the life out of the young Dreamer.

The old Dreamer was a subtle beast. Once Neru was dead, what web of deceit would Hakim spin to excuse the murder and get himself reinstated as Dreamer?

But they could do nothing. They were all standing now.

Even the Marshal of the Hunters, who had felt bound to remain silent while Neru's 'guilt' was being debated, did not step forward and put a stop to it. He was staring at Neru. His face was haggard, for he had misjudged his son.

Suddenly Hakim's body twisted; his left arm shot forward, his right hand wrenched Neru's hand.

The nomads heard the click of bone and the scrunch of sinew. They stared at the flame-lit figures. Then they saw a smile on the Dreamer's face.

'Thank you, Healer,' he said, giving Hakim a new title.

The old man looked into the boy's eyes with a smile. 'Wait,' he said with a richer ring to his voice.

Hakim walked to the Dreamer's Tent. He came out, shouldering aside the decorated tent flap. He was carrying the Dreamer's Cloak over his left arm and Halcyon's sky-blue Stone in his right hand. He had found the Cloak folded neatly on top of the Stone. Somehow he had known he would.

The nomads were surprised to see Hakim carrying the Dreamer's Stone so easily. They recalled the solemnity with which the Dreamer usually carried it. No one else was allowed to touch 'The Beyond Within'.

'It is as light . . .' Hakim answered their unspoken question, throwing Halcyon's Stone into the fire 'as a forgotten dream.' He turned to Neru and smiled. 'Cast your own Stone into the fire . . . Dreamer.'

Neru smiled back at the man, who had been called the Dreamer. Flexing his arm, he stooped and picked up the ruby Stone. He raised it above his head with both hands, as he had done earlier. Again it glowed, as if radiating inner power. Caught in the flickering firelight, tongues of flame leapt from the Stone into the starlit sky. For many of the nomads it had the effect of crowning the boy Dreamer.

'The Dreamer names the Stone,' Neru's young voice rang out for all to hear. Again, thrills ran up the nomads' spines: they remembered that each Dreamer gave a name to his Stone. 'It is the Dragon Pearl.'

A moment of awe was followed by respectful clapping, and murmurs of 'The Dragon Pearl.' 'The Dragon Pearl.'

In one of the firebright myths of the tribe, the Dragon who dreamed the world into creation, began weeping over the slowness of mankind to waken from the dream of Life. He sacrificed the ruby pearl that was his third eye, plucking it from his forehead and squeezing a tear of his own blood into the heart of every creature. This is their soul. Those who discover it realize they are One with the Dreamer.

The young Dreamer tossed the Dragon Pearl into the fire of the phoenix. Somehow the nomads felt sure that no one else could have lifted the Dreamer's Stone.

Something else hurtled through the air and into the flames. Not with his ordinary eyes, but with his Dreamer's vision, Neru saw it. An old crone in her black 'tent' had thrown another Stone, a shark-tooth in the shape of a crescent moon, into the fire. The former Dreamer had *seen* how her successor was going to assume the Mantle.

With paternal gentleness the man they had called the Dreamer removed the deerskin coat from Neru's shoulders and replaced it with the Dreamer's Cloak.

Neru saw the Cloak and the invisible Mantle merge into one. He was the Dreamer in both form and substance.

The Day of the Rainbow

When he awoke, he knew himself.

Most of the tribe had already gathered in the Circle. Some stared at the dawn sky, glowing red beyond the Hills of Heaven; others looked at the grey ashes of the fire. They squatted on their haunches, waiting for their Dreamer.

Rainbows were sparkling in the dew when the man who had regained his memory came out of the tent. For it had been his own Dreamer's Tent to which the Chief had led 'Hari' on his return to the nomads, after disappearing one month before. It had been his own Dreamer's Stone, the Dragon Pearl, on which Hari had slept – as the Healer had suggested.

This had been the last action of the old man, whom the Dreamer had taken to be the Dreamer. Hakim did not regain consciousness, though his lips moved in the night, mumbling the verse with which he had relinquished the role of the Dreamer 17 years before. The lines vanished from his face. The soul dropped the body and fell like a raindrop into the ocean of consciousness.

When they saw the man come out of his tent, the women sighed with relief, the hunters cheered. Their Dreamer was back! They all stood up. They could see that Neru had recovered his mind. Last night the man with one month's beard had been ordinary. But now, what lightness of step! Yes, the Dreamer had returned. How his eyes shone!

'Wake, Dreamer,' Neru called out, looking at them with the gaze that was a blessing.

'Wake, Dreamer!' the roar of many voices answered; the

nomads laughed, delighted with the appropriateness of the conventional greeting.

If Neru had been absent one day more, they feared it would have resulted in the dispersion of the tribe. After Neru, no one would have dared claim to be the Dreamer, unless they *knew* they were the one, for Neru had spoken of the inner transmission. No one had even hinted at having a Dream Contest, as the month passed by with no sign of Neru, although they thought he had disappeared like Halcyon.

'I'll have to shave off my beard,' the Dreamer smiled at some boys nearby, rubbing his chin. 'I never dreamt you'd run away when you saw it.'

The boys laughed, following him and watching with delight as Neru shaved off his month-old beard. He had been the Dreamer all their lives. He had been the nomads' Dreamer for 17 years – ever since that day of the Swim when, as a boy longing to be a Man, the son of Narad had failed in his most cherished desire, yet realized a goal beyond his dreams.

Awareness governed everything he did. Neru performed even mundane tasks – washing his face, folding a deerskin blanket, untying a tent rope – with poise: centred in a temple of the heart fit for the divine presence. His words and deeds were in harmony. His wisdom was such that they had given him the name, 'The Voice of Eternity'.

Neru had become a living legend, guiding the nomads with a certainty that eclipsed even the power and the glory of Halcyon. Neru's fame spread. People came from distant places to seek the Dreamer, as the fisherfolk from Shark Bay had come long ago, as Hari and Lina themselves had come.

Most came with sincerity. Some came with flattery, calling him 'The Shadow of God on Earth', 'The Centre of the Universe' and other flamboyant titles.

The Dreamer treated all of them like a kind father seeking only the best for his children. He saw the Dragon Pearl of their soul, rather than the mask of personality.

Those who could not speak the nomadic language slept outside his tent. The Dreamer appeared to them in the night, revealing the dreams they needed to go forward, answering the questions they did not know how to ask.

Sometimes seekers from afar came into his dreams asking for help, and once a beautiful pearl-diver from Shark Bay appeared in his dreams.

And thus it had come to pass . . .

At the birth of the new moon the Dreamer left his tent and stepped out into the dark. The tribe was asleep. Neru was naked. He put himself into the trance that empowered him to use the Dreamer's Walk.

Barely touching the ground, with his arms out behind him, the Dreamer walked down from the Hills of Heaven. He ghosted across the river, more fluidly than, two weeks later, Lina would glide down the Temple steps and into the Palanquin waiting to carry her to the Great Shark. He was on the way to save her.

Three days after the Swim, 17 years before, Anil had gone to Halcyon to leave the body, as instructed by Neru.

Halcyon had guided the soul through the nameless realms to its rebirth as Lina in Shark Bay.

And he gave it a special mission: to redeem the village from the annual tribute of a living virgin – caused by the original sin of the pearl-diver who had broken her promise to the Shark Prince. Despite the Sacred Soup, all the previous girls had gone to the Sacrifice reluctantly. The ancient Dreamer had not told the Headman that the Shark would be completely appeased only when the Bride went willingly.

On the plane of the Dreamer, Auntie, Neru's predecessor as Dreamer to the nomads, saw the death of Lina's mother in childbirth. Auntie deemed that the special baby needed someone special to look after her. *With clothes and pearls and fishing knife She'll save the girl from death-in-life.* When she saw the old lady from the island die of a heart attack,

211

watching the typhoon smash her husband's boat against Shark Rock, Auntie rushed into the body. For reasons best known to herself, she decided to forget – like Hari – that she was herself the Dreamer.

With the Dreamer's Walk Neru was able to cover in one night the distance that would take Hari and Lina two weeks on the return journey. He 'walked' till he came to the meeting place of earth and sea and sky. Then he lay down, naked of mind and body, on the beach below the pine tree at Shark Rock. He was no longer aware of his power.

As there is an exception to most rules, there was a limitation to his will: Tradition said that the Dreamer could not leave the tribe for more than one month – or the nomads would be dispersed. In divine trance Neru saw that it was a true Tradition.

'Very well,' the son of Narad decided. 'I have one month.' He used his hermetic powers to ordain his return on the eve of the new moon – whatever happened.

There was another limitation, self-imposed: within hours of throwing the Dragon Pearl into the fire of the phoenix, the boy Dreamer had realized that the mind can justify whatever it wishes. He had decided never to use his control of invisible forces, if he himself gained by doing so. That was why he had not been able to *see* Lina's escape and their marriage.

The Dreamer divested himself of his power so completely he no longer knew such powers existed. He shed the nomadic tongue and clothed his mind in the language of the Coast. He wore no clothes in case they gave a clue to his identity.

In Shark Bay, the next year, the priest selected a Virgin as usual. In his new boat Tao towed the Bride out, in the black and gold Palanquin, to sacrifice her where Shark Rock had been. But no Shark came. This recurred the following year, and the villagers decided to abandon the Sacrifice. However, the Shark Festival continued every summer with the

Palanquin careering down from the Temple to the beach at full moon. Over the decades the Chosen Virgin was translated into the Queen of Heaven, descending to earth to marry the Ocean.

As he finished shaving, the man who had recovered his memory looked up, hearing laughter.

He saw his sister walking towards him, wearing her black 'tent'. Plump and jolly, Maya was now the mother of four. How she had wanted Neru to marry, to be happy like herself! Maya had made him meet all the girls of the tribe who were 'illegible', as she put it, chuckling.

Then the Dreamer had said something that made her stop trying to find a wife for him: 'He could never be happy with someone unless he knew she was his soul-mate. The Dreamer would rather die childless than make any compromise.'

'Can't you dream her?'

Neru took her hand. 'It is strength to get what you want, but it is weakness to want it.'

'Oh, more of *his* riddles,' Maya laughed, her eyes dancing as brightly as ever. 'I can do them.' She set her hands on her hips, 'To grasp the Truth with your mind is as easy as to catch a ball with your ear.'

'There's a lot of truth in what you say,' Neru smiled.

'Thus spake Maya, holy sister to the Dreamer,' Maya added. She burst into laughter, giving her brother a push that would have knocked him off balance, if he had not been so light on his feet.

'If it will content you, woman,' Neru put his arm round her ample waist, 'I will shave off my beard. I will not grow it again until I meet my soul-mate.' The beard was a sign of manhood amongst the nomads. Its lack would be a constant reminder, even for the Dreamer.

'I caught you. You said "I", not "he".'

'*I* am not the Dreamer,' Neru pointed to his nose.

'Who is then?'

'*He* is.' Neru put his right forefinger between his own eyebrows, then Maya's. Pressing her third eye, he did something Maya would never forget. 'Which ear?'

'Oh, this one!'

Neru raised his left hand up to it. His forefinger and thumb took hold of her earlobe.

Maya felt paralysed. She was in agony! She wanted to scream! But she could not move, not even open her mouth to shout for help. The pain was unbearable. And her brother was smiling at her!

Suddenly Maya realized it was not pain at all, but the most intense pleasure she had experienced in her life – starting in her ear and surging in wave after wave down through her body, then up again to her head, as if she was experiencing orgasm after orgasm. Maya saw a moonlit ocean – and felt a joy more perfect than anything she could have imagined.

He took away his hand and she looked at him, her eyes wide with wonder.

'The Dreamer has no sister, woman. We are all One. When you can have that experience, at will, you have started to realize Oneness.' Neru smiled, 'And that is only a bubble of foam, compared with the ocean of divine bliss.'

The night before, as soon as she had seen Neru with a beard and a woman, Maya knew that the Dreamer had found his soul-bride. Whatever the state of his mind, the unconscious depths would not have allowed him to break his word. An inexplicable unease would have nagged him, maybe erupting into a physical disease, until he shaved.

When the Chief led 'Hari' away to the Healer, Maya and the women of the tribe had looked Lina over, as camel-dealers look over a female camel for breeding. They intended to pass their own judgement on the son of Narad's choice of a woman, particularly since he had gone outside the tribe. For she was to be his mate. The way he looked at the woman (who was lovely, they granted that) left no doubt about that. But they were not to be beguiled

214

by surface beauty. The Dreamer was merely a man, when all was said and done – and when it came to women, he was only a boy! Whatever his wisdom, if they did not find her suitable, her life would not be worth living.

They bantered and stroked and prodded her.

One crone hobbled forward and pinched the stranger's arms. Then she took hold of Lina's breasts and kneaded them. Whatever she said while she conducted this examination set the rest cackling with laughter.

Lina submitted to this treatment with quiet dignity.

And they approved. Yes, she would bear fine male children for the Dreamer.

'Lina,' the girl from Shark Bay pointed to her heart.

'Lina,' the women nodded, smiling.

Lina meant 'twice-born' in the nomadic tongue. Halcyon must have laughed when he named her: Neru meant 'twice-born' in the language of Shark Bay.

Maya led Lina to her tent. Banishing her thin-faced husband to Narad's tent for the night, Maya gave Lina the deerskin bedding that Neru had used in his boyhood.

That night Lina had an extraordinary dream: She dreamt she was Neru. The Dreamer was enjoying one of his long walks in the Hills of Heaven. In the dream she, Neru, had reached the age of three score years and ten. He had been Dreamer to the nomads for over half a century. He had never married. He was honoured by all, loved by many, worshipped by some.

The Dreamer saw the great stag bounding towards him.

'Anil!' Neru waited with open arms for the stag to gallop to him, then he threw his arms round that loved head and clasped it to his chest. Tears brimmed in their eyes.

Neru vaulted onto the deer's back. They were galloping to the summit. That joy again! He had not experienced it for 50 years. He was clutching Anil as tightly as he had when, entwined in loving enmity, the stag had been trying to throw him off.

Suddenly the hill became Halcyon's ledge. They were

215

racing towards the chasm. They couldn't stop! Anil reared up, throwing himself back on his haunches, pawing the air with his forelegs. The precipice gave way under the stag's hind legs. Rocks tumbled into the abyss.

Neru found himself falling, clinging to Anil in a loving embrace. He felt strangely calm.

Silence.

Neru looked down: he saw the bodies of an old man and his deer lying dead on the rocky floor of the chasm.

Then everything went black.

'Death blesses you.'

Neru looked up: in a garment of flame the Angel of Death was welcoming him.

'We seek the Light,' the Dreamer spoke.

In the darkness the Angel's fiery garment blazed: 'The response should be made in the singular.' After a pause the Angel added, 'You are judged by your life.'

'Let us be judged by the grace.'

Again, a moment of flaring hesitation before the Angel continued: 'Neru, son of Narad, Death welcomes you to eternal Bliss.'

'We bless Death.'

'Not the deer!' The Angel's flame garment crackled. 'Animals have no capacity for heaven. The stag must be reborn as a human being and progress towards perfection.'

'Anil comes with the Dreamer!' Neru used the voice-mode of command.

'Your powers carry no sway here.'

'The Dreamer will not go without Anil.'

'Death will turn you away from Heaven.'

'Then the Dreamer turns away from Heaven,' Neru answered. 'He will go with Anil, wherever that may be.'

'Foolish mortal! You have no imagination to conceive the pain and misery.' The flames blazed. 'Come with me. Enjoy the highest Bliss man can hope for.'

'The Dreamer goes with Anil.' Neru put out his hand to

216

touch the deer's cheek in a caress that said, 'We are united.'

The flames of the Angel of Death leapt high, transforming into an incredible Light, then into a rainbow. Neru heard a voice in the Heavens: 'That is the correct response.'

Shimmering in the rainbow light, a young woman stood where Anil had been. She was naked, apart from the white briefs the pearl-divers wear. Her flesh gleamed, as if she had just run out of the sea.

'Death welcomes you to Bliss.' The rainbow arched over the young couple, for Neru had been translated back into the prime of life.

Neru was not regarding the loveliness of her body. He was looking into her eyes . . . and there he saw her soul . . . One with his own in Bliss . . .

'Love of my life.' They ran into each other's arms. 'Life of my love.' As they embraced, Neru realized he was the pearl-diver. Their bodies melted into One.

She woke up.

Maya was leading Lina, wearing a black 'tent', towards Neru, as he finished shaving.

Now it begins! Neru caught sight of Lina. For the first time since he had found himself, he laid eyes on the woman he loved. She was his soul-mate. And he was the one, who knew her before she took birth in Shark Bay. *Heaven on Earth!*

Nomads are not given to exaggeration, but they said – dancing round the camp fire at the wedding – that when the two met, their hands touched, and sparks flew from the Dreamers.

Now it begins! Lina saw Neru and knew who he was. She woke from the sleep of Life. She saw who she was – one with all that ever was and all that ever will be. The Great Shark was her mount. Shark Rock was her Stone. *Heaven and Earth!*

Lina was Neru's twin-soul Dreamer, for sometimes it

takes two to realize a Dream, as both time and space are needed to spin our universe.

Experiencing the consciousness where all is One, Lina saw that Halcyon was the Dreamer. Maya was the Dreamer, though sleeping, as Hari had been. So was Hakim. And Narad and the Chief. Julian was the Dreamer, all but awake; so was Rat-eyes, sound asleep. And Danny and Tao and Ken and Katha and Anna and Older Brother.

Lina's heart leapt to her father: she saw Martin, dreaming away on the family altar. The Dreamer Auntie was placing a tiny brass bowl of rice before his black and gold memorial tablet, muttering about the fate that had defied the natural order and had taken Martin 'up there', while she, his elder, remained below with *them!*

Rita was the Dreamer, her name meaning 'Play of Truth'. The once pot-bellied Lovegod, at death emaciated by sickness, left the body with that holy word on his waking-Dreamer lips. And Rita died, after raving in agony for months, gasping: 'Help, stranger! Help, Hari!'

All, *all* are the Dreamer. Our planet is a chorus of dreams, winging in, singing out to the creator Dreamer.

Now it begins! Neru took Lina's hand. The Dreamers soared out of space-time into another Dimension, where All is One. They were dancing together with all creation . . . in the divine consciousness that guided him to the fishing village . . . that led her to reject all proposals of marriage . . . that cloaked him in her language . . . that gave her the courage to face death at the Shark Sacrifice, waiting for the one who knew her before she took birth . . . that cast him like a shipwreck on the beach at Shark Bay . . . that destined her to be his finder . . .

She was early that dawn, running across the sands. Her face radiant, Lina plunged into the waves. She began swimming towards Shark Rock, while the sun rose over the horizon like the Dragon Pearl. She dived and she played and . . .